junk mail

CW00486970

Also by Brian Gallagher

The Feng-Shui Junkie

BRIAN GALLAGHER

junk male

ORION

Copyright © Brian Gallagher 2001

All rights reserved

The right of Brian Gallagher to be identified as the author
of this work has been asserted by him in accordance
with the Copyright, Designs and Patents Act 1988.

First published in Great Britain in 2001 by
Orion
An imprint of Orion Books Ltd
Orion House, 5 Upper St Martin's Lane,
London WC2H 9EA

ISBN: 0 75284 5942

A CIP catalogue record for this book
is available from the British Library

Typeset at The Spartan Press Ltd,
Lymington, Hants

Printed in Great Britain by
Clays Ltd, St Ives plc

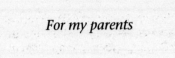

For my parents

monday

1

From one point of view having your wife inform you that she's pregnant can be extremely good for your health. But from another it can send you into a choking fit so severe that it leaves you wondering how you learnt to breathe in the first place.

Such was the effect his wife's announcement had on Joel.

He was playing saxophone in the lounge, one bright August morning, wailing out a frenzy of improvised notes, when Ellen entered in her nightgown. She came up to him, holding up a small plastic device with a tiny red light beaming on its tip. Normally, she would wait for him to finish a solo. This time she didn't. She brought her mouth up to his earhole and articulated two simple words, with the utmost clarity.

Joel got such a shock that he choked on his saliva, then embarked on a sequence of spluttering spasms so severe that he tried to remove the instrument from around his neck, but couldn't.

Ellen grabbed a glass of water from the coffee table and passed it to him. He sipped it, then spat it out in a diffuse spray, which missed her face by inches: he'd forgotten that he'd soaked a sax reed in the glass overnight to clean the cane and that it contained 3 per cent hydrogen peroxide. She fetched him some tap water that did not kill you, and after a few gulps he was okay again. He removed his Golden Goddess from around his neck, took the gadget from Ellen and stared at the tiny beacon, aghast. Seconds later, the red light went out. *'How can you possibly be pregnant?'*

'I'm not sure. I think it might have something to do with the

1

fact that we've been making love to each other.' As always, Ellen was distressingly calm.

'But I always wear protection. I always have.' And it was true: he wore it religiously.

'Well, they always say those things are never one hundred per cent.' She shrugged, nodding at the appliance. 'I suppose they must be right.'

Joel collapsed in an armchair. 'Ninety-nine would have been enough,' he croaked, 'like the small print said.' Holding his head in dismay, he watched Ellen sit down quietly on an armrest. She looked beautiful. Vulnerable. The early morning sunlight shining through the bay window augmented the blonde in her hair and the blue in her glistening eyes.

'And I have some other good news for you as well, love.' She was staring at him with deathly composure. 'You've got a whole *nine* months to find a regular income and get some savings together.'

Joel got up and started pacing. He was not a big earner, exactly. In fact, he was almost completely dependent on his wife financially, apart from the times he managed to secure a run of gigs, which was roughly once in a blue moon. Sure, husbands and wives helped one another out and vice versa, but in Joel's case it was always more versa than vice.

'We're going to have a lot of expenses,' she added. 'The pram, the cot, the nappies, clothes. We're living hand to mouth as it is. The last time we had a nice meal out was at our wedding breakfast.'

'I know that, I know.' He was roaming around the room, his brain feeling like a fly buzzing round in an empty jam jar.

'I can't do any more than I'm doing. I give eight piano lessons a week at the Conservatory. I'm up to the brim with rehearsals and recitals with the Trio. I'm already working flat out to cover all the bills. We have to build up our savings. You'll have to help out.'

Joel's head was spinning from the double blow. He wasn't exactly sure at this point which was the more distressing news. 'But don't we already have savings?'

'Our nest egg? That two thousand is all we have to fall back on. We're going to need every penny of it. Look, you'll find a proper residency somewhere. For goodness' sake, you're the fifth-best sax player in the country.'

'Third.'

'And you've got *the* best saxophone in the country,' she added, pointing at his precious, gold-plated Selmer, its honeyed lacquer sparkling in the strips of sunlight traversing the room. 'You'll have to find regular work. Playing the odd gig every few weeks just won't be enough.'

Joel went to the bay window, swung open a window and gulped in some fresh sea air. He stared down over the harbour, its two long pier arms clawing the deep blue water of Dublin Bay. *My God Almighty. A baby. I can't believe it. After all these years of not trying.*

Ellen came up behind him and wrapped her arms round his chest. She rested her chin on his shoulder and whispered: 'I may need to take time off, too. I don't know how I'll react. Some women go through it fine but others can be quite sick.'

Joel turned and held her by the arms. 'Why, are you all right?' He scanned her face for signs of illness.

'Yes, I'm fine, I've never felt better.'

'Are you sure? You look a bit pale. Can I get a cup of hot, sweet tea or something?'

'No, Joel. I was just making a point.'

'A hot-water bottle?'

'Joel, I'm fine.'

He cradled her in his arms and exhaled a shaky breath. 'Look, Ellen, I don't want you to worry, okay? I'll sort something out.'

'I know you will.'

'I mean it.' And he did.

'Your heart is pounding. I can feel it.'

'I think I'm in shock.'

Ellen kissed him. 'You'll be all right, Joel, it'll be fine.' She pulled away and stood up. 'I have to get dressed. I'm rehearsing in town at ten.'

She walked to the door, then she turned. 'Oh, by the way . . .' She looked suddenly grave. '. . . You're not to tell anyone about this, okay? Not yet. Not even your father. I don't want any fuss.' She brought her finger to her lips. 'Promise me.'

'I promise.'

'Good.' Ellen smiled.

She was just stepping out of the room when Joel called after her, 'Hey, Ellen.'

'Yeah?'

'Just had a brainwave. I know how we can make a lot of money fast.'

'How?'

'Sue the Durex Corporation for negligence.'

2

Ellen's fingers tripped to a halt just before the letter C. She glared at the Beethoven passage on the music rack in front of her.

The rehearsal wasn't going well. It was her fourth finger error in the last minute alone. She glanced over at a concerned-looking Ita, whose violin and bow were poised, ready to continue. Sean, the cellist, also waited for a sign. Ellen apologised and refocused, taking several deep breaths. 'From letter B again.' She counted them in and they were away once more.

Fourteen bars later Ellen came to another crash, cocking up at a relatively uncomplicated scale passage. She stood up, at the limit of her patience. 'I'm sorry, but I have to break for five minutes.'

She left the hall under the concerned gaze of her two colleagues and went out to the water dispenser in the corridor. She'd barely filled up her cup when Ita suddenly appeared beside her. 'What are you doing?'

'I'm getting a drink of water.'

'Come on, Ellen, I was watching you in there. You weren't even reading the music. You were a hundred miles away.'

Ellen brought the cup to her lips and sipped.

'I hate to remind you,' Ita said, 'but we do have a recital in four days' time. If we play like that in front of the critics, it might turn out to be our farewell concert.'

'I'm sorry, Ita.' Ellen stared at the Stravinsky print on the wall above the dispenser. 'But there's something on my mind and it's doing my head in.'

'What is it? What's the matter?'

'I was talking to Joel again, about starting a family.'

'Oh, not again! I've told you a thousand times, that man will never be persuaded to have children.'

'I just persuaded him.'

'*You persuaded Joel to have a child?*' Ita looked animated.

'More or less.'

'How on earth did you manage that?'

'I'd love to tell you, Ita, but how do I know you won't go blabbing?'

Ita mimed zipping her lips together.

Ellen began warily. 'Okay, but if you tell anyone, I'll never forgive you.' She stared warningly at her friend. 'I found a way that he wouldn't insist on wearing them any more.'

'Wearing what? The condominiums?'

'Yes.'

'Why wouldn't he wear condominiums? Joel *always* wears condominiums.'

'You're going to think this is crazy, Ita.'

'Try me.'

'I told him I was pregnant.'

'You did *what*?'

'That way, he won't need to wear them, see? I showed him my fertility test. I told him it was a pregnancy test. That's all. That's why I can't concentrate. It's unprofessional of me, I know, and I apologise. Now, let's go back inside.'

'Wait, wait, wait!' Ita's eyes had widened into wide pools of incredulity. '*You actually told him you were pregnant?*'

Ellen shrugged. 'It's a bit of a black lie, I know, but it will only be for a few days, maybe even one day if I'm successful tonight.'

'*Holy Jesus, Ellen!* You must be desperate.'

Ellen crushed her cup and flicked it into the bin. 'I want a child. I couldn't let it go on any longer. And I know he wants one himself. He just doesn't realise it yet. He thinks he's not ready. Of course he's ready, he'd be a great father. He's funny and he's kind and he's—'

'At home all day.'

'That too.'

'How many days have you got?'

'Four, counting today.'

Ita blew out a big breath. 'Did you try this morning?'

'No, he went into minor shock.'

'Yeah,' said Ita, 'I think I know how he feels.'

'He'll be all right by this evening, when I get home. I know he will.' Ellen linked her arm into Ita's. 'Come on, let's go back to the rehearsal. I'll concentrate better.'

She led Ita down the corridor, careful to hide her tightly crossed fingers.

3

Joel stumbled out of the sound booth on the ground floor of Quaver Instruments, bathed in perspiration. His armpits were on the point of detonating and his face was a trickling estuary of sweat. But for the guy who invented eyebrows, his eyes would now be splashing around in their sockets. It would have helped, too, had there been oxygen in that germ-ridden sweat tub.

Despite this, Joel had spent a highly constructive hour in there, experimenting with different brands of saxophone with a view to possible purchase. The King Zephyr Special came out tops. It was a great vintage horn. Not up to his own Selmer by a long shot, but definitely pro standard. Smooth, balanced action. Nice tone. Adequate intonation differentials, at different extremes of volume. And at three grand, it was just the right price.

Joel advanced with trepidation to the wind section counter. Trading in his Golden Goddess was going to break Joel's heart, but in the aftermath of the shocking announcement, he had decided it would be the appropriate thing to do. Up till then, he'd put virtually nothing into their joint account. Now he would put in a few thousand.

'Hi, there,' said the friendly ponytailed assistant in his fifties, 'how did you get on?'

'I liked the Zephyr. I'm tempted to go for it, but, eh, any chance you'd do a trade-in deal?'

'Depends on what you're trading in, son.'

Joel picked his sax case off the floor and laid it on the glass counter top. 'High-quality flight case,' he said, unfastening the four clasps. He opened the lid and swivelled it round. 'Selmer, Mark VI, entirely gold-plated. Paris 1926. Slick action. Beautiful warm timbre. De luxe scroll engraving. Pearl touches on the octave and G♯ keys. Collector's item. Also, I'm throwing in a clip-on microphone and one of my Meyer mouthpieces – five star, with a large tip opening. Crook savers, end plugs . . .'

The assistant removed the Selmer with due reverence. 'This'd be worth a lot more than the Zephyr, you do know that?'

'Absolutely, that's the whole idea. I want to sell the Selmer and buy a less expensive one. Be great to know how much cash difference I'd get.'

'I'd have to show it to the man upstairs.'

'Sure thing.'

The assistant squinted at Joel now. 'You're a jazz man, aren't you? I heard you playing there, across the way.'

'Down to my toes.'

'You look familiar!' The guy smiled cautiously. 'I'm sure I've seen you perform around.'

'Yeah? It's possible you have all right.' It felt good to be recognised. 'Though I haven't been playing too many gigs lately. I've been sort of off the circuit in Dublin.'

'I know where I saw you.' The guy jabbed his finger towards Joel in recognition. 'It was in Prague last June, at the jazz festival. I'd remember your face anywhere. You were playing with that jazz pianist, weren't you? What's his . . .'

'You mean Monk Lavery?'

'Yeah, that's the man. Still playing with him?'

'Not really. He's always on at me to join his band. Asked me to play tomorrow night in the Sugar Club, as a matter of fact, but I don't really want to because he's . . . you know . . .'

'He's an A1 asshole.'

'Well, yes.' Joel chuckled. 'How did you know?'

'I had to have words with him, over there, in Prague.' The ponytail's eyes were squinting again, but this time they didn't look too friendly.

'Oh? Guess they weren't very nice words.'

The man leant across the counter. 'I brought my sixteen-year-old daughter with me, right? She went up to him after one of the gigs to get his autograph. He signed it for her . . .' – he inhaled a snort at this point – 'guess where?'

'On a postcard of Prague?'

'On the inside of her thigh.'

'Sorry to hear that.'

'And put down his hotel room number too, the bastard. You don't mind me calling him a bastard, do you?'

'No, not at all. I do it myself all the time.'

'Good for you.' He picked up the Selmer. 'I'll get you that quote.'

Ten minutes later the assistant returned. 'Five thousand tops. Five two if you buy the Zephyr.'

'*Five?* Is that all? But that would only leave me with two . . . I bought the Selmer in London for seven, only a few years ago. It's solid-gold plate. Sidney Bechet played it in Paris. It's a quality piece. I thought I could make four, minimum.'

The man looked disappointed. 'I'm sorry, my hands are tied. But if you want my opinion I'd say this is the best price you'll get in Dublin.'

Joel slumped back, severely disappointed.

'Is it for the money you're selling it?'

'Yeah. For my wife. Something's come up. I wanted to surprise her when she got back home tonight.'

The guy squinted at him, as if he was trying to grasp Joel's predicament. 'Why don't you go back to the place where you got it? If they know its history they might give you a better price. Where did you get it?'

'Saxophone Boutique, in London.'

'I know it. Wait there a second.' He went in behind and returned a few minutes later with a phone number written on a piece of paper. He handed it to Joel. 'Give them a buzz, you never know.'

Joel thanked him, went outside the shop and called the London store. He instantly recognised the sleepy American voice of Hal, the man who'd sold him the sax a few years back. Joel introduced himself, introduced his Selmer and asked him what kind of trade-in price he'd offer.

But Hal refused to be drawn. 'I'd have to see it first, buddy. Why not bring it over, I'll have a look. Hell, even if we don't trade it, I've got some good horn deals going.'

'You have?'

'Absolutely. Some fantastic prices for top-notch horns. We've got Yamahas, Selmers, Kings . . .'

'You wouln't happen to stock the King Zephyr Special?'

'I have a vintage King at the moment. The Super 20.'

'You actually have a Super 20?'

'Just came in yesterday. Played it for two hours myself last night. Beautiful horn.'

'How old is it?'

'I have serial number listings here, so I can locate the exact year for you, when you come over. Certainly a better horn than the Zephyr. It's a top-line tenor, in ninety per cent of its original laquer. Superbly styled. Art deco engraving. Beautiful, warm tone. Hard case included. Going a-begging for one nine hundred.'

'Is that all?'

'Unless you want to give me more.'

Joel was doing some calculations in his head. Even taking into account the sterling differential, the Super 20 was way cheaper than the Zephyr. He grilled Hal about the instrument. Sturdiness. Balance of the action. Precise dimensions of the tube and location of the eye for the sling hook. Whether construction was ribbed or post. Joel asked about leaking pads and clattering keys, about dents, rust and odours.

Five minutes later, Hal said he really had to go.

'Wait! I like what I'm hearing,' said Joel.

'Then get yourself over here on a plane, man! Could be gone tomorrow! Bring the Selmer with you and I'll have a look at it. We close late, if you want to come over today.'

'There's just one problem,' Joel said, excited. 'If you can't match the Dublin offer for my Selmer, then I'll have no money to buy your Super 20.'

'Well then, get someone to lend you the money and pay them

back when you sell your Selmer. I don't know, buddy. It's your dilemma.'

'But where am I going to get two thousand?' Joel halted suddenly, as if awoken by a sudden revelation.

4

Two hours later, Joel was on the catamaran to Holyhead, saxophone strapped to his back.

It was shortly after midday and he was standing on the small viewing balcony at the rear of the craft. As it slid through the harbour, he gazed at his beloved town and port, receding rapidly before his eyes. Tree-lined seafront, church spires and Victorian terraces. The Town Hall with its clock tower and the Pavilion apartment block where he and Ellen had lived for the past three years: it was showing up nicely in the brilliant midday sun.

After leaving Quaver Instruments, Joel had returned home in a mad panic and grabbed his passport. He'd gone to their local bank, emptied their joint account of its two grand and exchanged it into sterling. Because these were Ellen's own accumulated savings, Joel didn't want to tell her a thing. What was the point? It would only freak her out. And with a baby in her womb, the last thing he wanted to do was freak Ellen out. So he'd simply left a message on her voicemail, reassuring her that he had everything sorted, financially, and not to worry because everything was going to work out like a dream.

Joel filled his lungs with the blustery sea air and admired the mountainous background of the city, now diminishing in size. He was still in a bit of a daze from this morning's news. Who would have believed it would come to this? They were going to be a family, minimum three. A real, pop-up family with squawking, vomitation and Sunday afternoon walks with the stroller. He was going to be a real live daddy. God, this was serious stuff. More serious, possibly, than he could imagine.

It wasn't that Joel had a problem with babies per se. Babies were cute to look at and fun to be with. True, they set fire to carpets and destroyed antique furniture, but they were basically good company.

They just cost a lot.

The catamaran glided through the channel between the two lighthouses and took a sharp right turn. Joel looked over his shoulder. There was no one but him in the viewing area. Impulsively, he bent down and opened his saxophone case. It might be his last chance to play it. It was worth a blow. He quickly assembled the glittering treasure, moistened a reed and put it into his mouth. A melody came straight into his head: Elton John's 'Sacrifice'. Soon Joel was playing and improvising with all his heart.

As the Irish coastline slipped away into the hazy distance, however, Joel's performance was becoming complicated: a powerful wind was blowing in from the starboard side, making ghoulish whistling noises in the bell. Also, gusts of air were sweeping thin mists of sea spray on to the sax: not even *Monk* could corrode better than salt. Worst of all, Joel now had company, apart from the seagulls whom he was entertaining overhead: a group of inebriated teenagers, who were conducting a crazed, free-form dance in the small space behind him.

Hurriedly, Joel packed up and went inside. The central area was a mayhem of people and noise. He felt nervous carrying two thousand pounds on his person, so he chose to sit in the secluded Club Lounge at the top of the craft. He settled into a comfortable window seat opposite a neat-looking woman who was absorbed in an illustrated book about Irish monastic settlements. She looked up and smiled. Joel smiled back, then stared out of the window at the great expanse of turquoise sea. He inhaled a deep breath of air and, as he let his head fall back against the comfortable headrest, an unexpected gust of relief swept through his whole body.

Sacrifice, he decided, was the wrong word. Nothing he could do to make Ellen happy would ever be a sacrifice.

11

5

'I didn't order that.'

Joel was pointing at a glass of champagne, which a waiter had just placed on the table in front of him.

'It's complimentary,' replied the waiter.

'You're saying I can . . .?'

'You can drink it, yes.'

Parched with thirst, Joel guzzled down the sparkly liquid so fast it practically exploded in his gullet. He replaced it on the waiter's tray, belched discreetly, then sank his jaw into his palm and stared out at the sea porridge.

'There's a charge of seventeen Euros, sir.'

Joel frowned. 'I thought you said the bubbly was free?'

'I meant, the charge for the Club Lounge.'

When it was explained to Joel that he was presently seated in the prime executive lounge, he groaned in acknowledgement, unzipped his jacket pocket and pulled out his wad of banknotes – discreetly, because he sensed he was being examined by the woman opposite. He gave the waiter a fifty, then re-zipped the banknotes.

The waiter soon returned with his change, which Joel stuffed in his trouser pocket for convenience. 'Can you bring me another complimentary glass of champagne, please?'

'I'm afraid it's not complimentary, sir.'

'You just said it was!'

'Only the first glass is.'

'Oh, right.'

'You're welcome to have mine,' said the woman opposite, when the man had gone. 'I'm not drinking it.'

Joel hesitated.

'Go ahead. It'll only be thrown out. Into the sea or somewhere.' She pushed her glass towards him. She was a friendly woman of over forty, with a slightly swollen but pleasant face and almost non-existent eyebrows.

He thanked her, then slugged back that glass too.

'Is that a musical instrument?' she asked.

'A saxophone.'

'Very good. I play keyboards myself.'

Joel was instantly aroused. *'Really?* Roland? Yamaha?'

'Nothing like that.' She laughed. 'No, I play the organ.'

'You mean, like, in a church?' Joel felt himself deflate.

'Yes, and also in our small convent chapel.'

'You live in a convent?'

She nodded and smiled. 'I'm a nun.'

Joel was perplexed. 'I'd never have guessed.'

'We don't tend to wear the habits any more when we're out in public. Sister Boniface.'

'Joel.' He shook her hand.

'Have you been playing long?'

'Since I was twelve.'

Once on to the subject of his saxophone, Joel couldn't be stopped. He told the nun how, when he was thirteen, he'd heard the tenor saxophonist Joe Lovano play in Paris. Joel was with his father, who was making vain attempts to break into the French snackfood market. The gig was a source of supreme inspiration to Joel, although his father was sorry he hadn't attended a string quartet recital in the Place des Vosges instead. Seeing Joel's interest in music, however, Henry bought him a clarinet on the rue St-Jacques, insisting that a training in classical music would be an 'ideal way of imparting the novel notion of discipline'.

Joel flunked every clarinet grade in sight, in the hope that his father would buy him a sax. In the end, he managed to palaver his old man into it, informing him that the school band required a tenor sax player. It was a complete fabrication, as was Joel's implication that the school had a brass band in the first place.

His old man was delighted at the idea of band practice, because he felt Joel needed to become a 'team player'. So he bought him a crappy second-hand saxophone for a miserly sum and, for the rest of his teens, Joel spent hours per day in the eggbox-insulated garden shed in Sandycove, practising on this heap of junk on which he was basing his entire future. He spent so much time transcribing and emulating old recordings by such sax greats as

Coltrane, Hawkins and Coleman that it wasn't too long before he was gigging with reputed geriatrics. Then, at twenty-three, he purchased the Selmer with money unexpectedly inherited from an aunt.

The nun was smiling approvingly when Joel concluded his tale. 'It teaches you one thing, Joel, doesn't it?'

'What's that?'

'The importance of nurturing and fostering one's inner vocation.'

The nun now told him a bit about herself and her order in Ireland. She said she was on a fundraising expedition to the head of her order in Devon, to renovate their chapel. Joel said he was on a fundraising expedition of his own. He told her he was heading to London in the hope of trading in his sax. 'Money will be tight,' he explained, 'now that there's going to be an addition to the house.'

'You're having an extension done?'

'We're having a baby.'

The nun was shaking her head earnestly. 'I think what you're doing is exemplary. Selling your saxophone like that, to help with raising your family.'

'You think so?'

'In today's world, I can tell you there aren't many people who would do a thing like that.'

Joel had to admit it hadn't been easy, going into Quaver Instruments that morning. Once upon a time, if he'd had to choose between parting with his saxophone and parting with his right hand, he'd have lobbed off the hand. 'Well.' He shrugged philosophically. 'I suppose priorities are priorities.'

'Is it your first child?'

'Yes. Ellen's wanted one for a long time. I didn't necessarily make it easy for her. I was hoping to make it in the music business first.'

'Lord, you can never tell what's around the corner.'

'Indeed you can't.'

'I'm sure you'll be very happy.'

'I have a gut feeling it's all going to work out. Oh, God!'

'What?' She looked concerned.

'I've just remembered – Ellen didn't want me telling anyone.'

The nun smiled. 'Don't worry, you can trust me.'

6

Ellen stared in through the shop window. It was lunchtime and there were quite a few people inside. She scanned left and right, but could see no one she recognised. So she went in.

To drown out the muzak in the store, Ellen upped the ear volume of Chopin's 'Tristesse', which she was studying in advance of her upcoming recital. Since it was her first time in the store, she did a general sightseeing tour of the clothing area, stopping at this rack and that. There were lovely red pinafore dresses, tiny stretch suits and cardigans. Pretty nighties and sleepsuits. Sunhats and tiny shoes in red, yellow and blue. Cute miniature gloves. Ellen checked the price labels. As expected, they weren't cheap.

At the far end of the store was a vast array of mobile equipment. Swinging cribs, baby gyms and techno strollers. Winnie the Pooh baby baths, baby feeders and snugglies. Cribs, carriages and pushchairs. Door bouncers and car seats.

She stopped at a row of prams and examined a so-called travel system – a pushchair which doubled as a car seat and tripled as a rocker. For babies up to nine months. A money saver, according to the promotion, but at 380 Euros, Ellen might have chosen an alternative description.

Ellen felt a hand on her shoulder. She swung round and was mortified to behold Imelda, a slightly nosy colleague from the Conservatory who specialised in teaching singing and spreading gossip. 'You gave me a fright!' she said. '*What?* Hold on a second . . .' She turned off her Walkman.

'. . . didn't know you were having a baby!' Imelda said.

'I am,' Ellen blurted. 'I mean . . .'

'When are you due?'

'What I mean is,' Ellen began, tongue-tied, 'I *hope* I am.'

'I'm sure you are!' said Imelda encouragingly. 'I'm sure it'll go fine!'

'No, what I mean is, I'm *not* pregnant.'

15

'Oh.' Imelda looked disappointed. 'You aren't?'

'No, but . . . we'll see.'

'Perseverence.'

Ellen pointed at the equipment. 'I just came in to see what they had. Three hundred and eighty for this techno stroller. Can you believe it?'

'You should ask behind the desk – sometimes they have damaged goods at a reduced rate.'

'I think I'd rather stick with what works.'

'How is your husband?'

'Joel? He's wonderful.'

'Still playing the saxophone?' It was the way she said it.

'Doing really well,' Ellen replied, smiling defiantly. 'He's doing a lot of recording these days.' It was a stock response.

'Well, as long as he can earn something from it.'

'He's earning a fortune. He's paying the mortgage now. I'm delighted.'

Imelda didn't seem too pleased to hear this, so she left the shop. Ellen waited five minutes and, when it was safe to do so, she approached the desk and asked a girl about any slightly damaged equipment that might be available. The girl listed a few articles. One that grabbed Ellen's attention was a combination carriage-stroller, for babies from birth. It reclined fully, so that it could be used as a cot. Downside was that the shopping tray at the base was missing, and the material was slightly grazed.

'How much?'

'I'd have to talk to the manager, but I'd say at least two hundred.'

'How much would it be new?'

'They're selling for four hundred.'

Ellen sprang. 'Can I see it?'

The girl brought it out. It was light blue, with horizontal pink stripes. The hood was a little frayed, but it was in good condition otherwise – apart from the missing tray. Ellen was eager. She asked to see the manager. She informed the young guy that without the tray, the article was practically worthless. She added a good deal of charm to her practical arguments and the manager

16

eventually caved in. Ellen knocked him down to less than half-price. He took her name and number, and promised to hold it for her.

She left the shop, poker-faced, feeling like she'd just ripped him off. She was delighted. Strictly speaking, she didn't yet need the pram but with the state of their finances, they were going to need every bargain they could find. She turned her phone back on. There was a rushed message from Joel.

Ellen? It's me – Joel. Em, you know what we were talking about this morning? I just want to let you know that I have everything sorted, okay? I'll tell you about it when I get back this evening. How are you feeling? Love you. Bye!

She pressed 'off'. Joel was upbeat, despite everything.
Hallelujah!
Ellen walked down Grafton Street, her guilt evaporating in the sunshine.

7

'What would you prefer?' Sister Boniface asked, as they drove down the ramp of the catamaran into the sunny port of Holyhead.
'Well, generally I prefer to have it off in the car.'
'Really?'
'Provided it's not too cold.'
'I was hoping you wouldn't say that: I get cold so easily.'
'Oh, in that case, turn it on. No probs.'
'You don't mind?'
'I'm just grateful for the lift.'
She switched the heat on full, then smiled. 'If it gets too warm, just take off your jacket and fling it into the back.'
Because Joel's armpits felt like they were about to enter melt-down stage, he removed his leather jacket and flung it over the saxophone case in the back seat. He might be roasting, but he wasn't about to complain. The ride to London was manna from

heaven. Maybe it was true what they said: when you put yourself out for other people, good fortune invariably boomeranged your way. Joel had put himself out for Ellen, and now this lovely nun was actually going to drop him off at the Saxophone Boutique in London, saving him both time and money. He was damn grateful to have met her. She was living proof that goodness still stalked the land.

'How will you be travelling back to Dublin?' she asked.

'There's a flight from Gatwick at eleven this evening.'

'That won't leave you much time to buy your new saxophone.'

'If I have to, I'll call Ellen and fly back home tomorrow. And you know what? If I get lucky, I might even travel business class.'

'Oh, Lord!' she shrieked out loud, hand to mouth.

'What's the matter?'

'*Water!*' she cried. 'I forgot water!'

'Does the gauge say you're out?'

'No, I mean mineral water, to drink. I always have some with me in the car, for the journey.' She looked a bit annoyed with herself. 'Would you mind awfully if I went back for some?'

She performed a surprisingly dangerous U-turn in the middle of the road – for a nun – and she sped back towards the town. A few minutes later Joel spotted a supermarket. They managed to find a place to pull in, three streets down.

She parked in front of an advancing green road sweeper. 'He probably won't want me stopping here,' she fretted.

'Don't worry, Sister,' Joel assured her. 'I'll hold the fort.'

She gave him a strange, wild-eyed look. 'You wouldn't mind awfully popping in for me? For two small bottles?'

Joel hesitated for some reason.

'In case he makes me move the car,' she explained, her face red. 'Here, I'll give you a fiver.'

'Forget it,' said Joel, stretching over to his jacket in the back seat. 'I'm loaded.' He undid the zipper to get at his money wad.

'I insist!' She poked a fiver into his palm. 'Please take this.'

He stared at the grimy note. It felt odd, taking money from a stranger, but then, nuns could hardly be classified as strangers. They prayed for your soul, for God's sake. 'Are you sure?'

'Put your jacket back. This is my call.'

18

'Fair enough,' he said. He re-zipped his jacket, flung it back and hopped out.

'Take your time,' she called.

Joel jaunted round the corner and walked towards the super-market, whistling 'On the Sunny Side of the Street'. Though only a few short hours had elapsed since Ellen's shock announcement that morning, Joel felt he was already well on the way to rec-overing. He went into the medium-sized shop and located two bottles of mineral water from a nearby refrigerator. He went towards the checkout, but halted when he saw a rack full of chocolate bars. He feasted his eyes on the heavenly offerings. Dairy Milk, Fruit and Nut, Yorkie Bar . . . Or he could be the purist and go for the jugular: dark Bournville. Or the heretic and dabble in a Crunchie, a Mars bar or a Turkish Delight.

Dilemmas.

He ended up purchasing an oversize bar of Bournville, a coffee and five packets of spearmint Wrigley's – as well as the mineral water. Outside, he sank in his teeth, rinsing it down with delicious coffee. Instantly reinvigorated, Joel proceeded towards the car, biting and sipping at a fairly advanced rate of compulsiveness.

When Joel reached the third left turn, he spotted the bright-green road sweeper. But where was the red saloon? He carefully scanned the road, his stomach turning. His saxophone and his money were in that car! Where the hell was it? Joel watched the sweeper progress slowly along the road.

Hold on, you thick eejit.

The council worker must have shifted his sweeper on to a different road, obviously, stupid. Joel backtracked, then forward-tracked, checking five left turns in succession. But he couldn't spot the red saloon. Joel crossed the road and checked the first four lefts. No luck. He crossed back over again and checked three succeeding lefts, just in case, but had no luck. This brought him back to the supermarket.

By now, Joel was in a seriously paranoid state. He gasped his way back to the original third-left street and ran up to the straw-haired council worker, who was guiding his sweeper gently along. 'Excuse me,' he croaked, out of breath, 'can you tell me which was the last road you were sweeping on?'

19

'This is my first one, lad. Just started my shift.'

Joel was now on a full-scale panic alert. 'Did you see a red saloon? It had a roof rack. Woman driver.' He pointed to the spot where he thought the car had been parked.

The man grinned humourlessly in recognition. 'Oh, yes. Friend of yours, was she?'

'No, no. I don't know her at all.'

'Good for you.' He continued sweeping.

'Did you see her?' Joel shouted, exasperated. 'Where did she go?'

'Around the bend, as far as I could make out.'

'Which bend?'

The sweeper brought the machine impatiently to a halt. 'As soon as I went near her, she accelerated and tried to run me over. Sped off like a maniac.' He flicked his arm up in the direction of the main road.

Joel felt warm coffee drain over one of his feet. The sweeper was shouting something at him about litter, but the words were a blur. Dazed, he walked to the corner and looked up and down the street, but he saw no red saloon. He staggered against a wall and slid uselessly into the concrete, lowering his head into his hands. When he looked up again, he noticed a uniformed man ambling in the opposite direction. 'Officer!' he shouted. '*Please!*'

The man turned.

Joel struggled to his feet. 'Officer, Officer, something's happened, someone's stolen my sax! A woman – a nun, my money, she gave me a lift from . . .'

'I can't hear a word of what you're saying,' said the man. 'Start again.'

'She's got my saxophone! And my money, my jacket, my . . .'

'What are you saying about a saxophone?'

'I've just been robbed.'

'You were robbed?'

'Yes. She took all my stuff.'

'So, what are you telling *me* for?'

'Pardon?'

'What do you want me to do about it?'

'You're a policeman, aren't you?'

The man laughed, as if he found the situation extremely

amusing. 'I'm a traffic warden,' he said, pointing to his uniform markings. 'See? Police station's up the town.'

Joel started running.

'Hello, there!'

Joel stopped.

'It's back that way.' He was pointing.

Ten minutes later Joel located the police station. He was taken into a room, where a kindly policewoman gave him some Kleenex tissues and offered him a cup of sweet tea for aftershock. He said no, thanks, and proceeded to narrate his gruelling experience. All details were written down, at a pace Joel regarded as criminally slow. Name, address and contact number. Amount of cash stolen. Serial number of the saxophone and other specifications. He was asked if the instrument was insured and replied – his wretchedness quadrupling in seconds – that he'd let it lapse due to financial concerns. Finally he gave a detailed description of the car and the vicious thief who, in the diabolical pose of a nun, had so casually suckered him out of his livelihood.

Because he was in such a wretched psychological slump, the policewoman returned him to the catamaran terminal in a police car. Joel purchased a one-way ticket with his remaining funds and returned to the same viewing gallery at the rear of the craft where he had stood only two hours earlier with his saxophone. He clutched the bar and stared at the hilly town of Holyhead, now bathed in an early evening sunglow, almost as golden as his treasured Selmer.

Soon his face began reverberating to the rumble of the loud engines. The catamaran slid out of port and he gazed at the receding town in a trance of disbelief, each passing second a coffin nail hammered into his weary soul.

Joel tried desperately to piece together the enormity of what had just happened to him, but he wasn't able to. All he could think about was that evil demon masquerading as a nun, speeding down the M1 to London with his valuables in the back of her car, cackling aloud in a mad revelry of laughter.

8

When he shuffled out of Dun Laoghaire catamaran terminal at nine o'clock that evening, he had no problem piecing it together.

He'd ballsed up big time.

Joel stood outside the sliding doors, staring at the huge rain pellets which shot up the paving in front of him like firecrackers. Over the tops of the wind-buffeted trees stood the straight, pale mass of the Pavilion. The bay window of their sixth-floor apartment was illuminated yellow. Ellen was at home, where warmth and love awaited him.

But Joel could not face her. Sure, she was kind and understanding enough to forgive him. But in the circumstances, it struck Joel as outrageous even to consider the concept of forgiveness. She must never know what happened to her nest egg. She would be devastated if she found out, and it would be unthinkable to upset her at a time like this. Sure, she'd find out the next time she went to make a deposit in the joint account but that wouldn't be until she next got paid.

The thought that Joel had little over a week to come up with a way of replacing the money left him cold. He had agonised over his options on the catamaran on his way home and he had come to the conclusion that he had precisely one and one alone. Awful as it seemed, Joel's only hope was an A1 asshole.

He ran up Marine Road into the waves of rain and arrived at Monk's place in Crosthwaite Park eight minutes later. He was breathless and soaked. He entered the open gateway and walked up to the two-storey Victorian terrace. To the left was the wooden stairway to Monk's basement quarters. Joel looked downwards.

Monk was standing in the doorway, his mouth was locked in tongue-sushi with a woman with a feather boa and he was massaging her behind with a free hand. Joel waved to attract his attention. While Monk's tongue was still stuck in the woman's mouth, he eyeballed Joel through a weirdly enlarged eye, pulled his hand off her behind and poked him the stiff-finger salute.

Joel removed himself, as requested, ascended the few steps to the main front door and rang the bell. Moments later, the heavy red oak door opened to reveal Monk's mother, a tall, elegant, ghost-worn lady in her sixties. Her sad face broke into a wrinkled smile.

'Hello, Mrs Lavery.'

She looked confused. 'Mrs Lavery? Who's Mrs Lavery?'

Joel stared at her closely, then lowered his eyes respectfully. He had no idea she'd gone this way. How well she'd concealed the onset. It was just too bad. He scratched his soaked head. 'Em . . . *you* are Mrs Lavery.'

She addressed him in a controlled, well-spoken voice: 'I think I asked you to call me by my first name, Joel, didn't I? Or am I forgetting myself?'

He reddened. 'Yes, of course. Hello – Miranda.'

'That's the one!' she said, her face cracking into a warm smile. 'Come in. Come in out of the rain. You'll catch your death.'

Joel wiped his soggy shoes on the doormat and stepped into the hallway. 'I just popped up to see Monk.'

She squinted down at him.

'I mean Myles, that is.'

'I'm afraid I can never accept that silly nickname. I don't know why he uses it, at all. I gave him a perfectly good one twenty-six years ago. He was getting along with it fine until he went to college.' She closed the door behind him.

'It's after Thelonious Monk, the jazz pianist.'

'Yes, I know.' She didn't sound impressed. 'I'm sure I heard him down there earlier.'

'He *is* down there. He's outside his door with . . .' Joel hesitated.

Miranda raised a sarcastic eyebrow. 'It's all right; he probably doesn't know her name either.' She led Joel through the warm hallway and opened the interconnecting door to the basement. Light bebop piano sounds emanated from below. She shivered at the draft and folded her arms tight against her thin frame. 'You should call up more often, love. You're a good influence on him. I remember when you used to call up, when the pair of you were back in school. It was always nice having you around. And then you stopped coming. You were a good influence on him, a normalising presence. Still are, of course. Just a normal, ordinary person. Thank goodness. Not like some of the other types he has around.'

Joel descended the cold, bare stairs, slightly disconcerted by her compliment. When he reached the basement passage he knocked on the door of Monk's quarters: three short, nervous taps. The piano stopped.

'One moment,' came the voice from inside. Footsteps approached. 'It's all right, Mother,' he said. 'His tray is clean. You can go back upstairs.'

'It's me, Monk. Joel!'

There was a lull. The door opened and an irritated-looking Monk appeared in a dark-green jacket and purple shirt. 'How did you get in?' he snapped.

'I let him in from up above,' Miranda cut in from the stair top, 'because he was too considerate to disturb you outside. And I cleaned Rufus's cage while you were out, so there won't be any doodle for you to be upset over.'

Monk closed his eyes and flexed his jaw. 'In!' he spat, poking an uncivil thumb backwards.

Joel went through the darkened rear room and into the front, but didn't get much further than the connecting doorway.

'*Stop!*' Monk shouted, shoving up a hand. 'Don't move!'

'What? What's wrong?'

Monk grabbed a towel from the floor by the futon and flung it at him. 'You're dripping on my carpet,' he said. 'Stand on that.'

'Oh, for chrissakes.'

'*Stand on it!*'

Reluctantly, Joel spread the towel on the floor and stepped on top. There was a screech behind him. It was Rufus, Monk's resident parrot. The orange-tailed and slate-coloured African grey was clutching a wooden perch on top of the piano, his beady eyes glaring at Joel with masterful disdain.

Monk sat at his piano and began playing tonal chords. He looked sour. 'I might as well make something clear to you now, O'Leary.' He smashed a minor chord into the piano. 'Just because I've been asking you to join my band, doesn't mean you can just

24

drop in without warning me first. That's the type of cheekiness I won't stand for.'

'Well, I'm sorry about that, Monk. Next time I'll send a telegram, I promise.'

'Don't act the smartass with me.'

'I had to come up. Because I want to tell you . . . I'm prepared to join your band.'

Monk's fingers came to an immediate standstill.

'But on one condition,' Joel added, clearing his throat. 'I need to be paid up front. An advance for six months' work. That should equal about four thousand, but I'm willing to settle for two. That's half the sum you'd normally have to pay me. You'd be saving a whole two grand. It's a great deal for you, Monk, and the only reason I'm offering it is that I need to turn over some money fast.'

A curious look came over Monk's face. He raised his eyebrows to Rufus. 'Pay you in advance?'

'Two thousand, cash or cheque. Excellent deal. For both of us.'

'Really?' Monk mulled over this, as if he were secretly intrigued by Joel's unexpected offer. 'And I suppose it will be an excellent deal if your fingers suddenly get horribly mutilated in an accident or you go deaf jerking off, or you develop Parkinson's disease. What do I do then? I'd be a bit stuck then, wouldn't I? But you wouldn't think of that, would you? Oh no. Too bloody selfish.'

'Monk. My sax was stolen today.'

The smile vanished. 'What?'

'I was in Holyhead and it was stolen. It was taken along with all my money.'

'Your saxophone?' Monk responded through gritted teeth. 'And what the hell are you going to play with tomorrow night in the Sugar Club, then?'

Joel shrugged.

'For chrissakes, O'Leary,' bit Monk, squeezing his forehead. 'Telling me you want to join my band and you don't even have a bloody sax to play with. Are you trying to make a fool of me, or something?'

'No, Monk, but just to get back to what I was saying, if two grand is too much to pay me all at once, I could always take

25

the payment in two instalments, over a period of . . . I don't know . . . say, a fortnight? That wouldn't be a problem.'

Monk was shaking his head. 'I don't know which I should admire more, O'Leary, your neck or your stupidity. Can you get a replacement sax for tomorrow night?'

'No.'

'Surely you know someone who can lend you one.'

'No.'

'Gobshite.' Monk stood up and strode around the room, fondling his jaw, then halted and clicked his fingers. 'Wait a second! I think I know where I might get one.' He put an arm round Joel's shoulders in comradely fashion. 'Come with me.'

He ushered Joel into the rear room and opened the door. He led him out into the cold passageway, then guided him to the front of the basement. He opened the door. 'After you,' he said respectfully.

Joel stepped outside, though it was bucketing down out of the heavens. He waited for his host to follow, but Monk didn't budge from the doorstep.

'I'll see if I can get one from McCoy. If I do, I'll call you tomorrow to let you know. All right? The gig's at nine o'clock. I expect you to turn up on time. And for God's sake, try to look presentable.' Monk stepped back into the hallway, glancing disdainfully at the rain sprinkles on his tips of his shoes.

'But, Monk, what about the money we were talking about? What about the two grand? I need two . . .'

Slam!

Joel jumped back as the door banged in his face. He stood staring at the wet wood, fuming.

Then, getting ever more drenched, he plodded back up the steps and trudged his way homewards.

9

Joel squashed his soaked ear to the front door of his apartment and listened.

There was no sound from inside: Ellen was in bed asleep. He crept into the dark hall, stifling the latest in a succession of sneezes. Their bedroom door at the end of the long passageway was closed. Joel tiptoed into the kitchen, stripped naked and emptied his pockets on to the table. He stuffed his wet clothes into the tumble-dryer and turned it on to twenty minutes. A red Christmas tablecloth was grabbed from a drawer and wrapped round his waist.

Joel collapsed at the kitchen table and stared blindly at the remains of Ellen's nest egg – a crisp tenner perched in the middle of the table like a chaise longue. As he stared at the note, Joel struggled to comprehend the size of the bonfire into which he'd just chucked himself. When he succeeded in doing so, he sank his face into his hands and moaned.

The calamity was total: Joel had exterminated every penny of savings Ellen had in the world and happily handed over his priceless Selmer to a crook. This was fuck-uppery on an unforeseenly vast scale, of which not even the word 'gross' adequately described the extent.

'Two thousand Euros,' he whispered in disbelief. 'And we're going to have a baby!'

Joel left the kitchen, driven to distraction by the revolving cycle of the tumble-dryer. He stood at the bay window in the lounge, peering through the rainy dots on the glass.

The canvas of black night and sea was adorned by a glistening necklace of orange, tracing a wide arc round Dublin Bay. A chain of white lights travelled up to the top of the east pier, where a beacon flashed green against the pitch-dark background of the sea. The lighthouse at Howth flickered just once and a low plane approached from the east, headlights beaming like those of a car.

Below him lay the catamaran terminal, empty and silent. Joel peered over towards Sandycove, its Martello tower a bright yellow stud against the night. Down the road from the tower was his father's residence. It was quite clear. Joel's back was so well and truly glued to the wall that he had no choice but to go to his old man and beg. It was going to be difficult, though. His father was the biggest tightwad in town.

Joel ran back into the kitchen as soon as the tumble-dryer buzzer sounded. He pulled the clothes from the machine and threw them on the table. He was separating them out from each other when he heard the door handle squeak. He swung round, his heart beating like the clappers. The door opened and it was Ellen, wearing a sexy silk negligée he hadn't seen in months. 'What are you doing in that tablecloth?'

'I was just drying my clothes.'

'Your hair is all wet.' She retrieved a hand towel from the drawer and started rubbing it through his hair. 'Where were you all evening? I thought you'd be home when I came in.' She pulled the towel round the back of his head and drew him in close to her.

Joel pressed his face on to her shoulder, trying hard not to become emotional. 'I was just . . . wandering around. Thinking about things.'

She pulled back, concerned. 'Joel, there's no need for you to be getting upset about what I told you this morning. Wandering outside in the rain isn't going to help things.'

'I'm not upset about that. I was actually getting used to it. I was thinking, hey, I'm going to be a father. I'm going to be able to support my child. This is okay!'

'It's the money, then? You're still worried about the money?'

He lowered his eyes. 'A little.'

'But you left a message this morning saying you had everything sorted.'

'I did?'

'You sounded really upbeat.'

'I *do* have everything sorted,' Joel insisted. 'At least, I *will* have everything sorted. I *will* get some money together.'

That, brooded Joel, would be a bloody miracle.

'I know you will.' Ellen's voice was kind. 'Even if you can't find anything for a while, it won't be the end of the world. The important thing is you're happy. In the end, that's what matters most. I didn't mean to upset you, telling you that this morning.'

Joel shook his head, feeling a little better for her comforting words.

'And anyway,' she added, trying to coax him into a smile, 'we still have our nest egg to fall back on, remember?'

A singularly attractive option occurred to Joel at that precise instant: would it not make utterly excellent sense for him to go to the balcony and chuck himself six floors over the edge? Instead, he pulled away from her, picked up his boxers and tried to put them on underneath the tablecloth, seaside style.

'You're not getting dressed again! Come to bed, Joel, you look bunched!' She led him by the hand to their bedroom. The room was in complete darkness, so Joel feelered his way over to the left side of the bed and dropped the tablecloth to his ankles. He rooted underneath his pillow. 'Where are my pyjamas?'

'Never mind about them,' she replied, making swishing sounds as she slipped under the duvet. 'Get in the way you are.'

'But I'm not wearing anything.'

'Neither am I.'

It was the way she said it: a whispered, erotic invitation for them both to spend a short amount of time together, getting hotly laid. It wasn't that Joel didn't want to get hotly laid. He did. It was all he wanted to do, right then: forget all about his mind-bending grief. But after all that had happened, he wasn't entirely sure he could get it up.

'I thought you were wearing your nightdress,' he muttered.

'I've taken it off,' she whispered in a very appealing voice. 'And you don't have to wear anything, either.'

'I'm not.'

'I mean, you don't have to wear your Durex.' She grabbed his hand, pulled him into bed beside her naked body and began kissing him. 'You know, I've never felt you properly inside me before, Joel.' She gripped his personal column. 'And I'd like to, now.'

'Ellen, I don't know if I can tonight. It's just that . . . I'm bunched.'

'That hasn't stopped you before.'

'Won't you be tired for your rehearsal tomorrow?'

She raised her head. 'You're very tense, love. Try to relax.'

'I really don't know if I can.'

'Try.'

But Joel couldn't relax. He was gripped by a combination of such crushing fear and guilt that he probably couldn't have got it up for Ellen had he been King Dong himself. When Ellen realised this she stroked his face. 'Some other time, then?'

'It's not you, Ellen, it's just . . .'

'I still find you very sexy.' She kissed him on the forehead. 'Do you know that?'

'Whatever.'

'You're the best husband a woman could have.'

'I wish I could believe it.'

10

Monk was sitting up in the futon, a Dutch Agio hanging from his mouth.

It was three in the morning and the butt of his cigarillo shone like a tiny orange beacon in the darkened room. Rufus was fast asleep under his cover, like the rest of the world above.

A beautiful peace and quiet would have reigned, but for one thing, which was now pissing Monk off big time: the persistent whining complaints of the girl lying in the futon beside him, punctuated by the occasional grotesque nostril-clearing snort. She'd been complaining and snorting since they'd had it off an hour ago, and Monk was considering getting the hell out of there and spending the night in one of his mother's spare rooms upstairs.

'I won't stop until you tell me,' she droned on.

He glanced down at the girl, the whites of whose eyes gleamed in the dim light that filtered through the curtains. He shook his head and took another drag of his cigarillo. Was she ever going to shut up?

'It was just a lie, wasn't it?'

'Look,' Monk said, exasperated. 'I told you I'd give you an audition and I was true to my word.'

'You lied to me. Just to get me into bed. I know you did. There were never any auditions.'

'That's not true,' he said, impressed at how quickly she'd

figured out how to use her brain. He stretched across her and grabbed the ashtray from the bedside locker. 'As a matter of fact, I saw a woman this evening, just before you came.'

The girl perked up a little and turned her face from the pillow into his hairy armpit. 'Who?'

'A short lady with a feather boa. Can't remember her name. Met her earlier in Temple Bar.' He sat back and put the ashtray on his belly, reflecting on events earlier that evening.

'Was she any good?' the girl wondered.

'Her oral technique was interesting, now that you mention it. Her mouth impressed me and also her tongue. You see, it's all about the size of the buccal cavity, I've told you that before. The larger the better. You have to know how to use it, of course.'

'How did she use hers?' she asked, looking concerned.

Monk shot up his eyebrows. 'Like a seasoned pro. Definitely very experienced.'

'You're going to give her the position instead, aren't you?'

'No, I don't think so.' He flicked ash into the ashtray. It would be folly, he decided, to tell her that there'd never been a vacancy for lead singer in the Leading Frights in the first place. 'Her mouth had one serious flaw. I got the distinct impression it'd turn out to be the type of mouth that wouldn't shut up harassing me with stupid, repetitive questions, that would refuse to give me a bit of peace and quiet, even in my own bed, when all I want in the world is just to smoke my cigarillo in peace.' Monk peered directly into the girl's glistening eyes. 'And that's the sort of mouth I could never work with. Do you understand?' He slipped his long legs from the futon.

'Then let me be the lead singer,' she insisted. 'Let me sing tomorrow night at the Sugar Club.'

'Look,' said Monk, astonished at her continuing display of blind stupidity. 'I'm going upstairs.' He got off the futon and grabbed his silk robe from the coffee table. 'Don't follow me up. Don't call me. Don't make any noise, all right? We don't want to wake Mother up.' He probed his way towards the door. 'She might decide to cause a scene.'

The girl huffed her face back into the pillow and Monk left the room.

He walked up the darkened wooden stairs to his mother's abode, barefoot and silent, so as not to disturb her, sleeping above. Entering through the doorway of the moonlit kitchen, he jumped. At the far end of the table he thought he could make out the form of a person, sitting deadly still. But he wasn't sure. He swished his hand against the wall, to locate the light switch.

'Leave it off, please.'

Monk jumped, instantly regretting he'd come up. 'Are you long up?'

'I didn't go to bed.'

'Oh.' When his eyes became accustomed to the dark, his mother came more clearly into focus. She looked wretched in the moonlight, which heightened the creases in her face. Her vexed expression said it all: migraine.

He moved quickly to the cupboard to get a glass.

'Is there something the matter with your friend?'

Monk grimaced. Clearly, she'd overheard the pubescent rant earlier on. The whiner in the futon downstairs had spent five minutes around midnight giving out at full volume about her college lecturers, her wealthy father and the impossibility of finding a decent band to gig with. To try to shut her up, he'd been driven to sticking his tongue into her mouth, but obviously not for long enough.

Monk poured out a glass of lemonade and loaded a plate with digestive biscuits.

'I sensed something was wrong, earlier,' she said. 'Did something happen?'

Monk sighed into his glass of lemonade and moved towards the door.

'He seemed very badly out of sorts.'

'*He?*'

'I didn't want to ask him. He was too upset-looking.'

Monk was confused. 'Who?'

'Your friend, Joel.'

'Oh, *him*.' Monk sagged.

'Did something happen to him?'

He shrugged. 'I don't know.'

'You wouldn't think to ask? Couldn't you see the way he was?'

He shrugged again.

'He looked like he was having a nervous breakdown.'

'Someone stole his saxophone, apparently.'

'Oh, dear.' His mother sounded concerned. 'And he never said anything.'

Monk opened the door. 'Better go back down.'

'Poor Joel. Where did it happen?'

'I didn't get the details,' he said.

'You didn't ask him?'

'No.' He left the kitchen.

'Wait!'

Monk popped his head back in. 'What is it?'

'Why don't you have your biscuits up here? If you go back down you might wake that girl up. And I'll probably have to listen to all that whingeing and moaning again.'

He delayed at the entrance.

'You'll have to forgive me, Myles, but I find it so depressing to have to listen to it.' She rose and went to the cabinet to remove a glass, speaking as she did so. 'People like that are so horribly self-indulgent, not caring who might hear.' She took juice from the fridge and poured it out. 'She doesn't know how lucky she is. Did she tell you that her father has just bought himself a yacht? I mean, a big one.'

Monk flexed his mouth. How could his mother *possibly* know who he had in his futon downstairs?

'Tinted glass. All covered. He has it moored in the marina. I saw it yesterday. We were all looking at it.' She sat back down and sipped her juice. 'My head is easing, I think. I really should eat something. Hand me one of those.'

He held out the plate, disgruntled.

'I was speaking to Lizzie today on the phone,' she said, taking a biscuit.

'*Lizzie?* Do I know a Lizzie?' Monk scaled through the mental-ised entries of women in his address book. He couldn't place a Lizzie, though.

'Your aunt in Australia,' said his mother.

'Oh.' He sipped his lemonade.

'Stephen is getting married.'

33

'Who's Stephen?'

'Your cousin.'

'Oh, really? How interesting.'

'In September. To a girl from Howth.'

'I'll make sure to send him a sympathy card.'

'Why do you have to make a joke about it?' she said. 'I didn't tell you so you could make a joke of it.'

'I wasn't making a joke, but you're right: I won't send him a sympathy card. He doesn't deserve any sympathy.' He drank down the rest of the lemonade in one.

Miranda returned her unbitten biscuit to the plate. 'Why do you always say those things, Myles?'

It was time to go.

'You don't know what you're talking about,' she continued. 'Degrading marriage like that. You've never even fallen in love. Have you?'

'Goodnight, Mother.'

'That's right, run away. Don't dare face the truth whatever you do.'

'Here we go again,' he muttered, going to the sink. *The truth.* She hadn't a clue.

'What you do with that woman down there, and all the others . . . well, it's nothing. Nothing. Anyone can do that.'

Monk turned round, mildly curious.

'But to fall in love with someone and marry them,' she added, '*that* takes courage.'

You can say that again, Monk thought, rinsing his glass under the tap.

'To be brave enough to open yourself up to someone. You've never been able to do that because you've been too scared. And instead of wishing people well when they get married, you belittle them. But you only do that because you haven't found happiness in love yourself, and you're the one who's—'

'THANK YOU!' he shouted, slamming down the glass on the draining board.

The kitchen fell into silence.

He lowered his head and whispered down his chest, 'Sorry.'

But there was no reply. Monk turned round. His mother's eyes

34

were closed and she was rubbing her forehead with her long fingers: firmly, methodically. Her face was frighteningly taut. He apologised again.

'Go,' she said.

'Do you want painkillers?'

'Just go.'

He left the room. Back downstairs, he was relieved to find that the girl had miraculously fallen asleep. She was sprawled across the bed, lying with her head back. Her mouth was propped open and she was snoring through the back of her throat.

'To fall in love with that?' he whispered. *'Courage?'*

He crept across the room and drew open the curtains. 'They'd have to give me the Victoria Cross.'

He sniggered. Marriage! Surely his mother had learnt by now that he wasn't the marrying type. If he had a vocation, it was music. But no, his mother just couldn't bring herself to accept it. Ah! The world was full of misguided souls.

Monk snatched a folded letter off the top of the piano. *And talentless piss-artists, too.*

Praha, 31 July

Dear Thelonious Monk!

Hallo there from the Czech Republic!

I am writting to you because I am looking for a plays to stay in Dublin for the next six months time, because we are hoping to escape the terrible snows next winter, and I was wondering if you could by any chance accommodate me, my wife, and my extended family in your home, including nephues, nieces and cusins without charge?

No, seriesly, how are you keeping, Monk? I write because I don't have the address of Joel O'Leery, the sax player you brought over with you last Joon. We've been seeking for a new saxophonist, and we want to offer Joel a six week period in our band, trial basis, beginning September 1 next. To tell the truth, we were impressed with what we herd: his performance on the sax was almost as impressive as his performance with the nine glasses of Pils, in connection with our trumpeter.

We are offering Joel over a hundred thousand Czech crowns for the period, plus accommodation in a lokal brothal. Seriesly, though, our last sax player is going back home to Kazekastan, to be a rebel, leeving his apartment free for two months. There will be three residencies per week, a jazz festival in Budapest, and some recording required. I know he will be interested in the offer, because he told me in Joon that he wanted to leave Dublin because it was jazz death.

How is your own good playing, Thelonious? How can I forget the time Vaclav gave you a lecture on Czech beer while you were attempting to wiggal out of a pint of trosers on which a very pretty girl accidentally spilled a pair of Pils.

Anyway, could you please to pass this letter on to Joel, or tell him to contact me soon, if he is intersted? Thanks!

My wife and extended family all hope to hear from you soon,
    Jan Fuks

'Do you indeed?

Monk bunched the letter up in his hand and proceeded to squash it into a tiny ball between his palms. 'Such a shame,' he hissed, shaking his head in mock disappointment. 'Would have been the ideal career move for O'Leary. Would have made him so, so happy to go – specially since he's broke. And such a beautiful city, too. Yes, indeed. If only the prat hadn't bonded himself into my service.'

He flung the paper ball at a bin in the corner but it missed, rolling under the grand piano instead.

'Oh, well,' Monk concluded. 'He's always been an unlucky bastard.'

tuesday

11

Going to his father for a loan of several grand was not quite as humiliating as returning to Ireland after being taken to the cleaners by a nun – but it wasn't far off.

At eleven o'clock, Joel went through the glass doors of O'Leary Snack Foods Incorporated and walked up to the chessboard-floored reception, sparkling with a giant chandelier of five thousand pieces.

'If it's not young O'Leary!' said the receptionist. 'Your father called in to say he'd be delayed. You can go on up.'

Joel moved slowly up the staircase.

'How's the saxophone going?'

'Incredible.' He dashed up the remainder of the stairs and went through his father's oak-panelled door on the first floor. It was a large, dusty room, fitted out with antique trappings of luxury: desk as large as a car, arching ballet-dancers for reading lamps, mahogany furniture, studded leather armchairs, the forbidding portrait of his grandfather, Joseph.

That inventive entrepreneur had set up a business in the thirties importing peanuts from the Caribbean and toothpicks from Thailand. He'd married his third secretary and that union gave rise to his father, who in turn gave rise to him, via his mother.

Joel's old man had long regarded his own father as a decent bloke at heart, but a dreadful skinflint. While Joel was staring at the portrait of his parents on the mantelpiece, he couldn't help thinking that his dad suffered from an extreme version of moral blindness. Henry was such a tightwad that he used a single teabag three times before chucking it in the bin. Clearly, persuading him to part with a cheque for two thousand Euros was going to be sheer murder.

'*Dad*,' he would begin, '*I'm desperate: the only means I had to earn a living was robbed from me yesterday and I need a loan to replace it.*' 'Desperate'. That was a good word to use. Joel walked to the window, hands in his pockets. '*You see, Dad, jazz instrumentalism is a respectable form of self-employment.*' 'Respectable' and 'self-employment' – more good words. '*I want to be a responsible member of civilised society, like everyone else*' – another phrase he'd definitely keep in mind. Joel walked back to the connecting door. '*Oh, and I would insist on index-linking the interest on any loan you give me, with penalties for late payment.*'

And on the thorny issue of how and when Joel would propose to pay back the loan: '*Trust me, Dad, I swear I'll pay it back somehow.*'

At twelve thirty the phone on his father's desk rang. The receptionist informed a now weary Joel that his father had been spotted in the Oliver Goldsmith bar across the road, with another gentleman.

Joel's heart sank. He left the building and waited at the lights. As he was waiting, he spied a well-dressed man leave the pub. Joel recognised him at once – an old family friend, now acting for his father in the current divorce proceedings. Joel crossed the road and cornered him on the footpath. 'Hi, Liam. Is my dad in there, by any chance? He is? Is anything wrong?'

Liam told him that Joel's mother was suing for three-quarters of the rental income generated from Henry's luxury apartments in Galway, which he'd failed to disclose to his wife – or to the divorce court. 'Our hands are tied,' he concluded. 'We may have to sell.'

'How's he taking it?' wondered Joel.

'Hard to tell. He's been drunk out of his noggin since I told him. Go in and see for yourself.'

Inside, it was a busy lunchtime. Joel went upstairs and found his father on the upper level, slumped over a table in front of two whiskey glasses – one empty and the other full. Gradually, Henry became aware of his presence and looked up, readjusting focus. 'Joseph? Where did *you* hail from?'

'They said I'd find you here.' He hadn't seen his old man looking so drunk in ages. His eyes were glazed and bloodshot, his voice thick and hoarse. He seemed barely aware of his surroundings. He was frowning, now, pointing an unsteady finger at the full glass on the table. 'Want it?'

'It's a bit early in the day for whiskey, Dad, isn't it?'

'Suit yourself.' He leaned across and dragged the glass towards him.

Joel sat down, heavy-hearted. *Of all mornings!*

His father had been a regular patron of this institution up to several years previously, when he'd had it professionally explained to him that neither his wife nor his internal organs would put up with it any longer. To his credit, he'd given up the drinking at least in time to save his liver, but not to save his wife. She took up with a younger man possessed, very possibly, of a more vibrant set of organs.

As he looked on, Joel recalled the sorry story to mind. One cold November afternoon, several years ago, he and his father had decided to go for a walk on Dun Laoghaire pier. They'd bumped into his mother, who was being accompanied by a younger English guy with a sheepdog in tow. He was introduced as her personal trainer, despite the fact that he was puffing maniacally on a cigarette butt. His father was dubious, but he let it pass.

Then, on Christmas Eve, his dad returned home early from work with a large sackful of presents. Apparently, he recognised the Englishman from his arched buttocks over his wife on the late Victorian rosewood divan. That very evening he booted her out of the marriage, an hour after she'd already cleared off.

Joel's mother requested maintenance but his father refused her a penny, accusing her of desertion. Several days later she took her revenge by spreading word at a party that her former husband was impotent: socially, psychologically and spiritually. She alleged, furthermore, that he was sexually impotent and, in addition, that he was a stingy-clawed old stiff with a pole stuck up his ass. The latter precise formulation was reconveyed to Henry on the grapevine, via a mutual acquaintance. His father promptly sold the family dog, hours before she was due to arrive and collect it. When she did arrive, she pretended not to care about the dog, but went away with a priceless Jack B. Yeats masterpiece instead.

When, some months later, his father opened a solicitor's letter demanding maintenance, Henry called her and shouted down the phone, 'Sue me!'

And that's exactly what she did.

'Dad, you're only getting yourself drunk.'

'Good,' his father bellowed back, with dozy-eyed impudence. 'If a man can't have a drink when he hears from . . . from his long-lost wife, what's to happen? . . . Been all of . . . many, many months. Want to celebrate . . .' He raised the empty glass in the air and rocked it back and forth, swaying, as if to a silent sing-song in his head.

'Dad, put the glass down. You'll only make a fool of yourself.'

'Already made a fool of myself,' his father snapped, slamming the glass back down on the table. 'Married your mother, didn't I?'

'Shush,' hissed Joel, conscious they were making a public spectacle of themselves. 'Look, why don't I get a taxi for you? I'll ring the office and tell them you're not well. Are you listening?'

But his father wasn't listening. He was staring out through void grey eyes. 'It's a cruel world, Joseph. Never told you that. Wanted to shelter you. But it's all pointless. You won't escape. Nobody does. Might as well know the facts. Your marriage is destined for the scrap heap. Not to take it personally. They all are.' He took another gulp of whiskey.

Joel checked his pockets for some taxi fare.

'They do it behind your back, you see, when you're not looking. With a knife.' Henry mimed a sharp stab into the smoky air.

'Come on,' said Joel, locating a tenner in his pocket. His father was sure to have some more on him. 'I'll bring you to the taxi rank.'

'You don't believe me, do you?'

'Sure, I believe you, Dad, let's see if we can stand up . . .'

'Your wife could be seeing someone right now, behind your back.'

'I'm sure she is. Is this your coat?' Joel picked up his father's overcoat and held it out for him to put his arms through. 'Do you want to put this on?'

But his father had become suddenly agitated. 'What did you say? She *is*?'

'No, no.'

'But you said . . . you said . . .' He poked a drunken index finger. 'Who's she seeing behind your back?'

'Nobody.'

'Don't lie to me, Son. Don't accept it . . . have to talk about it, have to tell me. What's . . .?'

'Put on the coat, please.'

'No, no, what's she doing?'

'She isn't doing anything.'

'*What's she doing?*'

Joel didn't need this. He could have stayed at home and started writing his repentance speech instead.

'Tell me!' barked his father, swaying on the edge of his seat. 'What's she doing behind your back?'

Joel glanced up and beheld the scattering of nosy lunchtimers tuning in to their conversation. Embarrassed, he swivelled round and whispered sharply to his father, 'Will you put your coat on if I tell you?'

'Yes, yes . . .'

Again, Joel held up the open sleeve of the coat. His father pushed in an arm, but wouldn't move his other one.

'Put in your arm.'

'Tell me, is she seeing someone behind your back?'

'No.'

'IS SHE SEEING SOMEONE?' his father bellowed.

'*Yes, for God's sake, Dad!*' hissed Joel, glancing around the bar.

'When, where?'

'*Your coat!*'

'TELL ME!'

'*On the pier, okay?* On Dun Laoghaire pier. Every night after work. Are you going to put on your coat now?'

Henry stiffened. 'Oh, my God! What are you going to . . . to do?'

41

Joel managed to slide the second arm through the overcoat. 'I'm going to get you home. Let's go.'

'Can't ignore it, Son, no, I can't!' He spoke into Joel's face with drunken sincerity. 'Listen to me, goddammit! I've been there. I know. Same thing happened to me. Can't let her make a fool of you. Got to get out . . . *now.*'

'Just what I was thinking.'

'Before it's too late . . . the humiliation . . . it's no use, once the threshold is crossed . . . no going back.' His father's bloodshot eyes were rolling in their lubricated sockets. He slapped the table with a hand. 'Don't you understand? You've got to get out now! *Do you hear me?*'

'Yes, Dad, and so does everyone else.'

Joel noticed a barman looking over. If only his poor father realised how badly he was behaving. He would have been utterly mortified.

'You could stay . . . you can stay in one of my flats . . . in Galway. I *won't* see you on the streets. Far, far away.' His eyes were beginning to close. 'Make a fresh start, away from all of womankind.'

Joel tried giving his father a lift, but he stopped halfway off his seat, patting a jacket pocket. 'And you'll need money, yes. I'll have to give you money. I *won't* see you starve.' Semi-squatting, his father withdrew a red chequebook. 'No son of mine is going to starve on the street.'

Joel stared at the chequebook, stunned. '*You're going to . . .?*'

'A new life,' said Henry, fumbling in his pockets. 'It's the only way out.'

Slowly, Joel levered him back down on to the bench, still staring at the chequebook.

'To Galway,' his father chanted gruffly, producing a pen and clicking it open. 'Land of the free.' He leant forward over the table, hesitating at the line where the name of the recipient was to be written. 'What's your name?'

'Joel O'Leary.'

'What?'

'Joseph. Joseph O'Leary.'

Henry scrawled out the words 'Joseph O'Leary' with painstaking slowness – above, through and below the designated line. 'Make a fresh start,' he muttered, moving his hand down to the box. 'How much . . . did I say?'

'You didn't say anything.' Joel watched, fascinated, as the pen hovered tantalisingly over the paper.

'Well, how much do you need?'

'I dunno, I don't know what to say . . .'

'How much, man?'

'Ten thousand would do it, I suppose.'

His father inhaled sharply through pursed lips. 'Ten?' He didn't move the pen. 'Fancy that. The flat, Galway . . . costs ten, ten thousand per annum. Have to charge it, it's the going rate.' He wrote down ten thousand Euros – in a gently descending slope through the line. Then he tore out the cheque and held it up for Joel. 'All right?'

Joel was shaking with anticipation. 'Have you forgotten to sign it?'

Annoyed, his father scrawled his name in the general vicinity of the signature line, then jerked it at Joel. 'Here, you fill out the rest.' He dropped the pen on the table and sank back into the bench, picking up his whiskey. 'Stab you,' he mumbled, eyelids fluttering. 'Just where it hurts . . .'

Joel stared at his father for some moments in disbelief. Then he held up the cheque before his eyes, to make sure it was for real.

It was for real.

12

After the early morning rehearsal with Ita and Sean, Ellen left the main hall and strode past reception on the way to her twelve o'clock upstairs, her one and only piano lesson of the day.

She smiled at Tom behind the desk as she passed. It was reassuring to see his benign, contented face. No matter what was happening in your life, you could count on a pleasant greeting from him. Each Christmas, she would buy him a nicely gift-wrapped bottle of port. He would shake his head, as if embarrassed. Ellen loved people when they were just themselves and didn't puff themselves up with falsity or pretension.

Tom had been there as long as she could remember: from the day she first entered the music school for her first piano lesson at the age of five, holding her father's hand. Then, Tom was a young man with jet-black hair. Now, his hair was a shock of grey and his forehead was furrowed with tiny parallel canyons. But in himself he hadn't changed. And he hadn't forgotten her father, who had taught there for twenty years: often, he would speak fondly of him.

At the top of the stairs, Ellen walked along the corridor, criss-crossed by the diverse sounds of flute and oboe, piano and harp. Her pupil was standing outside room 26 – the precociously talented seven-year-old, Helen Kearney. She was fond of the shy, intense girl, with her aquiline beauty and her ponytail, though less so of her rather severe mother, who was determined to push her daughter into the role of concert pianist before the age of sixteen. She unlocked the door and they went in. Helen sat down on the left-hand stool.

'How's your mammy?'

'She's okay.'

'And your daddy?'

'He's fine.'

'And your Labrador? I can't remember his name.'

'Teddy. His leg hasn't healed yet.'

'Poor Teddy. Shall we warm up with a few scales?'

'Okay.'

'Let's try C♯? Left hand only, then try both hands.'

Helen performed to near perfection. Ellen reminded her to relax the wrists and shoulders, to lend her fingers greater fluidity. Helen played the scales of B♭ and A, then the corresponding arpeggios. These were better. After this, she went straight into the complicated scale of D♯, which she'd learnt off her own bat. Ellen reminded her to hold her elbows slightly away from the body and not to play too fast. Helen was so responsive and diligent, she was always a joy to teach.

Ellen made her principal living touring with her new Trio, playing in arts centres and old houses all around the country. But

44

the part-time hours were a crucial supplement. She was teaching assistant of concert pianist Ivan Beausang, a colleague of her father's who had taken her under his wing at the age of twelve. Nine years later, having sat her music degree at Trinity, Beausang and her father arranged for Ellen to study at the reputable academy in Prague, the Akademie Muzickych Umeni v Praze. For two years she studied under the renowned aged composer Miloš Jasny, who had himself taught Beausang a generation earlier in Paris. She completed a Fulbright scholarship at the Juilliard, New York, then returned to the Conservatory in Dublin as Beausang's teaching assistant.

This arrangement ensured that only students of the highest calibre came her way. And Helen was one of those students.

'Now. What note is the seventh note in F♯ minor?'

'E,' replied the girl, after a short pause. She played the scale, then the arpeggio. Then, familiar with Ellen's modus operandi, she played the two-octave chromatic scale, each hand separately.

'What were we working on?'

'The Bach.'

Moments after she began playing the two-part invention, Ellen's phone trilled. Castigating herself, she read off the text message: *Meet me 4 lunch in sambo bar on Dawson at 1pm, love, J.*

Instantly her mood lifted. She'd been worried about Joel all morning. He'd left a note early to say he was meeting his father. Stupidly she'd got herself into a small panic that he might spill the beans. But it was just the guilt. And it was beginning to corrode. It was bad enough deceiving your husband, without having to watch him turn into a nervous wreck as well. He'd been in such a state after what she'd told him that he wasn't even able to get it up – that was a total first. Now he wanted to meet her. That was good. She would calm him. Reassure him and not burden him with money issues until all this was over.

Certainly, Joel needed to earn money and get a car. He needed to learn what it was like to hold a credit card and share a mortgage. In short, he needed to learn responsibility and stop always talking about them both having to go away to some exotic foreign city where they could live comfortably and not have to worry about the cost of living. It was a pipe dream. If anything would change Joel, of course, it would be a child.

Ellen was paying scant attention to the Bach as she ambled over to the window and peered at the small picture of Joel on the adjacent wall. The pudgy nose and the dreamy eyes! There was no trace of that tortured artist's expression, so evident in other photographs. Here, he was facing the camera with a shy mischievousness, looking very like Bruce Willis.

She remembered back to their first ever meeting in the Conservatory, where Joel was taking sax lessons. It was at the water dispenser near reception, ten years previously. They'd got to know one another over the months. Joel was funny and scatty, and he made her laugh. Then, one day, he told her he was discontinuing lessons because there was nothing more he could learn.

They didn't meet again for several years. Then, one summer lunchtime, he came up to her in St Stephen's Green, where she was seated on a bench in the shade. It was as if no time had passed, as if she'd always known him. They merged into one another like music. He was intimate and easygoing, not at all like those arrogant guys who constantly pestered you, as if you were some sort of fiddly pick-up doll. He was even funnier than he used to be. He talked a lot. He wasn't exciting, in that sense, but who needed excitement? The point was, when she was with him she could relax from having to be constantly on her guard. She could be herself. And *that* was what love was about.

Ellen turned round and realised that Helen had called out her name at least twice. 'Sorry, love?'

'I've finished the Bach.'

'Shall we try a performance of the Chopin?' Ellen opened out the lid of the piano, then sat on the chair and scanned the Prelude in B minor, pencilling the manuscript in just one place: 'Try the third finger on that D.'

She stood behind her pupil. 'Focus on the melody, the feel of the piece as a whole. Also, remember what I said last week about making the left hand sing more?'

Listening to Helen play the prelude, Ellen's heart warmed once again to her task. Teaching had its compensations – if only she could concentrate her mind on it. There was always that little

46

thrill, hearing her students play something beautifully, where before there was little more than a hesitant jumble of notes. It was fascinating to witness young talent create something out of nothing, fashion raw material into a thing of genuine beauty.

Watching Helen's small fingers travel skilfully across the keyboard and hearing the beautiful sounds that emanated, it felt to Ellen as if her day had been suddenly graced by a miracle.

And, imagining that the pretty girl playing the piano before her was her very own daughter, Ellen desperately wanted to believe in miracles.

13

When Joel walked into the bank at ten to one, clutching his father's cheque, he felt like he was in seventh heaven. But when the bank refused to cash the cheque he tumbled straight back down to hell.

'Hold on a second.' Joel trembled. 'This is a valid cheque.'

'Valid or not,' said the teller, who was now ignoring him while he counted out banknotes, 'it has to be lodged.'

'Look,' said Joel, annoyed at the teller's arrogant attitude, 'my father's name is written here: "Henry O'Leary". This is my father's branch. He's an important businessman. Have you never heard of O'Leary Snack Foods?'

'The cheque has to clear.'

'The cheque's perfectly clear!' Joel was aggrieved, partly because he was staring jaw first into the worst example of customer service he'd seen since he'd walked into a glass door in Heuston Station on his way to the Cork Jazz Festival last year. And partly because he hadn't a shagging clue about the country's banking customs, given the fact that he'd never had sufficient money in the first place to consider them relevant.

He tried explaining that his wife was pregnant and that if she discovered the figure zero in their joint account, she might well suffer a miscarriage.

It didn't work. So he simply lodged the cheque and left.

*

Over lunch, Ellen dropped a bombshell.

They were seated at a table in a small sandwich bar in Dawson Street, consuming tuna rolls and coffee. 'I was looking at a carriage stroller round the corner yesterday.'

'Oh, yeah?'

'It's going for a song. I thought I might buy it.'

'How much?'

'One hundred and sixty.'

Joel became nervous. 'But don't we have to pay the mortgage this week?'

'Oh no, I'd just take it out of the nest egg,' she said casually, sipping her hot coffee.

'The nest egg? Our joint account?'

Ellen shrugged. 'Well, that's what it's there for, isn't it?' She sat back in her seat. 'All the effort I went to, building it up over the last few years. I'm really going to enjoy spending some of it. I can't wait, actually.'

Joel felt his ears burn.

'I know it's very early to be buying one,' she continued, but we'll be saving well over two hundred. There's a lot of baby things we're going to need, so we might as well start early. I thought I'd buy it this afternoon.'

'I don't think that's such a good idea,' said Joel, starting to panic.

'Why not?'

'Because . . . because . . .' The previously tasty tuna sandwich had turned into a dry and indigestible clump in his mouth. 'Because I want to buy it instead.'

'*You* do?'

'Yes. I'd like to buy it for you, for the baby. Please, let me do it.'

'Are you sure?'

'Yes, yes, very sure.'

'But you haven't any money.'

'I will, soon. Very soon, our financial situation is going to improve.' Guilty as hell, Joel lowered his head into his awful tuna roll and took a bite.

'But how soon is soon, Joel? They won't hold the stroller for ever.'

Joel grabbed her hand away from her bread roll and squeezed it tight. 'Please, just trust me, baby. I'll get it for you.'

Ellen smiled at him. Whether in sympathy or delight, Joel wasn't certain. But it didn't matter; she was cool about it. He lowered his face, drained with unspeakable relief, into his sandwich. *Change the subject, quick!*

'You know, I was thinking,' he began, doing his best to sound nonchalant. 'Do people still use those old-style terry nappies any more? You know, the plain cloths?'

She was surveying him with some humour.

'Be a good way to save a few bob,' he explained. 'Disposables are pretty expensive, especially if the baby goes a lot.'

'Would you be willing and able to do the changing?'

'Why not? Always been good with my hands.' He held them up in the air.

Ellen reached over and locked her fingers into his, palm to palm, her eyes unusually moist. 'Why don't we do it tonight, Joel?' she whispered.

Joel was puzzled. 'What? Change nappies?'

'Make love. I've got such an incredible urge, I swear I could do it right now on the table.'

Joel frowned and looked down at the pine table. 'But there isn't any tablecloth.'

'Then let's do it tonight, in bed.' She was squeezing his fingers tight.

'Just name a time. Better make it early, though. I feel like it could go on all night.'

'That's good,' she said, pouting sexily and rubbing the back of his calf with her foot. 'So do I. How about seven?'

14

'I wanted to tell you . . .' said the redhead.

Monk was lying on the futon in his wine dressing gown, an unlit Dutch cigarillo hanging from his mouth. Bright afternoon rays zigzagged through the barred window of his basement quarters and flickered against the wall above him, exposing a patch of mildew just below the ceiling. He stared curiously at the blemish, then glanced towards the disturbance at the other side of the room.

'I was thinking of asking him for a divorce . . .' she said.

He returned his gaze to the mildew patch. Should really deal with the problem now, he decided. Once and for all. Far too pressing to let go for yet another day. As a matter of fact, if Mother had any of that fungicide spray left, he might even clean it off himself.

A bell tinkled. Monk glanced over again. Clutching the bars of his birdcage was his trusty African grey. The woman was rattling the bells inside the cage, which rested on a table between his grand piano and the wall. He eyed her disdainfully in her unimpressive bikini, disappointed that Rufus would be so duped by the fake charm of a broad who knew damn all about parrots. He'd thought he'd trained the bird better than that.

'Well? Do you have an opinion about it, Monk?'

He surveyed her bare profile across the room, as she tickled Rufus's roving gullet. He eyed the creases of flab around her waist and considered the issue.

'My opinion', he muttered to himself, 'is that you should stop eating pastries as a matter of urgency.' He surveyed the cellulite on the backs of her thighs. 'And what's more – you've no right to be telling people you're only twenty-eight.'

Monk had spotted the redhead several weeks previously at the fruit stall of a Dun Laoghaire supermarket, chatting to the manager, who turned out to be her husband. Unlike the husband, she was English. She was also brash and fair game. When the man walked away to take a call, she leant over and plucked three bananas in a smooth, digital movement which aroused Monk to such an extent that he felt compelled to pursue her around the aisles with a bottle of orange juice. He bumped into her trolley, dropped the bottle and insisted on taking the blame for the resulting mess on the floor. Within minutes an exchange of numbers occurred.

When she'd gone, Monk approached the supermarket manager and asked him if he stocked condoms. 'It's for this delightful redhead I met recently,' he explained. The bespectacled greaseball

brought him over to the relevant rack and grinned conspiratorially. 'We have something in here for all our customers.'

The following night his wife was safely ensconced under
Monk's bed linen. She had become something of a regular fixture
there over the past few weeks, usually afternoons. Initially, he'd
imagined she was just in it for the sex, like any self-respecting
married woman. But lately he'd come to realise that her desires
were far darker. Rather hilariously, she'd told him straight out
that she wanted to live with him. It was, clearly, the end of the
affair.

'I'd like to hear your opinion,' she said from the far corner.
'Either I ask him for one or I don't.'

Monk leaned over and extracted a box of matches from his
jacket, draped over an adjacent chair.

'Well?'

He looked over. 'Are you addressing me? Sorry, I thought you
were talking to Rufus.'

'*I* think it would be a good idea. And, you know what? He might
give me one, too.'

Monk shrugged, as he flicked a match and lit his cigarillo. 'Why
not? He seems to give you everything else you ask for.' He took a
drag and exhaled into the large space.

It was a big black-and-white room, covered with posters of
piano legends like Thelonious Monk, Bud Powell and Keith
Jarrett. Separated by a sliding door was the rear room, which
contained most of the clutter: kitchenette, wardrobes and a CD
player plus a vast jazz collection. Monk slept in the front section,
within easy reach of an oak drinks cabinet and a ready supply of
porn. And from the futon he could not merely see his pièce de
résistance, but *smell* it: his boudoir grand, a six-foot Kawai, the
colour of creamy caffelatte.

'Your bird hasn't done anything into his tray today,' the
redhead said, more casually now. 'You mustn't be feeding him.'

'Seeds and shite are not my responsibility. Those tasks have
been assigned to my mother. My brief is limited to improving the
bird's vocabulary and affording him true companionship. Isn't
that right, Rufus?'

The bird squawked: '*Du ar halt vardelos.*'

'What language is that?'

'Did I never tell you? Rufus was once owned by a blonde Swede, who kept telling him he was worthless. My pet psychiatrist says he suffers from low self-esteem, but only in Swedish. In his native Spanish – according to my linguist neighbour – it turns out he's the greatest bird who ever lived.' He took a drag of his cigarillo. 'Rufus hates blondes, for obvious reasons, though he tolerates Mother's nearly yellow hair. He can get quite violent around redheads as well.'

She sat down on the futon beside him. 'I'd like to meet her some time. It's odd that I've been coming here for almost a month and we still haven't met.'

He shouted across the room, 'Rufus!'

'You're embarrassed, aren't you?'

'Rufus!'

The bird jerked towards him.

'Say something to the lady.'

'Something to the lady.'

'See? He does it every time.' Monk resumed his cigarillo, eyeing the tiny flower in the middle of her brassiere with some disdain.

She crossed a leg and was now staring at him with intent. 'You know perfectly well there's no point in me going ahead, Monk, unless I know where you stand.'

He frowned. 'Ahead?'

'Going ahead with the divorce. I need to hear your opinion!'

He gave himself a few moments to consider the issue. 'In my opinion,' he said finally, returning to the mildew, 'there should never be any need for divorce.' He blew out a smoke ring and watched it dissipate. 'Because there should never be any marriages in the first place.'

She averted her eyes to the piano and spoke softly. 'I know you don't like hearing this, but I'm not leaving him without some sort of . . . Look, I need to know you'd be here for me.'

'Goes without saying, darling. Course I'd be here for you.'

She watched him cautiously.

'Course I would. Doesn't matter to me if you're hitched or not. You'd still be welcome here any time. So long as you gave me advance warning, of course – I hate women who call up on spec.

Can get a bit awkward if the toilet's already engaged, so to speak.'

'Bastard.'

'Rufus! Close your ears.'

'The concept of fidelity doesn't mean a damn to you, does it?'

'Fidelity? Not really.' Monk lifted up her hand from the quilt and stared curiously at her huge diamond engagement ring. 'Perhaps you could explain it to me some time,' he said. Slowly, he advanced her ring finger to his lips, but she snatched her hand away before he got a chance to kiss it.

'I don't know why I come up here to you. I get enough abuse at home. You're just a bloody egoist.'

It took Monk some effort not to break into a shameless smile. He put on a poface. 'Oh, God, and a minute ago she said she loved me. I'm so confused.'

'How many women have you been with?'

'When? Last week, last month?'

'You probably haven't had a single meaningful commitment in your whole life, have you? You coward.'

'That's not fair,' said Monk, displaying visible hurt. 'You know nothing about my past. As a matter of fact I did make a commitment once. Long term, as you say. I was only sixteen. Went on for a whole year.'

She eyed him with doubt.

'Cost me a lot, too,' he added.

'Why? What happened?' She stared at him, guarded.

'I took out an annual subscription to *Playboy*.'

She stood up and got dressed. 'What the hell am I doing here?'

Good bloody question, Monk thought, hopping out of the futon. Far better that she left: if he didn't break for a few days, he could end up with orgasm burn-out. He checked his watch: already almost four in the afternoon. He slid on his silk dressing gown, went to the piano and donned his Thelonious Monk hat. He sat on the piano stool and started playing. He attempted a double-handed blues scale in E, at top tempo, but he made a hash of it.

He began again, but it wasn't great. His technique was abysmalising by the year. Totally his own fault. Thelonious would whip him, and rightly so. Better damn well get it together for the gig tonight.

'I knew there was something!' he shouted. He turned to the redhead, while still playing. She was sitting down, putting on her shoes. 'Listen, love, before you go, you wouldn't mind passing me my address book over there, would you? I have to call O'Leary about the saxophone you're sitting on.'

Monk was in the middle of playing in his Master's arrhythmic style – full of stops, starts and sudden twists – when he heard the front door bang shut.

15

It was not in Joel's nature to iron. But something deep inside told him that he'd have to get used to the idea pretty fast. It was one of the looming duties of parenthood which he suspected Ellen would shove in his direction, in a way that might well become permanent. Still, Joel was happy enough to learn – provided she didn't go telling anyone.

This was why, when he spotted the basket of clean clothes in the kitchen, he happily carried it into the spare room and set about his task. But there was another reason: with his father's cheque due to clear on Friday, Joel felt so buoyant he was game for anything.

Ironing was not easy. Joel was quite prepared to acknowledge this fact, without getting a huge guilt complex on behalf of all men for having left this task to women since the Stone Age, not, of course, that they had irons in the Stone Age. At first his progress was extremely slow. Where Ellen would scoop up a freshly ironed blouse in a couple of minutes, the first blouse Joel laid his iron on took a whole quarter of an hour. And even then he was unable to eradicate a network of creases on the front pocket, determined as he was to leave his mastery of the water-spray function to another day.

And it wasn't just blouses: it took Joel a whole five minutes to work out how to iron the top end of Ellen's olive-green trousers: the secret was to stick them into the end of the ironing board, as if they were attempting to swallow it wholesale, a bit like a shark attempting to eat a whale and getting stuck halfway. Socks were less complicated.

The second of Ellen's blouses took only ten minutes, proving that he was a fast learner. Now he was on to the third. So far, it had taken him a mere *seven minutes* and he was nearly done. Augured well for the future. Who knows, Ellen might graduate him to knitting baby woollens.

Suddenly Joel heard his mobile go off. He ran into the lounge and picked up. There was a lot of crackling so he switched off again. They'd have to phone back. He returned to the bedroom and lifted up the iron. The blouse came with it. Joel tore it away, leaving a large black burn in the middle of what was otherwise a well-ironed item. The burn was so efficient he could see the photo of Ellen's late mother on the dressing table through the triangular hole. He stuffed the blouse into the bin and made an attempt to conceal it underneath a heap of tissues. He hoped Ellen wouldn't notice. If she did, she might punish him by withholding sex tonight. You had to watch your step around women sometimes. They could get edgy.

Eventually Joel got through the small pile of linen. At the bottom of the basket was a medium-sized bath towel. It was white and furry. For some strange reason it reminded him of one of those old terry nappies he'd been talking to Ellen about in the restaurant earlier. A mischievous smile slid across Joel's face, while he spread the towel across the ironing board. He folded the corners inwards in an attempt to emulate the shape of a diaper. It was, he acknowledged, a ridiculous thing to be doing. But it was more constructive than burning blouses.

Joel made several attempts at forming a diaper with the white towel and eventually he was convinced he'd succeeded. Then he got a brainwave. He would play a joke on Ellen when she got home: he would wear the diaper himself. At lunchtime she had questioned his ability to put on diapers, relegating him to the Third Diaper Parent Division. This was unfair. He'd show her.

He found two safety pins on Ellen's dressing table, then wound the towel round his trousers and between his legs. He fastened both hips tightly with several pins, then had a look in the mirror.

God, Joel, you've surpassed yourself.

Wait till Ellen saw him! She wouldn't be able to stop laughing.

He put away the ironing board and went into the lounge in his diaper. All of a sudden that sinking, depressed feeling came over him once more, despite all the hilarity. Sure, he'd be able to buy another sax and replace the nest egg when the cheque cleared at the end of the week. But what was he going to do until then? Iron clothes? If Joel were to admit it, the only reason he'd done the goddam ironing in the first place was to disguise the fact that he had piss all else to do, except perhaps hoover.

Hoovering? Now *there* was an idea.

While Joel was pulling the hoover from the cloakroom, his phone went off again. He went out to the balcony for better reception. Just after he pressed the 'on' button, he caught a glimpse of Ellen in the distance, crossing the road opposite the train station. He waved happily at her, but she didn't see him.

'I'm looking for a Mr Joel O'Leary,' said a man in a heavy Welsh accent.

'Speaking.'

'Calling in relation to one Selmer saxophone.'

'*What?*'

There was an audible, almost *bored* sigh at the other end of the line. 'Is that Mr Joel O'Leary?'

'Of course it's me. I'm Joel O'Leary. Who's this?'

'Detective Inspector Burchhill, Holyhead police. We're ringing in respect of a missing musical instrument, mislaid yesterday in Holyhead. Does this apply to you, sir?'

'I . . . I . . . *yes.*'

'Could you recite your full address, please, sir?'

Joel obliged, his heart ringing in his ears.

'Could you *spell* your address, sir? Each letter, slowly and clearly, please.'

Painstakingly, Joel spelt out his full address. When he was finished, the officer told him the saxophone had been found in a rubbish skip in the harbour area and handed in by a concerned citizen.

Joel swallowed. 'Are you . . . are you actually telling me that . . .'

56

'According to my file, it's a 1929 Selmer,' interrupted the thickly accented voice.

'Oh, God!'

'Cream case, red felt interior.'

'Oh, Jesus. Thank . . . Jesus . . .'

'Pleased to tell you that it's in perfect condition.'

'This is amazing.'

'Also located was a large sum of money.'

At this point Joel's head went into a crazy, colourful, dazed kind of spin, something like what happened when you fell in love. He was so exhilarated he was barely able to comprehend events. The nest egg! His beloved, invaluable saxophone! Everything was perfectly okay again! Joel would now return to Holyhead in the morning and collect the sax and the money in the police station, then he would go to London and then . . .

Ellen suddenly reappeared at the top of the granite staircase that led up from the junction. She looked up, saw him and waved. Joel waved back down, beaming at her like a thousand happy suns.

'Also, we located something else,' said the police officer in a more stern voice. 'A large bag of white powder concealed in the bell of the saxophone, which we have determined to be high-grade cocaine, worth a total of fifty thousand pounds. Would you care to comment about that, sir?'

Joel turned faint. 'Officer?'

'Yes, Mr O'Leary.'

'I've . . . I've something to tell you.'

'I was hoping you would have.'

'Officer, I've been set up, I don't know what happened. I've been screwed by a kleptomaniac, posing as a nun.'

There was a short spell of stifled coughing, after which the officer returned to the phone, clearing his throat. 'And I've something to tell *you*, sir.'

'Yes, Officer.'

'We've issued an extradition order to the Gardai for your immediate arrest and deportation, so I'm ringing to let you know that the law will be calling round to your apartment to cuff you any moment now, you balding, sweaty, little leprechaun.'

Joel stared at his mobile phone. An evil laugh crackled out of the handset. He slumped against the balcony wall in total disbelief. '*Monk*, you . . .'

'Screwed by a nun?' The scumbag was sniggering evilly. 'I'd say that was a first, O'Leary.'

'. . . *bastard* . . .'

'Good accent, isn't it, boyo?'

Joel deflated like a giant balloon punctured by a spear. He clasped his forehead. '*What the hell do you want?*'

'The reason I'm calling, you cocky runt, is that McCoy is cool about lending you his sax. I want you there tonight at nine.'

'Bugger off, Monk, I never want to see you again. I don't need the gig. I don't need the residency. I don't need the money. Now piss off.'

'What's the matter, O'Leary, can't you take a joke?'

'*Shite!*'

'Thought it was rather good, myself, though you do make it easy for me, you're such a gullible sap.'

'*Shite,*' Joel repeated in a low moan.

'O'Leary,' Monk said in a puzzled voice, 'do you really and truly have such little regard for your testicles?'

But Joel wasn't listening. He was stiff with fright because he'd just spotted his father on the terrace below. But it was worse than that: the old man was having an animated conversation with Ellen. Joel dropped the phone on to the slats. '*Oh, God, no.*' Slowly he backed away from the railing and groaned, 'He's going to tell her!'

Joel tore through the lounge and made for the front door. He stopped dead when he spotted himself in the hall mirror, wearing his brilliant white diaper. He tried to remove the safety pins, but his fingers were too puffed up and sweaty to get a proper grip. In a panic he pulled out his long winter coat, threw it on and buttoned it up to his collar. Then he pelted out of the apartment as fast as his legs would take him.

16

He left the lift on the ground floor, running. He practically mowed down his family in the lobby. He stared at Ellen and his father, one to the other, stiff with fear.

'Are you on your way out?' asked his father, whose breath smelt strongly of whiskey and mint.

'No.'

They were both looking at him and at his overcoat, although only his father had his eyebrows raised.

'Why don't you come up and join us for some dinner, then, Henry?'

'No, no, I won't, Ellen, thank you. I just want a quick word with the man himself.' He slapped a hand down on Joel's shoulder. 'I'll send him up to you in a minute.'

'Are you all right, love? You look pale.'

Seeing her warmth and concern, Joel immediately pulled back from the brink. It was perfectly obvious nothing had passed between them. 'Must be all the ironing I was doing.'

'See you in a minute, so.' She smiled secretively at him and slid a sexy glance down his buttoned overcoat, then got into the lift and pressed the button.

'I'll be at the concert Saturday, by the way,' his father shouted, but the doors had already closed.

'Dad, what are you doing down here?'

'I don't look so good, do I?' He rubbed his eyeballs in their sockets, stretching and squashing the wrinkly skin. 'She was looking at me funny.'

On the terrace, his father leant his palms on the parapet and gulped in the air. 'Woke up at home on the couch, an hour ago,' he said. 'Slept all afternoon. I rang the office and they told me you'd called to say I wouldn't be going back in.'

'I thought you'd want me to.'

Henry stood up straight and stuck his finger into Joel's chest. 'So you *must* have been with me this morning, then?'

'You mean you don't remember?'

59

He began massaging his face and temples again. 'I remember going to the Oliver Goldsmith with Liam. After that is a blank. Can hardly remember a thing. I just woke up.'

'You need a walk, Dad,' said Joel, scared that the blanks might start filling up.

'I've just walked up here, haven't I?'

'I mean, a walk back home. It would do you good.'

'I shouldn't have touched that stuff. My head is killing me.'

'You need to go back to your bed and lie down.'

'I told you, I slept all afternoon!' His father went to the edge of the terrace and they watched a large woman in a green tracksuit and a ponytail jog past them in a slow canter below. 'I got some bad news this morning, Joseph. About the divorce proceedings. That's why I succumbed.' He looked sheepish.

'Forget about this morning, Dad. Put it completely out of your head. You shouldn't have come down here. Better just to go home. If you don't want to walk, you can get the train. I'll bring you down to the station. Have you change for the ticket?'

His father, still looking sheepish, patted his coat pocket. He patted it again, as if something was troubling him. He reached into his inside pocket and withdrew a familiar-looking chequebook.

'Oh,' his old man said, blinking hard, 'now I remember why I came up.' He frowned at Joel. 'Did I give you money this morning, by any chance?'

Joel's mouth went bone dry. 'You mean . . . as in . . . *cash*?'

His father opened the chequebook. 'There's a cheque missing,' he said. 'But the counterfoil isn't filled in. I don't remember writing one.'

Joel swallowed dry saliva. He sensed his father's bloodshot eyes staring impatiently into him.

'What is it, son? *What?* I can see it in your face. Come on. Tell me. Did I give you a cheque?'

Joel pulled a blank face.

'Did I give you a cheque, Joseph?'

'Well you, you, you . . .'

'Did I?'

'Yes.' He sagged. It was no use.

60

'Oh, thank God!' Henry puffed out his cheeks in a gust of relief. 'I thought someone had stolen it on me.' But the frown soon reappeared. 'How much did I give you?'

Joel scratched his head.

'How much did I give you, Joseph?'

'Ten . . .'

'*Ten Euros?* Why would I write a cheque for ten Euros?'

'Not ten, Dad. Ten thousand.'

His father exploded.

'I didn't ask for it,' Joel pleaded. 'You gave it to me.'

'What are you talking about? Why in the name of goodness would I give you a cheque for ten thousand Euros?'

It was a tricky question and Joel would have liked time to consider it, but his father now perked up, as if in the grip of a new vision. 'Wait a second. There was something . . . I'm remembering now. It's on the tip of my brain, what was it?'

'Look, Dad, it's getting cold here. I have to get back up to Ellen.' Joel was praying hard.

'*Ellen!*' His father's eyes shot wide open. 'That's it! You told me something about Ellen. You told me . . . Oh, no. I must be imagining it.' He grabbed Joel's arm desperately. 'Am I imagining it? You told me that she was having an affair.'

'I did?'

'The pier. Some fellow on the pier. That's why I gave you the money. Yes. To leave her.'

Joel took his father's arm and led him towards the steps down to the junction. 'I'd better bring you to the station, Dad, you look sick. You need to get home and rest.' He ushered him across the junction.

'I want to know, Son. I demand to know what's happening!'

'I can't talk about it right now. I'll talk about it next weekend, okay?' Next weekend, he would tell his father the truth: that Ellen's supposed affair was no more than a stupid misunderstanding. But before he could tell him that, the cheque had to clear.

In the station Joel bought him a ticket. They went through the turnstile in silence and descended to the platform. He kept his eyes riveted on the red digital display: two minutes till the next southbound train.

'I can't believe she'd do such a thing,' his father said, morose and creased with distress. 'I had such high hopes for the two of you. Not like me and your mother. I'd never in a million years have thought it'd happen to you as well. This is shattering. Absolutely shattering. It's enough to push you back to the bottle.'

Joel was alarmed when he heard this. 'Look, Dad, there's no point in getting upset about all this. I really don't want you to . . .'

'*Upset?* Is that all marriage means to you? You're not even allowed to feel *upset* about it?' He placed his hands on Joel's shoulders and squeezed them together. 'For God's sake, boy, don't you love her? Don't you feel anything for her?'

'Of course I love her.'

'Then how can you be so unmoved?'

A trickle of sweat itched Joel's temple.

'Has she spoken to you about this other man?' his father asked pleadingly.

Joel shook his head, feeling little better than shrivelling dung.

'Then how do you know about him?'

Joel peered up the track. To his utter relief, he spied the train emerging round the corner, lights on. 'Dad, your train is . . .'

'How do you know about him?'

'I dunno, eh, some people told me. I was told by some people that she meets a guy down on the pier, as you said and, Dad, your train is coming and if you want to avoid the crowd, you should go to the far end of the platform.'

His father clenched Joel's arm in vice grip and glared. '*Some . . . people . . . told . . . you?*'

'Your . . .'

'Forget the damn train.' He shook Joel. 'Who are these people?'

'I don't know. I don't know them.'

'You don't know them?' His dad looked like he couldn't believe his ears. 'And you didn't even ask her about it?'

Joel pointed towards the train, now rolling to a stop. But his father wasn't moving.

'Jesus, Mary and Joseph, Joseph, what are you thinking of? You were going to pack up and leave your wife *because some people told you*? And you didn't even ask her if it was true?'

Joel's voice was breaking. 'Dad, for God's sake, it's going to go off without you.'

Henry was fulminating. 'What was I thinking of, giving you money? What the hell was I doing?' He held out his hand.

'What?'

'Give me the cheque.'

'I haven't got it.'

'Give me the cheque.'

'I lodged it into my account this afternoon.'

Henry now strode down the platform, peering into the incoming train.

'Wait, Dad! I could go back to the bank first thing in the morning, if you wanted. I could try to withdraw some of it, if you wanted some of it back . . .'

The train doors opened and a flood of passengers milled out.

'Oh no, don't bother yourself,' his father said. 'And don't bother trying to withdraw any for yourself, either, because I'm cancelling it first thing tomorrow morning.' He stomped on to the carriage and swivelled on his heels. 'You may want to make an idiot out of yourself, Joseph, but you're not going to make one out of me. *Some people told me*. Pah!'

Joel gaped at his father, aghast. 'But . . .'

The doors swished shut.

He looked down the carriage at the line of gawky passengers grinning at him from the windows. Some less kind souls gave him a wave as the train pulled out of the station, but did his father?

He did not.

Joel walked backwards, stunned, until he banged against a wall.

17

He plodded up the road to the Purty Kitchen, to drown his tragedies. After three quick shots of gin, he'd drowned himself as well.

Despite the mental torpor which this inebriated state induced, Joel had no problem subjecting himself to an honest self-appraisal. To put it colloquially, he was an incompetent jerk. It could no longer be argued that this was not an incontrovertible truth. The evidence lay scattered all over his past like open sores. The clarinet lessons. His Leaving Certificate. The driving tests. The wedding-ring fiasco. His failure to renew the saxophone insurance . . . The list went on and on.

He couldn't even wear a decent condom.

In thirty-six weeks, Joel would be a father. He and Ellen were, fundamentally and disastrously, penniless. What was he to do?

It was obvious what he had to do.

Yet again, he had no choice.

It was to be that A1 asshole.

Joel reached the Sugar Club, almost as drunk as he was late, but not quite.

At the entrance door, he had a tough time trying to convince the bouncer that he was in Monk's band. He had an even tougher time with Monk when he walked out on stage, moments after the band had finished playing a rhythm changes number to wild applause from the dense crowd ranged upwards on tiered seating.

'So,' said Monk, sporting a bored, deadpan look. 'Your lordship has decided to join us after all?'

'He has. He may be interested in the residency after all.'

'May he, indeed?'

'He may. Where's the sax?'

It was by the piano. He picked it up and brought it over to where an empty music stand stood, away from Monk's laser glare. On the way, he tripped over a flex, but luckily only landed on his knees. There was some brief laughter from the band, during which Monk started hammering the A key with an index finger. This was the signal for Joel to begin tuning up, despite the fact that he was barely getting up off his knees.

Ignoring the provocation, he started assembling the saxophone. He fitted a suitable reed – under the full heat blast of Monk's continuing derision – and blew a few scales to accustom himself to this slightly crap instrument. Finally he decided to play the note which Monk was still hammering like a nail into his head. The sax was sharp, so Joel wriggled the mouthpiece out by a millimetre. He blew again, achieving a perfect pitch. He attached the mic to the bell and consulted the trumpeter's sheets to see what was coming up next. Before he had time to take off his coat, the drummer counted in. Four beats later, the whole band were into a rhythm changes number called 'Oleo', a Sonny Rollins number based on 'I Got Rhythm'.

The music wafted over him like a warm, comforting blanket and soon all Joel's woes were vacuumed straight out of his head. When it came to his solo, he did not hold back. Despite Monk's presence in the background – and the fact that the drummer only sporadically hit the correct beat – Joel was swept up into a crazy outburst of improvisation, machine-gunning notes at the crowd from some deep space inside himself. He was seesawing up and down like a yo-yo and now the bell of his sax was scraping the ground. He jerked upwards and spiralled into a Spitfire volley of notes. He was spewing out such a frenzied shitload of pent-up repression that a voice deep within told him he was in danger of becoming *fantastic*.

While he was playing, Joel got a sudden flashback to Prague. That was the last time he'd played this well – during the festival last June, when he'd caught Jan's attention. And it was catching, here in the Sugar Club! Look at everyone! The dance floor had gone ape! The vibe was feeding him like a drug. He played three choruses in all, then traded eights with the cocky but technically firecracking trumpeter. He played another two choruses and soon it was over.

Joel was now baking hot in his overcoat. He peeled it off and flung it behind a speaker, then returned to his spot. He readjusted his reed and blew a scale to test it out. There was a loud clamour of voices in front of him and he looked up. This was a new vibe. A group of girls down left of stage were shouting and waving up at him, but he couldn't hear what they were saying because the trumpeter was blasting stuff in his ear. Other people on the floor were simply staring up at him, as if entranced, and others again were laughing in his direction.

In Joel's experience it was rare to find such an appreciative crowd. More often than not, jazz bewildered people. The audience this evening, however, seemed to understand jazz. They seemed to have grasped exactly what he'd been trying to express in his solo. That took maturity. Joel was profoundly moved. It was a deep support and comfort to know that – despite the fact that his life was going down the shithole in most other respects – he still had the capacity to move people.

Ah, yes, the maestro had arrived!

Joel allowed himself a small bow, as a mark of appreciation for all the compliments. And he glanced over at his collegues to see how they were taking it all. They were standing loosely on the stage holding their instruments, staring over at him in silence. Could it be that they too were stunned by his masterful technique?

He hoped so. He *sincerely* hoped that Monk was paying attention to this rare mark of respect from the crowd. Because as long as Joel had known him, Monk had sneered at his playing, despite numerous positive reviews. One critic had used the term 'genius' in reference to Joel's ability to sense the background chord pattern, while flying along miles above (*Hot Press*). And another had compared his playing to that of a 'tortured artist manqué' (*Irish Times*), whatever that meant.

'What's next, lads? How about something bluesy?'

Only Monk was looking directly at him now. The others seemed to be having a private joke at someone's expense.

'What's the matter? Prefer a bossa nova?'

The laughter and shouting were growing in volume and intensity. More and more people were joining in. One or two people were pointing at him. Joel turned to the other band members. 'What's going on, lads?'

Monk eyed Joel from his piano with an expression of profound distaste. Joel signalled to the trumpeter to tell him what the hell was going on, but the man just lowered his head and grinned, as if embarrassed. The bass player pointed straight at him, but then broke down into a heap of laughter.

The laughter was now spreading like wildfire across the venue.

Monk rose from his piano. He walked stoically across the stage towards Joel. He came up close to him and with his back to the audience he spoke calmly into his ear, in deadly earnest. 'Take that bloody thing off,' he said.

Joel froze. He looked down to see what was the problem. To his great shock, he realised that he was wearing a brilliant white nappy over his trousers.

Illuminated and humiliated in simultaneously vast measure, Joel unhooked the sax from his neck and put it down. Then, very wearily, he trooped backstage and removed the offending garment.

It was just like the time in primary school, when he was paraded by the Brother in front of his classmates with a dustbin over his head for botching up his Irish conjugations. Only this time it was way worse: there wasn't a dustbin anywhere in sight.

After the gig, Joel joined the band backstage for payment. There was a certain amount of predictable teasing over what Monk termed his 'glamorous' nappy, but Joel tried not to make too much of it. Also, he tried to hide the desolation he felt over the cheque débâcle earlier on. Embarrassment and misery weren't popular. Joel just wanted to collect his money and go home. And maybe find a way of making it up to Ellen for ransacking her evening.

'Wad!' shouted Monk, arranging banknotes into five neat piles on a table. Everyone huddled around immediately, as if they were in awe of Monk's 'charisma', as he himself once ridiculously baptised it. Joel ambled over last, but when the counting was over, he grabbed one of the piles like it was gold bullion.

'General announcement.'

Everyone looked up.

'Any of you killer sharks fancy winning some easy money off me?'

There were suspicious grins all around.

'Lads, I'm organising an all-night poker session tonight in my boudoir. Any takers?'

'What's wrong.' The drummer grinned. 'Got no company tonight?'

Monk ignored the nervous tittering from the others.

'Who's going to be there?' wondered the trumpeter.

'So far only *moi*. I won't sleep tonight, I just know it. Any of you interested? First one gets a free ride back in my Jag. Come on, lads, don't rush me, now.'

There were vague mumbles of 'don't think so' and 'some of us have to work in the morning', amid general shaking of heads.

Monk shrugged, clearly unimpressed. 'Jesus, lads.'

'I'm in,' Joel shouted. 'What time's it starting?' He realised that everyone in the group was staring at him, all except Monk.

'What time is *what* starting?' he asked, casually removing his wallet.

'The poker.' Joel held up his cash as proof of his bona fides. He couldn't let the opportunity slip. It was a chance to increase his meagre pot. It had to be grabbed.

'What poker?' Monk was behaving with deep indifference, as he placed his cash in his wallet.

'Lavery, you swine.' The drummer laughed, amid general tittering.

'There's a challenge for you, Monk,' said the trumpeter. 'Are you chickening out?

Monk eyed Joel's earnings with contempt. 'Is that all you have?'

'That's all I'm going to need,' Joel fired back.

'Ooo,' came the chorus from the band members.

'All right, glamourpuss,' said the swine, sniggering. 'I'll let you come, provided you don't piss on the carpet.'

Joel peered up at him, confused.

'I don't trust you when you're not wearing your nappy,' explained Monk, flinging the white towel in his face.

They all laughed raucously.

18

'*You mean, he couldn't get it up?*'

Ita was standing in front of the piano in her flowing purple evening garments, holding her violin aloft.

'I didn't tell you that to have it shouted back at me,' Ellen said, glaring at her with indignation.

'Of course you didn't,' Ita replied, chalking her bow insolently, 'but if your husband couldn't even . . .'

'Let's continue the piece, shall we?' Ellen placed her hands over the keys at the ready. 'We need to do a bit more on the eight-bar phrase, from letter E.' She counted to four and the two of them continued with the Shostakovich.

They were in the front room of Ita's house in Blackrock, rehearsing the hauntingly sparse sonata for violin and piano. It was a more relaxing rehearsal space than the Conservatory hall and had a reasonable acoustic on account of the woodblock floor. As they played, Ita's violin whipped through the room like a slick blade. The Blüthner upright – almost as good as her father's Steinway – was in perfect tune. The sole problem was that Ellen was playing abysmally.

The only reason she was in Ita's place at all was that Joel hadn't returned home from being with his father. Nor had he called her. And so, after waiting a full hour, Ellen lost her patience and drove to Ita's pad, having posted a note on the kitchen door telling him to phone her the second he got home. The two women ended up playing the sonata together.

'Feck!' she said at one point, her fingers stumbling.

'Wait here.' Ita put down her instrument and went out.

'I'll shoot myself!' Ellen shouted, standing up.

'Can you postpone that till after the recital?' came the voice from the hall.

Ellen wandered around the room to try to distract herself, admiring its various oddities. Hanging over the windowsill was a large blue crystal, supposed to yield calm and serenity. On the opposite wall was a tarot card chart and a large reflexology diagram of the soles of the feet, subdivided into different coloured sections. Incense burned from the mantelpiece. She picked up the packet. Extracted, it said, in the Tibetan Himalayas from six ancient plants and roots. Ita's house was like this: whenever she walked in, she felt she was disturbing some ancient Wicca rite.

Ita returned with a lavender aromatherapy candle and a pot of camomile tea. They sat in the comfortable blue armchairs by the coffee table.

She regarded Ita unenthusiastically.

'It seems to me you're going to have to prime Joel first, to bring him on.' Ita started pouring out the tea into two multicoloured cups. 'And the best way to do that is to use the natural method.'

'What's that?'

'Chinese medicine. It never fails. He'll be *up* till the crack of dawn.'

'That's all right, thanks, Ita. I have my own natural method. It's called taking my clothes off.'

'Didn't work for you last night.'

'He was upset. I think that's understandable after the shock of the announcement. He was more himself today. And he'll be himself tonight.' Ellen tried to sound convincing despite her doubts.

Ita looked disappointed. 'Oh well. I suppose there's no point in preaching to the unconvertible. And I suppose you'll say no to my crystals, too?'

'No, Ita.' Ellen sighed. 'What about your crystals?'

'Right. I can select a crystal for him and ask that my choice be for his highest good. Selanite, for example. That's gypsum.'

'Go on.'

'I know what you're thinking, Ellen, but hear me out. Selanite is excellent for loss of fertility and sex drive.'

'Ita, there's nothing wrong with Joel's fertility or sex drive, as far as I'm aware. The problem is getting him to turn up for dinner.'

'It certainly won't do him any harm.'

'Okay, then. Select a crystal for him. Any chance of some more of your delicious camomile tea? Don't mean to change the subject.'

'If you give me your cup, I'll interpret the leaves for you.'

'I think you're teasing me.'

'Don't you believe in *anything*? If you let me interpret your leaves, I can try to find out where your beloved husband is right now.'

Ellen decided to assume her friend was joking. She pulled out her mobile phone instead. 'Thanks, Ita, but this is why they invented phones.'

19

'This is deeply distressing,' said Monk, surprised at O'Leary's unexpected winning streak. 'I'd never have believed you had such a talent for . . .' The sod looked up hopefully from his bean-bag. '. . . for having such incredible good luck,' Monk concluded. 'That's two on the trot, isn't it? How would you like to play Twenty-One?'

'Don't know how.'

'Yeah, that's what you said about the poker, you lying little shyster. How much am I down?'

O'Leary surveyed the large pile of toothpick splinters which he'd painstakingly broken into chips with his plump fingers and began counting them out.

'You were never up to much, O'Leary, when it came to maths.'

'I don't mind counting when I'm whacking you,' O'Leary shot back. 'Nine, ten, eleven . . .'

Monk eyed him with a modicum of respect. He could surprise you at times, so he could. There he was, bent over the coffee table, revealing his balding pate and counting furiously.

'. . . twenty-one, twenty-two, twenty-three . . .'

Let him, Monk thought, sitting back in his chair and balancing a beer can on his knee. Let him have his little pleasure.

'. . . forty-five, forty-six, forty-seven . . .'

'I'm hungry.' Monk got up, craving something salty. He went into the kitchenette and pulled out several packets of O'Leary Dry Roasted Peanuts, which O'Leary had dumped on him last June in Prague. He tore them open and searched out a clean bowl to put them in.

'. . . eighty-four, eighty-five . . .'

He walked back in and held the bowl under Rufus's beak. The bird wasn't even slightly interested. 'Shunning an O'Leary peanut!'

He shoved the bowl under O'Leary's nose instead, who scooped up a handful and stuffed them into his mouth.

'. . . hundred and eight, hundred and nine . . .'

Monk sat down at the coffee table.

'One hundred and . . . one hundred and . . . ten thousand . . .' O'Leary was muttering oddly to himself. '. . . ten thousand. *Ten thousand.*'

'Well?' said Monk. 'How much am I down?'

O'Leary suddenly looked ill.

'What's the matter? Something wrong with your father's peanuts?'

Monk was startled when he saw the man drop his head into his hands. He brought the bowl of peanuts to his nose and smelt them. No. They smelt okay. What the hell was this, then? O'Leary sank back down into the beanbag, his head still hand-locked. He looked as if he was about to start bobbing up and down any moment. Suddenly he let out a stifled sob.

'Sweet Jesus!' exclaimed Monk, horrified. 'What the hell's wrong with you?' He hadn't felt so uneasy since that evening, two years ago, when the local parish priest caught him on the smooth grass behind the priory with the mistress of the auxiliary bishop.

O'Leary muttered something indistinguishable.

'Speak up, man . . . *Jesus!*'

'Ten thousand!'

'Ten thousand what?'

'I nearly had it.'

Monk frowned down at the pile of toothpicks. 'You did on your arse.'

'Two more days and it would have been mine.'

'You're off your head, O'Leary. What are you on?'

In a low, lonely voice, the emotional mess started talking.

20

'Let's get this absolutely clear,' said Monk, frowning. 'Your father was willing to give you a cheque for ten thousand Euros because he assumed she was having an affair?'

Joel nodded at Monk, who was pacing up and down in front of the two-barred windows, both fists in his pockets.

'And the only reason he withdrew the cheque is because he didn't witness the adultery on Dun Laoghaire pier with his own eyes?'

'How many times do I have to tell you?' shouted Joel, miserable. *Ten thousand Euros . . . ten thousand Euros . . . ten thousand Euros . . .* The words were still rotating like a crazy mantra in his head.

Monk went to the drinks cabinet. 'Well, then, why are you looking so miserable?'

'Huh?'

He pulled out a bottle and closed the cabinet. He walked over and tweaked Joel's nose.

'Hey!'

'Try to be more optimistic about life, O'Leary. Champagne? I like to keep some for special occasions.' He held up a bottle.

'You think this is a special occasion?'

'You haven't lost ten grand, you conehead. You can get it back.' He shook the bottle and took aim at Joel, who protected his face with his forearms. When the cork popped into the wall, he yelped out loud, and Monk and Rufus laughed raucously in unison.

'How can I get it back?'

Monk managed to get most of the escaping foam into a chipped mug. 'Simple: you introduce me to your wife. I'll talk her into walking down the pier with me.' He shrugged in a gesture of pure obviousness. 'You call your old man down to your sixth-floor apartment and he can see us with his own four eyes.' He poured the fizzy liquid into a crystal glass and took a taste. He hesitated, then tasted it again and purred.

Joel frowned in disbelief. 'I couldn't lie to my father like that.'

Monk put down his glass, then filled the chipped mug and passed it to him. 'Lying isn't so hard, trust me. All that's required is a little honest application. Eh, Rufus?'

'*Bollocks!*'

'You rude bird!' exclaimed Monk with exaggerated dramatics. 'Have you been talking to Mother again behind my back?' He picked up his glass once more.

'Why would you want to do that for me, anyway, Monk?' Joel asked warily.

'I wouldn't be doing it for you, flakehead. I'd be doing it for a cut of your old man's cheque.'

'Forget it.'

'We could negotiate it. I'm a fair-minded man.' Monk strode over to the piano with his bowl of peanuts. 'As long as I get at least half, I won't complain.' He prodded a bass note. 'Even less, if she's any way pretty.'

73

'Dream on,' said Joel, sipping his champagne, chafing his lips against the rough edge of the mug.

'What she look like, anyway?'

'Drop it, Monk.'

'Why, are you ashamed of how she looks?' He ambled round to the back of his seat. 'That must mean she's ugly and small then, like you.'

'She happens to be very attractive,' Joel shot back. 'And tall, too.'

'Anyone would seem tall to you, O'Leary. Figures, man, give me figures.'

'Five foot seven in her bare feet.'

'Five foot seven, really? And how tall are you?'

'Five foot four and three-quarters.'

'Bullshit. You're five foot four and seven-fifteenths in your cowboy boots, and don't deny it. Go on.'

'Well, she's got long, blonde hair.'

'Are you listening, Rufus? Natural?'

'It's black, originally.'

'Oh, a woman of many colours?'

'She's also slim.'

'Flat-chested, you mean?'

'I didn't say that. She has a nice figure.'

'Is she good-looking? No, you needn't bother answering that.'

'Why not?' said Joel, annoyed.

'Well, she's married to you, isn't she?'

'Piss off.'

'And I suppose she works at home as well, does she? Doing your washing and ironing and cooking for you? A domesticated wife?'

'Actually,' said Joel, flushing in annoyance, 'she works as a music teacher in the Conservatory. She's highly sought after. And she plays in a chamber trio. As a matter of fact, they're giving a recital this Friday, at the National Gallery.'

'Really?' Monk winked conspiratorially at Rufus, who nodded in reply.

'Look, Monk, can we talk about something else?' Joel picked up the cards from the table. 'Your idea is crazy. And even if it *wasn't* crazy, it would never work because my father would never in a

74

million years believe Ellen could have an affair.' He tried to shuffle but the cards went all over the place.

'He believed you this morning, didn't he?'

'He was drunk this morning.'

'So get him drunk again.'

'Ellen isn't the adultery type, so let's just forget this. Now, your deal or mine?'

Monk sat across his futon and balanced the bowl of peanuts on his knee. He wore a caustic leer on his mug. 'Don't be so pessimistic,' he said. 'Every woman is that type, given the right circumstances. I mean, she's married, isn't she?'

'Exactly.'

'Ergo, she's the adultery type. By definition, you can't commit adultery if you're not married.' He crunched a handful of peanuts between his teeth. 'You know, O'Leary, there isn't a single married woman who doesn't secretly desire to be seduced by a handsome stranger, trust me. Rufus can attest to that, he's met enough of them. It's just that there's so few of us around, so the theory's impossible to prove.' He ran his hand through his heavily gelled hair. 'Think about it. Why else would marriage have been invented? Obviously, so people could commit adultery.'

He rubbed his greasy hands on his jeans, obviously pleased with his slick reasoning. 'It's a unique pleasure that could never be experienced otherwise.' He grinned, then flattened his hair at the back, while examining Joel with precision. 'Your wife having an affair? Oh, yes, it would be believable all right.' Monk raised the crystal glass to his mouth. '*Very* believable.'

'Let's just continue with the poker, shall we?'

'And very profitable for you, too,' Monk added with meaning. 'But I don't want to insist, if it makes you feel insecure.'

'What's that supposed to mean?'

'It means, you gork, the only reason you don't want to go ahead is because you're scared my theory of adultery might prove correct.'

Joel watched him crunch a fresh mouthful of peanuts, wondering if there were any limits to the man's unscrupulousness. 'Topic closed, Monk, okay?'

'Suit yourself, peanut man.' Monk shrugged and flung a nut at him. In an effort to catch it before it hit the table, Joel crashed into the table, scattering the neat arrangement of toothpick chips on to the floor.

Monk chuckled. 'Did you want to start again? No problem.'

'I was winning!' Joel protested. 'You owe me at least sixty!'

Monk rose from his stool. 'And by the end of the evening you'll be owing me six hundred. I'll be back in a minute.' He went out of the door, shaking his head and moaning at a loud volume, 'Ten thousand Euros . . . ten thousand Euros . . . such a terrible shame.'

21

'Do I have your permission?'

Monk lay across the top of his six-foot Kawai, a thick velvet cushion under his head. 'All it means', he told his confidant, 'is that I'd be bringing her here to show her the true meaning of marriage. How does that grab you?'

There was no reaction but, this late in the evening, Monk knew the response rate would be slow. 'Don't worry, I won't do anything to her,' he said, raking his fingers through the peanuts in the bowl at his hip. 'At least, not in the first ten minutes. God, that ceiling needs a paint, eh?' He popped a peanut into his mouth.

'Funny thing is, I still haven't a clue what she looks like. I bet she's delightfully plain. Then again, when the lights are out, delightfully plain women can become delightfully delicious women. Let's make a bet.' He grabbed a single peanut and held it up. Beanshaped, like O'Leary himself. Matured in the Caribbean sun, my arse. They tasted like salted mud. 'I bet you I'll have her moaning with pleasure on the futon by the weekend at the latest. *Well? What do you say to that?*'

The total lack of response surprised Monk. He turned his head, feeling the piano surface hard against his left cheekbone. No, his companion wasn't asleep: his eyes were still wide open.

'Fine, you want to plead the Fifth, that's your business. But take note: I am going to interpret your silence as approval.' He picked

76

up a half-nut and held it over his nose, closing one eye. He focused on a spot on the ceiling directly above his head and took aim. He jerked his arm and the nut flew straight up into the air, dropping down into his mouth. 'Five foot seven.' He crunched. 'Slim. Blonde dye, black roots.'

He grabbed another nut and dropped it into his mouth. 'Classical pianist.' He chewed.

'You're very quiet over there. Care for one?' Monk flung a nut over, but it was a wasted effort. 'What's the matter? Don't tell me you disapprove?'

Zero response.

'Or are we sulking? Do you begrudge me my pleasure, just because you don't get any yourself?'

No, you just couldn't talk to him.

Monk took a cigarillo from his silver case and lit up. He blew a ring up into the air, a thick and well-defined band of smoke which dispersed after about an arm's length. He blew another and that too dispersed.

'How am I to explain it to you, you inarticulate creature?'

There was still no response.

'Imagine . . . yes. Imagine you woke up one morning without your orange tail and found yourself grey all over, like a slate roof, okay? Now. Imagine that the only way of putting the colour back into you was if you slept with the chief parrot's wife. *Now* do you understand?'

Monk looked over. The brown eyes blinked, but still Rufus did not respond.

'No, I don't suppose you do.'

He took another toke of his cigarillo and blew another ring. 'You seem traumatised. Are you traumatised?'

Rufus began stretching his neck.

'I swear to God, if that little droob upset you before he left just now, I'll add his testicles to your grape feed.'

The parrot closed his eyes.

'Teaches piano.' He took another toke and blew another ring. 'At the Conservatory.'

Monk grinned at his mute companion. 'Could it be more perfect?'

22

When he got home the first thing he smelt was garlic.

In the kitchen Joel discovered two pieces of chicken coated in sauce under a tinfoil wrap in the oven. Cold solid. On the hob was a saucepan in whose depths wallowed a yellowed puree of potato. Joel went into the lounge. When he saw what lay before his eyes, it made him want to weep.

A slim candle was burning low over the dinner table, casting dancing stars on to two wineglasses and projecting a solitary flame reflection on to the black window-pane. In the middle of the table stood a bottle of cabernet sauvignon, the cork lying on the table.

Joel went into their bedroom, sweet-perfumed and dark. 'Ellen?' he whispered into the darkened space, but there was no reply. He listened to the ebb and flow of Ellen's breath, which spilt like soft feathers into the still air of the room.

He went over and lay down beside her, slowly, so as not to wake her up. Just to hold her in his arms and kiss her tenderly, that was all Joel wanted to do. To tell her he was sorry for standing her up without so much as a phone call. They'd planned the evening together. They were going to have dinner, spend time, make love. Instead, Joel had entertained a scumbag at poker – and hadn't even had the wit to collect his winnings.

As his eyes grew accustomed to the dark, Ellen's pale face gradually separated itself from the shadows. It was warm in the room and the duvet was thrown down over her hips. She was in the same sexy negligée she'd worn last night. Her face was dim, but beautiful. Joel lightly caressed her hair, but she moaned and shifted in the bed. A narrow wisp of light from the kitchen now illuminated her cleavage and threw Joel into a state of serious arousal.

Why the hell did I go to Monk's? I could have come straight back. Look at her. She was waiting for me!

He ran his hand gently over her silk-sheathed hip. Was it too late to make love? It was half-one in the morning. Would she not be fit to devour him? She'd given him enough hints, that was for sure. Last night, when he'd proved as impotent as a sausage in a pot of boiling water. This lunchtime, too, she was on for it.

Joel began pulling his trousers down his legs. Then he halted. He spent a few moments watching Ellen's pale face, listening to the quiet rhythm of her breath.

No.

It wasn't right. He couldn't possibly do it to her. Ellen had needs beyond the purely carnal. Needs he had to respect. For a start, she needed a good night's sleep to be fresh for her rehearsals tomorrow. Sure, she desired him. Lusted, hungered and craved after him. But still. She was asleep right now, and in that state she could hardly be aware of the fact that she lusted, hungered and craved after him.

Chances were if he woke her up she would kill him. And if she didn't kill him she wouldn't speak to him at breakfast.

Joel dragged himself off the bed, leaving Ellen to her peaceful slumber. He crept from the room and closed the bedroom door. Sacrifice for your partner. That's what marriage was all about.

In the kitchen, he fetched the red Christmas tablecloth from the drawer, returned to the lounge and extinguished the flickering candle. He lay down on the couch and pulled the tablecloth over himself. He stared at the ceiling, his pulse slowing. He closed his eyes. As soon as he did so, the image of Monk's callous face presented itself to him.

You call your father down and he sees us with his own eyes.

It was a sick, lunatic idea. Although it might well work in principle. Would his father cough up? Probably would. Would ten thousand Euros solve all their financial worries? Certainly would.

But what if she found out?

God, can you imagine?

Joel bent down and hauled the sheepskin rug up over his body. He turned on his side. It was a crazy idea, utterly wacko. And he had to push it straight out of his mind.

And never, ever think about it again.

wednesday

23

Drifting on the edge of sleepy consciousness, Joel overheard sounds of clanking cutlery coming from the kitchen.

He opened his eyes. Yellow light beams were shimmering on the ceiling above his head. It was morning and Joel was surprised to find himself lying on the living-room couch, fully dressed, underneath a tablecloth and a sheepskin rug. He rubbed his neck, stiff from its crooked overnight perch on the armrest.

You call your father down and he sees us with his own eyes. Joel tried to sit up, but his lower back felt like it was about to give. He collapsed back down on the couch, stupidly unable to extinguish the evil voice from his head. *What the hell is the matter with me?*

The door opened and Ellen entered the room. 'Joel, are you awake?'

Now, hearing her voice in the cleansing light of morning, Joel felt shame for having discussed his private life with that slimeball, who had as much principle as a molecule. He tried to answer his wife, but couldn't. He coughed. She sat down beside him on the couch and leant over him. She was in her sexy silk nightgown. 'Where were you last night, love?'

'Huh?'

'Your dad told me he left you at the train station. I thought something awful had happened.'

As soon as his voice returned, Joel apologised profusely. 'There was a gig,' he explained. 'I had to go to it. I tried to call you, but I left my phone on the balcony and I had no change.' He strained his head upwards and attempted a hug. He lay down again, then, stroking her arm and gazing up at her. 'God, you look beautiful,' he said.

'I do?'

'Yes, you do.'

To his surprise, Ellen slipped effortlessly out of her skimpy nightgown. Her breasts swelled before his eyes, yellow in the light beams of morning. Joel ogled them, fascinated.

'How do I look, now?'

'*Mmm.*'

She pulled the sheepskin rug and the tablecloth off him, then leant down and started kissing him on the neck, repeatedly, softly. While she was doing this, Joel found himself staring up at the ceiling, unable to quash Monk's outrageous suggestion from his mind. *What the hell is the matter with me?*

'What's the matter with you, Joel? You're all tense,' she whispered, unzipping his trousers and sliding in a hand. She kissed him on the mouth. 'Come on, Joel.'

'Sorry,' he said, 'everything's still asleep.'

'Well, let's see if we can wake it up then, shall we?' She straddled his thighs and pincered him on both sides with her knees. While she was undoing his buckle, her hair was trailing down in front of her face. She grabbed his trousers and tried to reef them down over his hips. To oblige, Joel lifted them sharply off the couch, but suddenly felt his back spasm in pain. He froze on the spot, arched in the air like a gymnast, unable to move an inch.

'What's wrong, Joel?'

'My back,' he groaned. 'My back!'

'Oh God, no.'

'It's okay,' he spat through gnashing teeth. 'Nothing serious. Be fine.'

But she looked frightened.

'It's all right, baby,' he gasped, 'you didn't cause it. I slept crooked on the couch. Just . . . help me on to the floor, will you?'

They moved together, one inch at a time. Eventually he managed to slide off the couch and down on to the floor. Ellen placed a cushion underneath his head.

'I'd better call a doctor.'

'*No doctors!* I'm in enough pain as it is.'

'You might have slipped a disc.'

'No, just a spasm,' he panted. 'Happened last week. Was shifting amps. Got better.'

'How long did it take to get better?'

'Few days only.'

'*A few days?*' She appeared on the verge of tears.

Seeing Ellen upset, he tried to move upwards, but his back wouldn't let him. He lowered himself carefully on to the floor. 'See? I can almost sit up!' He was gasping. 'I'll just lie here for a while. You get ready for work. I'll be fine.'

'You should have slept in the bed,' she said reproachfully. She stood up and left the room, trailing the nightgown behind her.

When Ellen returned, twenty minutes later, Joel was seated in an armchair, on to which he'd managed to drag himself without causing another lumbar catastrophe.

'How is it?' she asked.

'Better,' he lied.

'I'll go, so. If it gets bad again, call me, won't you? Here's your phone. Do you want anything from the kitchen?'

'A pulley?'

She kissed him on the forehead. 'I'll see you later, then.' On her way out she stopped and turned. 'Oh, by the way . . . you know that stroller we were talking about? Well, the shop phoned and told me that I'd have to pick it up before Saturday, if I'm still interested. I know you wanted to buy it yourself, Joel, but I think I'd better buy it today just in case. You could always buy a snuggly instead or . . . *Oh, my God, are you all right?*'

'Nothing,' he groaned, clutching his sides with two hands. 'It's nothing.'

She hurried over. 'Are you okay?'

'Yes,' he panted.

'But you're in pain?'

'Yes.'

'Is there anything I can do?'

'Yes.'

'What?'

82

'*Don't get the pram.*' He was staring up at her, petrified. '*Not today.*'

'What?'

'I want to see it first, before you buy it. Please.'

Ellen looked perplexed.

'It's our first purchase for the baby together,' gritted Joel. 'And I want to be there with you when it happens.'

'Well . . . we'd have to go in on Friday afternoon, then, together.'

'Okay,' said Joel, looking up at her now.

'Because any later . . .'

'Fine!' he gasped. 'It's a date.'

'Will your back be better by this evening, do you think?' She looked very apprehensive.

'Absolutely. I think so, yes.'

She studied him uneasily for a few moments, then twinkled a goodbye with her fingers and sauntered out of view. The moment the front door closed, Joel struggled to his feet and staggered to the phone. He put his hand on the receiver but he couldn't pick up. He took several deep breaths and tried to get a grip on the crisis facing him.

Sure, Monk was a conceited, perverted, ten-timing, scum-sucking womanising cad, who regarded women, especially married women, as a connoisseur would regard a rack of fine wines. This was an unquestionable fact. But that Joel needed a lot of money fast was even more of an unquestionable fact. *For God's sake*, he reasoned, *Dun Laoghaire pier is a public place! He wouldn't dare try anything.*

For a start, Ellen wouldn't let him away with a thing. She despised falsely charming creeps like Monk and she was not like those other women Monk manhandled. She had high moral standards. She would never do anything untoward behind his back. She was dedicated to Joel, as a wife and now as a mother.

And she was completely broke.

Joel's trembling fingers lifted the receiver. 'Just do it,' Joel whispered. 'You've got everything to gain!' He input the numbers of his father's direct line at HQ. It was ringing. 'Just keep calm and make it sound convincing. She's meeting him on the pier. She's meeting him on the pier.' The phone was picked up.

'Dad?'

'Joseph.'

Joel's mind went completely blank. It was as if the bottom had fallen out of his brain and all that was left was a gaping void. He had absolutely no idea why he had rung.

'Can you make it quick, Son? I have a client waiting.'

'Just a second.' Joel put a hand over his eyes and tried to remember. While he was trying, he could hear the squeak of his father's leather swivel chair at the other end of the line. Twenty seconds later he remembered. 'Dad. That thing we were talking about in the train station yesterday evening.'

'That thing? You mean your ridiculous accusation?'

'She's meeting that guy tonight.'

There was no sound at the other end of the line.

'Dad? Are you still there?'

'How do you know this?' He expelled a sharp gust of air into Joel's earpiece.

'Never mind,' Joel replied. 'Just be at the apartment this evening at seven, okay?'

'But how . . .?'

'Seven o'clock sharp. That's the time, unless I call again to change it, okay?' He hung up before his father could ask any more questions and left the phone off the hook. Stiff-backed, he tottered out to the balcony and swallowed a lungful of fresh air. The adrenalin had begun to pump, the back pain to numb. Joel combed his hair over his head with his fingers.

'I've got to get that damn ten grand,' he swore, through closed teeth. 'And to hell with the consequences.'

He picked up his mobile phone and called Monk to arrange a rendezvous.

24

At the appointed time, Joel made his way into Quaver Instruments.

He found Monk upstairs, seated at a digital piano at the far end of the store, concentrating on a manuscript open on the rack in front of him. As he approached, Joel recognised the piece. It was Chopin's 'Tristesse', which Monk was playing in a syncopated, jazzy rhythm definitely not intended by that fastidious – if safely dead – composer. It was one of the pieces on Ellen's concert programme for Friday. Weird coincidence!

Joel walked up to him. He stood by the piano but Monk continued playing. His long, bony fingers flickered like a spider's legs over the keys. He was in his smart green velvet jacket and he smelt of expensive aftershave. He stopped playing only when he came to the end of the piece. He pulled out a wallet. He produced three twenties and slammed them down on the piano top. 'You don't deserve it, O'Leary, after chickening out on me like that, before I had a chance to win it back. Now get lost.'

Joel scanned around the general vicinity before speaking, to make sure there was nobody there who knew him. 'Monk,' he said in a low voice, pocketing the money, 'that thing you were talking about last night.'

'What thing?'

'The cheque. The pier. The walk. My father. Ellen . . .'

'And me.'

'Yes.'

A smile trickled across Monk's lips. 'I knew you'd come round, sooner or later.'

'I haven't come round,' replied Joel, 'it's just that . . .'

'You've had a rethink?'

Joel nodded, preferring that formulation.

Monk resumed playing, shaking his head and tutting like a kangaroo. 'I'm shocked, O'Leary. That's all I can say. There I was, imagining you were such a loyal and considerate husband.'

'Hear me out, will you?'

'With an unshakeable faith in the sanctity of marriage.'

'Will you stop playing for a minute?'

'Please accept my sincere apologies,' Monk said, turning the page. 'I'll never judge another man so harshly again.'

'Look, Monk, all you have to do is take her for a walk on the pier with a dog, like we talked about. Okay?'

Monk slowly removed his fingers from the piano.

'See, Ellen likes walking on the pier – she used to go walking there with her old Jack Russell. Here's my idea: this afternoon I get hold of a Jack Russell, somehow, and I bring it over to your place. This evening, at a quarter to seven sharp, you and the dog wait for me and Ellen at the ice-cream van by the pier. We all buy ice-cream cones. I introduce you to Ellen. When she sees the dog, she'll go ape. We'll all go down to the pier. Now for the key point in my strategy. Are you ready?'

Monk's face was a picture of bemused curiosity.

'I tell Ellen I left potatoes on the boil. She's paranoid about apartment fires. I tell you both to continue on without me, that I'll catch up with you in five minutes. Meanwhile, my dad calls round at seven. I bring him upstairs, where we have a telescope. He sees the two of you together. Get my drift?'

'Brilliant!' Monk cried, for everyone to hear. 'What a truly stunning plan! Oh, tell it to me again, please. It's so clever. O'Leary, you've got a military mind. You're wasting your time in jazz – you should be out on the battlefields.'

'Monk, will you keep it down, please.'

'How much are you going to pay me for my services?'

Joel knew it would come up so he was prepared. He'd grown up watching his father haggle with a host of charity organisations and he'd picked up a few tricks along the way. The key was to throw out the lowest offer you dared, without making yourself sound drunk, and hope to hell the other guy was stupid. 'Okay,' he began. 'I'd be willing to give you, say, two . . .'

'Two thousand.'

'*What?* I was going to say two hundred!'

Monk laughed. 'Get real. This piano costs two thousand: I can accept nothing less.'

'I can't give you two thousand.'

'Four thousand, then.'

'Come on, Monk!'

'Your old man's going to pay you ten so what are you getting all greedy for? I just want my fair share. You're asking me to go for a walk on the pier: I have a phobia about piers. You're also asking me to bring a dog. Have you any idea how much I despise dogs? I'll do it for three thousand Euros.'

'Four hundred.'

Monk shrugged. 'You'll end up with nothing anyway.' He turned back to the piano.

'Okay. One thousand.' As soon as he said it, Joel regretted it.

'Two point eight thousand.'

'I'll give you one and a half thousand, Monk. That's my final offer.'

'Two point five thousand.'

'One point eight.'

'Two point two.'

'Jesus Christ,' said Joel. 'One point nine.'

'Two point one,' said Monk dismissively. 'It's my final offer.'

Joel knew he was serious. 'Two grand.'

'Done!' Monk stood up and shook his hand, grinning evilly. 'Could you not have agreed that in the beginning and saved us all this trouble?' He sat back down. 'Now, if you don't mind, I'm trying to get some music practice on my new upgrade.'

Joel was fuming. 'I want you to be quite clear about something, Monk.'

Monk completely ignored him, turning his manuscript back to the opening page.

'I'm paying you to take her for a walk with the dog, nothing more, nothing less. I don't want you touching her.'

'You don't?'

'She's got high standards of hygiene.'

'Really? Well, why the hell did she marry you, then?'

'Also, I want you to keep the conversation decent. I'm paying you good money, Lavery. It shouldn't be too much of a problem for you to dream up clean conversation for a change. And no bad language.'

'Wouldn't fuckin' dream of it.'

'You can talk about the dog. Talk about diet, training, breeding. Talk to her about music. She likes theatre, too. Payments to politicians, I don't know. Just make it polite and clean, have you got that?'

'Yes, General O'Leary! And will there be anything else, sir?'

'No, I'll call you later. I have to get out to Shankill. There's this dog I'm going to have a look at.'

'Well, best of luck on your mission, sir!' Monk grinned, exposing a row of perfect, gleaming teeth. He gave a sharp salute with his left hand. And then an equally sharp stiff finger with his right.

'Yeah.' Joel pulled away and went back down the stairs.

25

After her two o'clock lesson, Ellen left her room and went downstairs. Rehearsals were over for the day, despite her protests. Ita and Sean had excused themselves by saying they had other things on and that one marathon session per day was quite enough. So Ellen decided to go shopping instead.

Passing reception, Ellen noticed that the poster advertising the Friday recital had disappeared, leaving a rectangular gap in the middle of the green noticeboard. She brought it up with Tom.

'Some fella came in here this morning,' he told her, shaking his head with disapproval. 'Arty-looking guy, you know? I think he took it down. I called after him but he walked off.'

'I can't believe someone would do that.'

'Don't worry, Ellen,' he told her, bending down. 'I have a spare.'

'I'll put it up myself.'

'Thanks, love.' He handed it to her.

She went over and pinned the top corners of the poster to the noticeboard.

Chamber recital in memory of distinguished pianist and conductor Hugh Butler will be held in the Shaw Room, National Gallery of Ireland, on Friday, 25 August at 1.05 p.m.

Beethoven	*Piano Trio No. 7 in B♭, op. 97 (Archduke)*
Shostakovich	*Sonata for Violin and Piano*
Chopin	*Etude No. 3 in E major – Tristesse (piano)*

The East Coast Trio:
Ellen O'Leary (Butler), piano
Ita Mulrooney, violin
Sean Knowles, cello

Ellen attached the bottom two thumbtacks.

'I'm sure you'll play a blinder for him,' Tom said.

She waved farewell to Tom and left the building. Outside, she stopped to check how much she had in her purse. Forty Euros. This, together with what was left in her current account, made a total of ninety. She had just enough for the book on fertility and the CD she was hoping to buy. Her fortnightly cheque wasn't coming in till next week. Ellen was running low. She didn't want to have to withdraw money from their nest egg this afternoon, to finance current expenditure. But if she had to she would.

Passing Brown Thomas, Ellen couldn't resist a visit. She tried on a few expensive dresses, not that she had the slightest intention of buying one. None of them could match her black Chanel number for looks. When she left the department store she walked to a bookshop on Dawson Street. Upstairs, in its own separate area, was the health section. She flicked through a few books on female reproduction and finally found one with an interesting-looking entry in the index: 'fertility: time span 47'. Quickly, she turned to the relevant page and started reading. It didn't take her long to find what she was looking for. She read the section eagerly. Yes! That confirmed it in black and white! *Only three to four days after the fourteenth day before the next cycle.*

At most, Ellen had two nights left to try with Joel.

She put the prospect of failure out of her mind. She had to look on the positive side. Chapter 3: Increasing Your Chances of Conception. She turned to page forty-three. A healthy, balanced diet, yes. Plenty of fresh fruit and vegetables, yes. Avoid added sugar and refined grains, yes. Avoid refined oils and fats, yes. Cut down on caffeine. Oops! Cut down on alcohol, which can damage sperm and eggs – she'd better tell Joel to go easy on the booze. Smoking – neither of them ever smoked.

Ellen suddenly felt a strange sensation behind her. She was no longer alone. Someone had entered the small enclosed area. There was a strong whiff of aftershave. She heard a page turn. She knew she was being watched. She was used to this but, quite frankly, she was sick and tired of it. She panned her head slowly and spotted someone in the corner of her eye. She returned to her book, shielding it close to herself and hoping the presence would go away.

It did not go away.

Ellen was now unable to concentrate on the page. She felt a tingling of nerves chill her spine. Alone with a strange man in a quiet area of the bookshop. But she was more pissed off than apprehensive. If they could clamp illegally parked cars, she reasoned, why the hell couldn't they clamp illegally parked eyeballs? Ellen wanted to turn round and give the guy a withering stare, but heaven only knew the consequences of that particular tactic.

After a while, the indistinct presence disappeared from the corner of her eye. But the smell of expensive aftershave was still present, all around her. She cocked an ear for creaking sounds behind her. There were none. There was absolutely no sound in the room. Ellen suddenly got an awful, creepy sensation that the man was standing directly behind her.

She slammed the book shut and turned sharply on her heels and . . . and . . . oh dear . . . the room was empty. Except for a whole load of books and the lingering scent of aftershave, she was completely alone. 'Stupid!' she whispered, feeling utterly foolish. Had she gone paranoid all of a sudden? Probably the guy hadn't even noticed her.

Ellen bought the book, then walked to her favourite music store to chase up Ivan Davis's reputedly soulful interpretation of the 'Tristesse'. She went up the stairs, stopping at the corner of the stairwell to read a poster promoting a festival of world-famous tenors coming soon to Dublin. Ellen loved opera. She would have made enquiries, if the tickets hadn't been so expensive. She continued up to the first floor and entered the quiet classical music section, cordoned off by glass.

The second she closed the door she had the weirdest experience.

That aftershave again. Was she going mad?

She scanned the room. There were three men in all, idling around in separate sections. One was accompanied by a woman. Of the other two, one was a scruffy young chap of about eighteen and the other, whose face was partially hidden, was a well-dressed guy in his twenties, holding a black envelope case.

Ellen acknowledged that, in the broad scheme of things, the source of the aftershave was a matter of complete irrelevance. And yet she was overtaken by a crazy urge to find out whose it was. So she moved towards the eighteen-year-old, who was consulting a CD at the compilations section. She walked up behind him and paused briefly to inhale. She moved on at once. No, certainly wasn't coming from him.

Ellen did a U-turn and approached the accompanied male, who was standing at the counter reading a brochure and expounding on Wagner to a younger woman. She took a leaflet off the counter, then walked away slowly, pretending to read the leaflet. She passed behind the man and sniffed. His was a sweaty whiff, but not a hint of aftershave.

She left the counter. Other people had entered the room, but the third guy was still at the far corner, checking the CDs in the A–Z section. Was he the man with the aftershave? She figured it must be him. He was smartly dressed in a dark-green velvet jacket and a pair of black trousers. His hair was jet black, gelled all the way down to a short ponytail. He was reading the back of a CD case, his free hand resting casually on a hip.

Ellen ambled towards him, along the long A–Z composers section. He was standing at the Cs. She slowed down when she reached the Ds, picked up a Debussy CD and waited. Then, at the appropriate time, she replaced the CD and moved closer to the guy.

The scent was *unmistakable!* How incredibly amusing!

Without warning the man whispered an apology and moved politely sideways to make room for her. She thanked him, though he seemed too engrossed in his CD to notice, and stepped into the vacant space. She picked up the first CD she saw. To her surprise, it was a Chopin. What a coincidence!

A cursory glance established that the guy was extremely good-looking. He had olive skin and shrewd green eyes. There was an energy coming off him, a presence, a certain sexual . . .

'Excuse me.'

Ellen jumped and the man leant across in front of her to replace the CD. 'Sorry,' she muttered. She turned and watched him saunter through the room, glancing around in an assured and somewhat cool manner.

A thought now struck Ellen and brought a blush to her face. Ten minutes earlier in the bookshop, Ellen had lambasted this perfectly civil person for coming up behind her and gloating lasciviously all over her body like some criminal pervert. Obviously she'd been mistaken.

But what had she gone and done *herself*? She'd come up right behind this poor man, here, in the music shop, like some perverted stalker. She'd shadowed a total stranger for no better reason than that she'd taken a fancy to his aftershave. What on earth was *wrong* with her? *She* was the one who needed a shrink, not him.

Shaking her head and vowing herself to better behaviour, Ellen turned to the rack and fingered through the Chopin études, to see if she could find the recording she was looking for.

26

Monk ambled through the classical music section, perfectly aware that he was being watched. Therefore, he projected his most confident image. He went over to a square column in the middle of the room and took up position behind it. He picked up a Puccini opera from a large low-price bin. From here, he had a discreet and first-class view of O'Leary's wife, who was still standing at the Chopin rack.

He had to admit it, he'd been completely taken aback by her. So taken aback that he found it almost impossible to believe this was O'Leary's wife. But it was. He'd established that beyond all doubt that morning.

Monk had penetrated the Conservatory before lunch to check her out. He'd done this from no motive other than naked curiosity. He'd gone to the main office and charmed his way into the knickers of the gullible young secretary with giant earlobes. Monk told her he was interested in taking up piano lessons and asked if there was a yearbook, or the equivalent, to give him some idea of what the college and staff were like, before he made a commitment. She passed him an annual, full of pictures and photographed musical events. It took Monk only two minutes to find the name 'Ellen O'Leary' located below a group photo.

When he picked out her face, he was instantly impressed. It had a certain austere, detached and determined beauty. She was blonde and slim, and had high cheekbones. Type of woman who stood out from a crowd. Principled? Hard to know.

With minimal lying and manipulation, Monk managed to establish from the secretary that Mrs O'Leary had a lesson at two o'clock that afternoon, then she was finished for the day. He handed back the annual, thanked the woman and left. In the lobby, he scanned the noticeboard. At once he spotted a blue poster advertising a memorial recital next Friday for one Hugh Butler, obviously her father.

When he was certain that the nosy turd at the reception desk wasn't looking his way, he immediately removed the pins, folded up the poster and stuffed it in his pocket. The man called him back, but Monk simply left the Conservatory and went straight to a music store. There, he requested Chopin's Etude in E major – opus ten number three – and listened to the piece at the head-phones station. The slow theme was vaguely familiar to him. It was simple, but moving. 'Tristesse'? If anything, it was romantic rather than sad.

He went to Quaver Instruments, then, to buy the correspond-ing sheet music and to pay O'Leary his poker winnings from last night. He spent the next hour learning the slow section of the 'Tristesse' on the digital piano, informing that interfering geezer with the greasy ponytail that he was considering adding the article to his private collection. Then General O'Leary made his swashbuckling entry and let Monk into his dastardly masterplan.

By two thirty, Monk had gone to the Conservatory and located himself behind an electricity box on the far side of the road. Ten minutes later the General's wife emerged from the building and stopped to check inside her handbag. He eyed her from head to toe and had a positive reaction. She was as tall and as slim as her husband had promised, and she had an attractive feminine movement, which Monk felt instinctively would transfer nicely to the bedroom.

He'd given her a ten-yard head start, shadowing her down Grafton Street and up Nassau. It was a pleasure following her from that short distance, like some perverted, unemployed private detective. And she totally blind to his advancing pleasure. What an exciting prospect, taking a woman under such wonderfully false pretences. It would be truly delicious!

At one stage Monk dared to walk so close behind her that he could smell her perfume. It was a fruity scent, but it contained a definite hint of soap. This made perfect sense, of course: having to share the same bedclothes with the permanently glowing O'Leary could give any woman a keen interest in soap.

He'd followed her to the department store, then to the bookshop. He could have started up a conversation: it was the perfect opportunity. They were alone. He'd come up right behind her. He'd been sorely tempted to take down a nearby paperback guide to lovemaking, with full-colour plates, and open it up in front of her at the most explicit page he could find. To see how she'd react. But a sixth sense told him it would be better to wait. And so he left the room quietly before she turned round. He continued following her outside, anticipating that she'd go in somewhere to eat. But then, unexpectedly, she'd cut into the music store. Instantly Monk conceived a brilliant plan.

On her way up the stairs she had paused to consult an opera poster on the stairwell. Monk swerved past her unnoticed and entered the classical music section, assuming this to be her most likely destination. He'd been absolutely correct: moments later she entered the section after him, innocent as a lamb, though a good deal more sexy.

Monk had gone to the Chopin collection and picked out the first CD he saw. From the corner of his eye he saw the woman pause at the doorway and survey the room. Then she moved across the room and did something so bizarre that Monk guessed something was drastically wrong with her marriage. She began this extraordinary little game.

She walked up behind a spotty adolescent and paused for a few moments, before moving off. She then approached a middle-aged ponce with a moustache, who was rambling on to some bird about the opera house in Bayreuth. For some odd reason – he was a fat slob – Ellen delayed even longer behind this particular bore. It looked very much as if she was *inhaling* him.

Next, it was Monk's turn. O'Leary's wife moved along the composers' rack by the window, manoeuvred her way slowly up to him and paused. He politely made room for her, careful to ignore her whispers of gratitude. She picked out a CD and, feigning interest in the container, she discreetly subjected him to a thorough visual examination. He knew this because he could sense her gaze on his skin, while he stared at the *Chopin Favourites*, and, *hell*, the gaze had lingered. Ha! Hardly a surprise that he'd finished first in her erotic survey.

Monk grinned. He found this behaviour rather horny, particularly from a woman who, in all other respects, would have struck one as extremely well bred.

He was still standing at the low-price CD bin by the column, awaiting Ellen's next move. As he did so, he surveyed her slender form. She was impressive. Monk was flabbergasted that such a woman could end up hitched to a loser like O'Leary, to whom the term 'sexual magnetism' was medieval Swahili. For chrissakes, the guy looked like he'd been processed in a sausage factory.

Monk would have to go to O'Leary, his tail between his legs. 'Look, O'Leary,' he would say, all humble, 'I was wrong about you all along and I humbly apologise. Your good wife resembles you in no conceivable way. She is not overweight, greasy or putrid. She is slim, clean and well dressed. And she is surprisingly attractive.'

Monk peered admiringly at her long blonde hair, which formed a straight line across her lower back. He surveyed the contours of her cellulite-free body through her jacket and skirt, and imagined how she might appear without such useless impediments as clothes.

She now bent down to inspect the CDs at the bottom of the rack. Monk tilted his head accordingly and became instantly aroused. He looked away and took a deep breath. Who would have credited it? If he'd known she could do that to him, why, he might have offered a reduced rate.

Mind you, Monk had to admit, the issue of money was not now at the forefront of his mind. Her hot, feminine beauty had pushed it well out of the way.

O'Leary's wife strode across the room and joined the long queue in front of a female assistant. Monk dropped the Puccini CD and scanned the scene. There was another assistant working behind the counter, a skinny squirt who did not look too bright. Monk went straight up to him. He was foostering around in an open drawer of discs. 'Excuse me,' he said to the squirt, at some volume. 'There's something I need to ask you.'

Monk was glad to note that all eyes in the queue were on him.

27

'I'm fairly sure it's a Chopin piece, but I just can't recall the name.'

Ellen stared at the guy with the aftershave, who had gone up to make an enquiry. She listened in, curious.

'It's a slow piece,' the man explained. 'Might be an étude. Do you know what an étude is?'

'A two'd?' repeated the assistant, looking puzzled.

'I've often heard my mother humming it. I don't even know what key it's in. Sort of goes like . . .' He began to whistle, softly and with the precision of a seasoned performer.

Instantly Ellen recognised the tune. She was mortified, then dumbfounded. It was her very own 'Tristesse' – the piece she'd been rehearsing all week. She stared over at him in amazement. He paused at the end of the second bar, then closed his eyes. He continued into the third bar, sustaining the high C, then travelling down again, sounding out each note in perfect pitch. He stopped at the beginning of the fourth bar and opened his eyes – directly at her. She glanced away.

'You don't know that tune, do you?' he asked the assistant.

'Sounds like the European Cup theme,' barked a skinhead type in the queue in front of her.

The man smiled politely. 'Never mind. Do you know of any place that sells sheet music?'

'Quaver Instruments have a good collection. They're in Wicklow Street.'

He left the counter and went towards the door.

Ellen turned and watched him as he walked from the room, empty-handed. *Why didn't I say something? What's the matter with me?*

Why the hell didn't she say something?

Monk made his way slowly down the stairs, cursing the lost opportunity. She couldn't take her eyes off you, goddammit! You had her transfixed! So why didn't she speak up?

He slowed down, in case she tried to follow. Give her a chance. Stop and check your watch. Don't look round. Look at the display in the corner of the stairwell. Look indifferent. Look at the stupid posters.

He stood in front of the poster of the three tenors. What he should have done was address a general enquiry to the queue instead. She'd have spoken up if he'd done that. But no, he took the tosser's word and walked out! What was he *thinking* of?

Soon it became clear that she wasn't coming after him. Annoyed, Monk descended the staircase past a herd of American tourists moving up like low-lying buffalo. Unfortunately, it would have to wait till tomorrow. Today he'd blown his luck wholesale.

'Excuse me,' said a tentative voice from behind.

He turned round. It was her.

She was standing several steps above him, breathless. 'That piece you were whistling . . .' She pointed back up the stairs.

Monk said nothing.

'I know it,' she said. 'It's a Chopin étude, it's his third, in E major.'

Monk stared at her, taken aback. It was the first time he'd heard her voice. He didn't expect her to sound so . . . so . . .

'Opus three . . . No. Opus ten.'

'Opus . . .?'

'Ten, number three – the "Tristesse", that's what it's known as.'

' "Tristesse"?'

'Yes.'

Her eyes were stark and intense.

'Well, thank you very . . . How do you spell "Tristesse"?'

As she was spelling the word, Monk searched in his pocket and withdrew the folded-up poster advertising her upcoming concert, which he'd nicked earlier from the Conservatory. He scribbled on to it, repeating the spelling out loud.

'Stupid!' she exclaimed. Monk raised his eyes, but she was in fact rebuking herself. 'I ran out without paying for this. Look: it's written here . . .' She held up her CD and pointed out the sixth entry. 'Etude number three in E.'

'I appreciate you coming out after me.'

'I'd better go back up and pay for it, before they arrest me.'

She smiled, waved and turned on her heel. She reascended the stairs and disappeared. Monk hurried back up the stairs himself and returned to the classical section. She'd rejoined the queue. He went straight to the Chopin section, located a copy of the CD she'd shown him and queued up directly behind her. He could not think of anything decent to say. That perfumed, soapy scent was fogging his brain.

Unexpectedly she swung round and smiled. 'Did you find it all right?'

It was the way she was looking at him. *Into* him. It threw him. Perhaps it was his own dumb guilt because he'd been following her around for the past hour but all he could do was hold up the CD for her to see.

'I'm told it's a good interpretation,' she said.

'I probably wouldn't hear the difference.' Excellent . . . she's buying it, modesty is good. Gets you everywhere . . .

To his annoyance, she turned back to the cashier. There were now just two people in front of her. Then she would be gone. He had to think of something. But what? Monk stared rigidly at her blonde, clean hair, his mind a total blank. He could think of nothing to say. Where were all his tried and trusted lines? They'd completely deserted him. Say something, goddammit! Anything!

'Do you play piano yourself?'

She turned round. 'Yes, as a matter of fact, I play in a trio.'

'Oh, really?'

'What about you?'

'I get by on the piano, very poorly. I can't read music, but I'm determined to learn the "Tristesse". Sort of a present for my mother's birthday. She lives for music, but she's not well.'

She looked concerned. 'You're learning it off a *CD*?'

'It's all I've got.'

'You must have a good ear.'

'I hope so – her birthday's next week. I should probably look for piano lessons, someone who would sit beside me and show me the notes of the main theme. I'm a fast learner, but I've left it a bit late.'

'Haven't you ever had a teacher?'

'Had one when I was six – put me off for life.' You lying bastard.

'That's a pity,' said Ellen.

'They'd want me to practise scales or something. Which is a shame because I can tell you I'd pay a good fee to learn how to play this piece.'

She still sported that look of concern.

'Anyway' – he shrugged, dropping his eyes to her cleavage – 'I'd imagine it'd be difficult to find a good teacher who'd be on for having a one-off session in private.'

The queue had moved forward two spaces, though she hadn't yet noticed.

'I feel like an illiterate', said Monk, warming up, 'who's hopelessly in love with literature, but can't find anyone to teach him to read.'

'That must be frustrating.'

'I don't suppose you know of any piano teachers, offhand?'

'Actually,' she said, 'you're not going to believe this, but I happen to be a piano teacher myself.'

'*You?*' He paused for dramatic effect. '*A piano teacher?*'

She nodded.

Cashier: 'Next please!'

She stepped up to the counter and made her purchase. When she was finished, she stepped aside. Monk watched her fold a note into her purse, while he was paying for his CD. She put the purse into her bag and browsed at a nearby rack. The assistant offered Monk his seven Euros change. Ignoring him, he grabbed the CD and strode towards the door.

'Your change, sir.'

Monk continued to ignore the assistant and walked straight past Ellen. 'Nice talking to you,' he said, with a small wave. He opened the glass door, as if to leave.

'Excuse me?'

He turned round.

Ellen was looking at him, pointing in the direction of the cash register. 'You forgot your change.'

'Gosh, so I did!' Shaking his head self-effacingly, Monk walked back through the room and collected his change at the counter. He thanked Ellen. 'Stupid of me,' he muttered.

'I was just thinking,' she said.

'Always doing dumb things like that.'

'I have a small suggestion to make.' She seemed slightly hesitant, as if she were sussing him out. 'It's just an idea. I teach piano at the Conservatory.'

'You mean the music school?'

'Yes. And I was thinking, I might be willing to offer you a one-off music lesson, if you were that keen.'

'Oh?' Monk stroked his chin, doing his best to seem surprised, even a touch embarrassed.

'I don't wish to put you on the spot,' she remarked.

'Oh, no, no.' He gathered himself. *She certainly sounds eager.* 'But how soon could you see me, do you think?'

She shrugged. 'Would today be too soon?'

'Today?' He tried not to smile. 'Well, why not? Today would be wonderful!'

'Actually, I have a free space in an hour, after my three thirty. How is four o'clock?'

'Four is perfect.' He stuck out a hand. 'My name is Myles, by the way.'

'Ellen O'Leary.' She took his hand and shook it.

'Very glad I bumped into you, Ellen.'

'Well, so am I.'

100

Monk held her hand for as long as was decent, staring deep into her eyes as he did so.

28

It was a dirty kip of a place.

Before he even got to see the kennels out back, Joel suspected that the dog owner in front of him had a woeful track record on dog care. Joel made this inference from the obvious fact that the guy barely observed minimum standards of dog care on his own person.

But Joel was desperate. He'd consulted the 'Dogs for Sale' section of the *Evening Herald* earlier that afternoon and three ads had caught his attention. The first was for the sale of a Jack Russell. This would have been perfect, except for the fact that the dog, to Joel's extreme annoyance, had died in a motorcycling accident that very morning.

The second ad appeared two entries down in the same section. Male, one year old, brown, house-trained and nurtured from its earliest days in a 'caring, supportive environment'. When Joel rang up, he learnt that the owner had forgotten to specify that it was a chimpanzee.

The third ad boasted a 'variety of dogs'. Joel called the number and was told they included a Jack Russell. Without further ado he took the bus to Shankill.

The man now brought him out to his backyard, from where Joel had a good view of the Sugar Loaf mountain. 'Here's your beloved Jack Russell,' said the man as they approached one of the kennels.

'I'll take it.'

'Don't you want to see it first?'

'A Jack Russell is a Jack Russell. It's my wife's favourite dog. She had to give hers up when we got married.'

The man frowned. 'Too much competition, was it?'

'Actually, no,' Joel replied. 'It was in the apartment regulations.'

'Here it is.' The man opened the wooden door and barked in a greeting.

The dog would have been white, with brown patches, had it not been for the fact that its ludicrously overgrown coat of manky hair was caked in dried mud. It had small, sharp teeth, and did not appear to have a particularly positive angle on other life forms.

'Very nice,' remarked Joel, hesitant. 'Any chance I could take her out, just for the evening? Could I do that?'

'Ah, now,' the owner said, eyeing Joel as if he had a screw loose. 'They wouldn't make the best dating companions.'

Joel laughed politely.

'Liable to embarrass you in a restaurant,' the man added.

'I guess so.'

'Very poor table manners.'

'It's for my wife,' Joel explained. 'I'm encouraging her to go walking on the pier. A dog is just the thing she needs.'

'For one evening?'

'Well, if she likes the dog . . . What's it called?'

'Doesn't have a name.'

'Right. If she likes the dog, she might want to keep it. I'd just be afraid she'd be stuck with something she didn't like.'

'A trial basis is not something I normally do.'

'I'm sure she'd like to go for a walk.'

'Who, now, your wife?'

'No, your dog.'

'The dog hasn't mentioned anything to me about a walk.'

'I'd pay a good rate for the evening.'

The owner peered at Joel, making him feel like a bit of an idiot, then he clawed sweat off the back of his neck. 'Well, when you put it that way,' the man said grudgingly, 'I suppose she could do with a bit of exercise. She's a quality breed, of course.'

'Of course.'

'Once was a show dog.'

'Is that a fact?' Joel peered in at the piece of mobile muck staring aggressively up at him. Well, why not?

'I'm just a bit reluctant to let her out to strangers. There's some queer types around, you know. No offence.'

'Well, I can assure you absolutely nothing will happen to the

102

dog, except she'll get a walk. My wife is particularly good with dogs.'

The owner was sizing him up. 'Hmm. Just for the evening, you say?'

'That's all. I can have it back before midnight.'

'All right,' said the man, opening the kennel. 'But I'll have to charge you the full rate. See it as a deposit.'

'How much?'

The dog started barking viciously and the owner bent down to attach the leash. Joel repeated his question, but was again ignored. The man stood up, red-faced. 'Just be gentle with her,' he said. 'She can get a bit nervous around humans.'

Joel felt a bit nervous himself. 'I don't suppose you've got anything more tame?'

'Sorry, we don't keep horses here.' He handed Joel the leash. 'Only dogs and humans.'

'You wouldn't happen to keep a spare muzzle?'

'No need for muzzles. The motto is: feed her right, and she won't bite.'

That pretty much disposed of that. Joel took the leash and the Jack Russell growled at him, but for the moment avoided his flesh. '*Good dog!*' he prayed.

'Seventy Euros.'

'*What?*'

'Summer rates.'

'I haven't got seventy Euros.'

'How much do you have?'

'Forty.'

'Deal.'

Joel produced two of the three twenties he'd got off Monk earlier, careful not to reveal the third. The man snapped them from his hand. 'Sure you don't want to keep her?'

'Well . . .' Joel eyed the dog for a moment. 'I don't think so.'

'Course you do! Save you the trip back. Anyway, isn't she the perfect pet? All she needs is the right home to bring out her true nature. Here.' He laughed. 'I'll show you out.'

The dog led the way, dragging Joel up the side passageway to the front of the house. Once there, the mutt paused at a rockery to piss.

'And you can keep the obnoxious cur from crapping on my flowers, if you don't mind. She has a bad habit of doing that when she gets excited.'

'Good dog,' said Joel, pulling her away. She was growling and drooling in the direction of his ankles, and Joel was glad he was wearing his cowboy boots today.

The man grinned. 'All right, then?'

'Grand,' said Joel, unsure what precisely he'd let himself in for.

The man squatted down and ruffled the cur's ears. 'You be good, now, Killer; you could have a whole new life ahead of you.'

29

Monk walked into the empty restroom of the hamburger restaurant, placed his stylish black satchel on top of the hand dryer and subjected himself to a close visual examination in the mirror.

He liked what he saw.

Not least, the dark-green jacket, the black trousers and the blue silk shirt. Physically, too, there was not a lot to fault. Teeth: pristine white, as usual. Eyes: surprisingly clear, despite the lack of sleep. Monk raised his head and inspected his neck: lean as always. He examined his face: no unwanted nasal hairs or bits of skin; a decent designer stubble today.

He removed his silver cigarette case and opened it up. He angled the tiny mirror against the mirror of the restroom and got a perfect left-profile shot of himself, from behind the ear. He repeated the procedure for the right profile and straightened a flank of hair at the back. He put away the cigarette case and checked the black mop for grey hairs. There was only one. He twisted it round his finger and pulled. Shaking it on to the floor, he checked his hairline. Still no change since he was eighteen.

Monk took a minute or two to consider the overall impression his face was likely to make on your average Dublin female. Duly satisfied, he bent over and squirted soap from the dispenser. He thumped the tap lever and washed his hands in the outgushing water. He struck the hand dryer and a gust of warm air blasted into his face, dishevelling his lacquered hair. Monk jumped backwards and thumped the funnel downwards. Some gobshite, he cursed, washing his face in a hamburger restaurant. When his hands were dry, Monk returned to the mirror and rearranged his coiffure.

He was ready for O'Leary's wife.

Monk pondered the events of the afternoon so far. She had been a total and complete pushover. On her own initiative, she'd come down the stairs after him. Then she'd offered him a piano lesson. Monk had barely to suggest it, yet she was tripping down the steps to indulge him. Obviously dying for a bit of excitement in her life. And who could blame her?

He brought his hand to his mouth to check his breath.

'Ellen,' he uttered. The name had a pure and innocent ring to it. As far as he could remember, he'd never had an Ellen before. No, he was sure of that. He'd certainly had a couple of Helens, but not an Ellen. He wondered where she was from. She was well educated and refined.

'Ellen O'Leary.'

The surname jarred horribly. The contagious association with her husband did her no favours. Ellen Butler – now that sounded finer. Butler had a nice ring to it, like Lavery: Anglo-Irish; more in tune with her ascendant nature.

Monk recalled the precise moment this Ellen Butler opened her mouth, on the stairwell of the music store. Her voice contained something unfamiliar, which had thrown him off his guard. He wasn't used to that sort of . . . directness, self-assuredness in a woman. And he had to acknowledge that it did give the proceedings a special flavour.

A toilet flushed behind him and a spike-haired teenager exited a cubicle. Monk watched him through the mirror. The disgusting creature strode straight out of the door without washing his hands. As he left, a grubby-looking old man pushed his way in and shuffled to a cubicle, banging the door behind him.

'Base degenerates,' muttered Monk. He checked his watch: two minutes after four. He adjusted his tackle, walked out of the Gents' and crossed the road towards the Conservatory.

30

It was nearly five past four.

Ellen flicked through her sheet music collection and pulled out her old 'Tristesse' manuscript. On the top corner of the folio was the name 'Hugh Butler', in faded handwriting. Shortly before his death, her father had given her the folder, which contained many of his favoured pieces.

The 'Tristesse' was the special piece she'd chosen to play in his honour. It was he who had taught the piece to Ellen. Learning it as a child marked the point in time when her love for the piano blossomed and merged into a deeper appreciation for her father. It had been a favourite of his. His mother had bought him the sheet music when he was ten and demonstrated it for him on the Steinway upright. He, in turn, had used the same manuscript to teach Ellen this piece as a child, on the very same piano, which now resided in their apartment. The piano and the manuscript were two of the most precious heirlooms she had.

The more she thought about it, the more stunned she was by the coincidence in the music shop. It was almost as if Myles had been brought her way for a reason. But what reason?

There was a knock on the door.

'Come in!'

Ellen's gracious new pupil entered the room and pulled a small white envelope from his pocket. 'For the lesson,' he said, placing it on top of the piano.

Ellen decided not to object. 'I'll be with you in a moment. You can sit at the piano.'

He sat down, opened the piano lid and began playing the scale of C with both hands, at a moderate pace. He appeared to be concentrating very hard, moving his eyes back and forth between his hands as he played, keen not to err. Listening to him now, Ellen didn't see how he could hope to learn the slow section of the 'Tristesse' in time for his mother's birthday next week, considering he couldn't even read music. Had this been a mistake?

Why had she offered him a lesson? Had it something to do with the fact that this classy guy was a dead ringer for Adonis? No, hardly. She'd made the offer from a simple desire to help. It was so rare to find a student so keen to learn – whatever his motives. And it was even rarer to find a student so keen to pay for the lesson, although she'd purposely avoided the topic of payment.

Ellen went over and placed her copy of the 'Tristesse' on the piano rack.

He then produced a manuscript from his black case. 'I didn't realise you had your own copy,' he said. 'I purchased the sheet music just now, in case. Never mind.' He put it on top of the piano and opened her copy instead. He peered at the music, flexing his mouth.

'Don't let it put you off,' she said. 'It only looks complicated.'

'It certainly does.' He looked bewildered by the complicated design of black dots and horizontal lines.

'Since we're only doing the slow melodic section, it shouldn't take too long. You say you have a good ear?' She sat down to his right. The musty smell from the folio brought her right back in time. Her father. Playing the piano in the living room of their Glenageary home. The way he would move backwards and forwards on the stool, looking down at her through thick glasses, his seemingly lazy fingers flitting like lightning across the keyboard.

'So! You wanted me to show you the fingering, didn't you?'

Ellen was about to begin playing, when the door to the corridor pushed open. It was Ita.

'Tom told me you were up here . . . oh . . .' She stopped when she saw Myles, took in the situation and winked at Ellen. 'Just to say I can't make tomorrow's rehearsal until ten thirty. Okay?'

'That's fine.'

Ita pointed to Myles's back and made a suggestive erotic movement with her eyebrows. Then she left. Again, Ellen adopted the position and brought her hands to the keys. 'I'll just play the melody. Slowly, first, to give you an idea.'

She stared at the page and remembered.

'**Study**', it said at the top, in bold. 'Op. 10, No.3.' On the top right corner, 'F. Chopin.' Below this, '*Lento, ma non troppo.*' Her father had shown her the meaning of these mysterious words many years earlier. He had sung the word *Lento* to her. It meant slowly. He had sung the word slowly. *Ma non troppo.* But not too slowly. He had sung those words more rapidly. For a quick moment Ellen allowed herself to recall the paternal smile, the eye-glimmering wink. Then she began.

'*Piano,*' she said, while playing, 'that means softly.' She played softly, then got louder at the hairpin. 'The numbers are for the positions of each finger. *Ritenuto.* That means you must hold back a little here . . .'

As she was playing, Ellen glanced briefly at the strange man sitting beside her. He looked sombre and attentive, and his eyes were glued to her fingers.

Monk stared at her hands, fully aware that he was being scrutinised.

Her wedding ring glistened in the bright light streaming through the window, as she moved her slender fingers across the keys with a fluid, fragile sensitivity. Her nails were carefully manicured and varnished. Monk gave her the once-over, when it was safe to do so: the slender shoulders and arms; the pale skin; the thin lips and pronounced chin; the long, clean hair, with not a split end in sight.

He peered through the gap in her blouse. Milk-white breast. 'Lovely,' he said, immediately lowering his eyes to her fingers and somewhat surprised by his second mild sexual arousal of the afternoon.

She finished playing the slow passage.

'Beautiful,' he said. 'You practically played it with your eyes closed.'

'I've known it a while,' she told him.

'I can't even play it with my eyes open.'

'Well, maybe we can rectify that now. At least you know the melody – you certainly whistled it nicely. You must have performed in public before.'

'Oh no,' he said. 'I only ever perform for my own pleasure, Ellen.'

'All right, then,' she said stiffly. 'Let's start. You don't read music at all, do you?' She shifted her stool sideways to give him more room. 'See if you can play this.'

She played the first bar very slowly with her right hand, giving a running commentary as she went. Index finger for the introductory B, then thumb and small finger pressing down the G and the E simultaneously. Back to the B, which led into a simultaneous G and F, using the thumb and *third* finger this time. The last three semiquavers, the A, the B and the A, were easy: they were played consecutively by the thumb and index finger.

'It's not as difficult as it seems. I'll play the first bar one octave up. See if you can follow me as I play.'

As the lesson progressed, Monk imitated her every finger move like some dumb retard. But he had to concede it was fun. Not since kindergarten had he got such a harmless kick out of doing something so totally redundant. Each bar that she got him to repeat he replayed virtually without error. The compliments served only to intensify his enjoyment. After five minutes they'd covered the first third of the principal melody.

In time, Ellen turned her attention to the left hand. She clapped out the rhythm for several bars, stressing the appropriate beat: '*One-two*-three-*four-five-six*-seven-*eight* . . .' Now she played the melody with both hands.

Monk followed her, at a lower octave, and in five minutes flat he performed the first five bars with both hands – virtually without error.

Ellen sat back in her chair and sighed.

'Is something wrong?'

'Are you sure you haven't played this before?'

'Scout's honour! Never saw the piece in my life before today.'

She smiled for the first time since he'd produced the envelope, then shook her head, clearly impressed by his mind-boggling talent. Over the next ten minutes they covered the first two lines. As a cautionary measure Monk decided to spice up his playing with some excellently convincing cock-ups. And he discovered a most interesting phenomenon: the more cock-ups he made, the more she brimmed with encouraging words. Blunderbussing into the keyboard seemed to put her into a most congenial mood. Was this a female thing, or was she just a natural teacher?

'That's really excellent progress, Myles,' she said after a while. 'I don't think this is going to take too long after all.'

Monk peered into the corner of her eye, mere inches away, and grinned shamelessly. 'No,' he agreed. 'I don't think it will, either.'

31

'That new student of yours with the ponytail is certainly a bit of a ride,' remarked Ita.

They were in Café Rio, after Ellen's piano lesson. 'Not on my horse, he isn't,' she replied, sipping her latte.

'You mean to say you don't find him extremely attractive?'

'Not particularly.'

'Looked like a bit of poseur, from where I was standing. You know the type. Great that he's always available for sex – too bad it's not always with you. Bit of a shark. What was he like?'

Ellen shrugged. 'He was very civil, but it's hard to tell – it was a one-off lesson. He gave me a fifty, imagine.'

'God, Ellen, what did you have to do to earn that? He must like you.'

'I don't think so. I got the feeling he was deeply in love with someone else.'

'Oh? Who?'

'Himself.'

Ita cackled aloud with laughter, but Ellen was only able to give half-hearted support. She was worried, seriously worried – and not only about the recital. It was Wednesday afternoon. It was two and a half days since she broke the 'news' to Joel and they hadn't even come close to making love. Her clock was ticking. She would simply have to do it this evening and do it well.

'Something's on your mind, Ellen.'

'I wish it were on his.'

'You're worried about his back pain, is that it?' Ita leant forward over the table towards her. 'I could work on him a bit, if you wanted.'

'I beg your pardon?'

'Reflexology. What's his feet look like?'

Ellen claspsed her friend's chunky forearm. 'Ita, it's okay. Thanks anyway.'

'Maybe you should bring Myles home for a piano lesson, then, and make him jealous, rouse his loins.'

'Who?'

'Myles, Myles Lavery. The fellow you gave the lesson to this afternoon.'

'Hold on a sec,' said Ellen, staring at her friend.

'What?'

'How did you know his name was Myles? I never told you.'

'It's written on the Chopin manuscript.'

'What Chopin manuscript?'

'The one that's sticking out of your satchel.' Ita pointed at her bag. 'See, his name, on the corner?'

'*What?*' Ellen whipped the manuscript from her satchel, examined it and sat back, relieved. His name was written on the manuscript all right, but it wasn't her manuscript. It was his. On the upper corner, scrawled in neat black ink, was the name 'Myles Lavery' and just beneath, his address and mobile phone number. 'Thank God!' she cried, relieved to see that her precious copy had not been defaced.

'You have a right neck, Ellen,' teased Ita, 'pinching his manuscript on him, so you'd have to call him up later. I knew you fancied him.'

Ellen was barely listening to her; she was too busy trying to work out how it had happened. How could she possibly have taken his copy from the top of the piano without noticing it was his?

She leafed through the small pile of sheet music in the bag, searching for her father's prized copy. Oddly, there was no sign of it. She pulled the folios from the bag and went through them individually. No. It wasn't there.

A thought suddenly crossed Ellen's mind. Her faced creased up and she recoiled in horror. '*Oh, no!*'

'What's wrong?' asked Ita.

'Blast him, Ita, I think he's got my "Tristesse".'

32

All was quiet in the room.

Not a sound anywhere to interrupt his concentration. Just the occasional creak of floorboards from his mother in the living room above. Even Rufus had been lulled into immobility by his quiet presence.

Monk was seated at the grand piano, his arms folded. He was staring at her Chopin manuscript, standing on the rack in front of him, closed. On the top corner was the name in faded handwriting: 'Hugh Butler'. It had been sinfully easy. He'd casually lifted her copy at the end of the piano lesson and slipped it into his satchel while her back was turned – only to place his own copy on the rack. It was a cruel but highly inspired move, so perfectly executed that she hadn't noticed a thing.

Monk's cellphone was perched conveniently on the piano top in front of him. Very soon now, he figured, she would phone him. She would phone him the split second she copped on, because it was obvious what the 'Tristesse' signified to her. *I've known it a while,*' she'd told him during the lesson, in a melancholic voice. It was her father's copy. Her father was dead. The Friday recital was for her father. Oh, yes, she would call him all right.

And the ball would be back in his court. They would discuss how it should be returned. Monk would invite her over to collect it. Once he got her into his den, he would subject her to his spell. And the parrot – who'd suddenly become restless – would live to tell the tale.

'What's the matter, Rufus? Want a breath of fresh air in the garden?'

But it seemed like something else was on the bird's mind. Now he was flapping his wings and craning his neck. The garden gate creaked outside.

It's her! Monk sprang to his feet and pounced over to the window.

But the vision outside was not what he had expected. It was something altogether more unpleasant. It was O'Leary, scrambling down the steps to the basement, rebuking a filthy-looking dog like a deranged pensioner. His face was all red and sweaty, and his jacket was tied round his waist. He leant on the bell.

Monk stormed out and opened up. 'What the hell are you doing?' he snapped. 'You'll ruin it all!'

'Here's the Jack Russell for this evening, man! Take it.' He held out the leash for Monk and nodded approvingly, his eyes closed.

'I don't need it.'

'Course you need it. Remember our conversation in the music shop this morning?'

'You have thirty seconds to get yourself and your brute creation off my property.'

O'Leary calmly tied the dog to the railing, then breezed past Monk into the basement, slapping him amicably on the shoulder. 'Got to get a drink,' he said, vanishing inside.

Monk stood, holding open the door, stunned by O'Leary's brazen confidence. He glanced at the tethered dog, a plain – if filthy – Jack Russell with a likely attitude problem. He pointed a finger into the dog's face and gave her a dire defecation warning. Then he slammed the door and went in. In the kitchenette, O'Leary had his neck twisted under the tap, from which he was gurgling water like a suction pump.

'Did you hear what I said?'

'I got her from this dog man in Shankill.' O'Leary belched and proceeded into the front room. 'Tried to rip me off, too.'

Monk took a few seconds. 'And he failed, naturally.'

'I pulled the wool over his eyes. He thought I only had forty, but I actually had sixty. You have to be up to these guys.'

He collapsed on the futon, perspiration steaming off him like a mushroom cloud. 'Took me almost an hour to get here with the dog,' said Joel, mopping his brow with a large handkerchief. 'God, though, she has a temper. Every animal we passed, she either sniffed their backside or tried to bite their head off. One decent old grandad with a chihuahua threatened to sue me. She's a bloody animal. No wonder they refused to take her on the bus.'

'*Out.*'

'Take it easy, man! The plan is in motion. My dad's coming down for seven. I need you down with the dog at a quarter to. You know the score.' He grinned at Monk. 'Don't worry, man, it's under control. This is General O'Leary, remember?'

Monk shook his head, trying to work out what planet O'Leary resided on. It was almost as though the man had a pathological need to fail. 'You really are the most incredible person I've ever met, you know that?'

'Thanks, man.' He shrugged with comic modesty. 'If you want, I'll jot you down some tips.'

'Get out, O'Leary. I don't need the dog. I had a strategy of my own.'

'What?'

'A piano lesson.'

O'Leary let out a guffaw of mockery. 'You're joking!'

'I'm serious.'

'Forget it. That idea is a non-starter. She's booked out solid for months. It's not going to happen.'

'Is it not?'

'No.'

'Really?'

'Not a chance.'

'Well, would you like to take a small bet on that, perhaps?'

'I'd love to.' He produced a twenty from his pocket. 'This is all I have to bet with, but I'll go for it.'

Monk whipped the note from his hand. 'Done!'

'Hey, that's mine!'

'Too late.'

'Give it back to me!'

Monk held the twenty up in the air, out of O'Leary's reach. 'It's already happened.'

'What's already happened?'

'The music lesson,' he said, putting the twenty in his own pocket. 'She's already given me a lesson, you jackass! In the Conservatory this afternoon.'

'What? *No way.*'

Monk picked up the Chopin folio from the piano and showed him the signature: 'Hugh Butler'. 'This look familiar?'

O'Leary's casual demeanour evaporated in a flash and his face went white and scared. He lunged at the manuscript. 'Give me that!'

But Monk held it up in the air, out of reach. 'Ah, ah . . . no touching. We don't want any sweat marks.'

'Give it to me! That's hers!'

'She might think they were mine.'

'How did you get that?' he snapped.

'I switched copies, conehead.'

'It's one of her most treasured possessions!'

'The more treasured, the better.'

O'Leary pursed his lips, making him look even more comical than he already was. 'You bastard, Monk. I told you we were going for a walk on the pier. That was the plan.'

Monk put the manuscript safely out of O'Leary's reach on top of the wardrobe. 'Plan's been changed.'

'You had no right to do that without telling me.'

'I'm telling you now.' He sauntered into the kitchenette, out of view. 'You see, I was thinking about it. And it seemed like I ought to get to know her first. It would be more convincing when your father sees us together if we looked like we're . . .' Monk re-appeared in the doorway with a canister of air freshener. '. . . the best of friends.' He was grinning widely.

O'Leary simmered, his sweaty hands clumped into two podgy fists.

Monk approached with the canister. 'Now, if you want my advice, I'd suggest you take yourself and that thing outside off this property.' Monk checked his watch. 'Because your good wife may be walking up here to collect her manuscript at this very minute. And if she comes in here, she'll smell you like a rat. You'll have some explaining to do then.'

'Shit.'

'Exactly.'

Before O'Leary left the basement, he glared at Monk with almost comic menace. 'You'd better not try anything, Lavery. If you do she'll knee you in the balls.'

'Don't worry,' replied Monk, spraying the air freshener at

O'Leary. 'They're well used to it.' He patted him on the back and guided him to the steps. 'Out you go.'

O'Leary grabbed the dog off the railing, muttering curses, and trudged up the steps.

'And if that animal does anything on my property, I warn you, you'll be getting it in the post.'

33

Joel walked up the hill towards Sallynoggin with his pet ogre in a state of severe disgruntlement. It made him almost nauseated to think that Monk had been sitting next to Ellen, alone in an empty music room, only hours before, while he was struggling along with this . . . this font of urination.

But Joel was too hot and sticky to get bothered about it now. He had more pressing things on his mind. Namely how he was going to return the Jack Russell to Shankill without going lame.

The dog, for sure, wasn't making it easy. It was every pole. She couldn't seem to get enough of them. Electricity poles, standing signposts, wooden poles (trees) and postboxes (probably counted as poles to a dog). Even a slim walking stick was used on one occasion, planted on the concrete by this auld one, seated on a bench by a bus stop.

Bus-stop poles were the most depressing of all. Not only because the dog never missed one, but because they were a fair indicator of the distance that lay ahead of them, given their even distribution. Joel had counted the number of bus stops they'd passed on their recent hike from Shankill to Dun Laoghaire. Eight in all, along two bus routes.

After bus stop number two, they bumped into a burly man with an Alsatian, coming in the opposite direction. It wagged its lupine tail and Joel's mutt insisted on saying hello. She sniffed up the bigger animal, then attacked. Joel had some trouble hauling her away from the scene. He dragged her twenty metres up the street where, luckily, there was a fresh pole – number three.

By the time they reached bus stop four, Joel felt like he had a furnace in each pore. Not only that, but his feet were hurting and his lower back felt just millimetres away from slipped-discing. Every time a bus passed him by he wanted to cry. He might have been able to convince an exceptionally understanding bus driver to let him and the dog on, but without the twenty Monk had just stolen off him Joel had no bus fare.

Still, he'd have enough bus fare for the return journey: the dog man would certainly give him back some of his money.

Five.

Joel was having a dreadful time, pulling the quadruped this way and that, speeding up, slowing down, halting while she sniffed or urinated or barked or growled, or otherwise generally made a 100 per cent arse's nuisance out of herself. He tried to keep a permanently safe distance of three feet from the cur, because he didn't fancy getting his feet enmeshed in the jaws of a live animal who regarded Alsatians as dead meat.

Six.

Eventually he came to the end of his fifty-minute trek. Rounding the corner, he immediately recognised the dog man's bungalow, set back off the road on the left-hand side. You could hear dogs barking now. The dog was getting all excited at the prospect of rejoining the only beings in the world who regarded her with deference.

Exhaustion hit him as he walked up the stony driveway. His feet burnt. He slowed to a halting stagger and, without warning, his mobile went off. He accidentally let go of the lead and the dog started circling him. Joel cursed, pulled out his mobile and inspected the digital display: Monk's number was flashing. The dog ran between his legs. The phone fell through his fingers like a bar of soap and landed on the driveway, still ringing. He bent down to pick it up, but the dog got there first. She clenched it between her jaws and ran. He ran after his phone, which was still ringing through the dog's teeth.

Joel made a dive for the moving leash, but ended up on the grass. He stood up, covered in green bits, and jerked the leash so hard that the dog dropped the phone. He picked it up and pressed the 'on' button.

Monk was on the other end. 'Slight change of plan,' he said. 'Your good wife just called. She wants me to bring her Chopin manuscript to the Pavilion instead. Looks like I'm going to need the dog after all.'

'*Fuck off!*' Joel roared, his legs buckling.

'We're going to do things my way, O'Leary. I'm calling down to the apartment at six thirty, so I'm going to need the dog by six at the latest. I don't need you involved: she knows me now, so she'll come out walking off her own bat.'

'*I hate you, you bastard.*'

'Not my fault. She said she couldn't drop by my place because she's busy this evening.' Monk hung up and Joel stared uncomprehendingly at his phone.

He looked around. The dog was over by the hedge, destroying flowers. But all Joel cared about was another four-mile trek through hell, his feet blistering like lava. He sagged to his knees and slumped on to the carpet-soft grass, his legs aching like hot pikes. There he lay, half dead, under the blazing sun.

The dog came over, sniffing and panting beside him, in a gesture which Joel interpreted as solidarity.

'Get the hell off my property!'

Joel sat up, shading his eyes. It was the dog man.

'I didn't sell that dog to you to destroy my flowers! If I catch it, I'll put it down!'

'I didn't buy the dog!' Joel implored. 'It was only a loan!'

'Get off my property!' he bellowed.

'Look,' said Joel, pleading. 'How about I give you back your dog and you only have to give me back, say, twenty Euros, quits? How's that?'

The dog man literally chased Joel and the dog off his property. As he walked down the road, Joel felt a damp patch on his thigh. He knew instantly that he'd just been urinated on. Oddly, however, Joel didn't care. He was simply too exhausted to care.

34

Monk finished off his last forkful of roast beef and mashed potato, leaving one sole surviving pea on his plate. He rolled the pea round and round the empty plate with his fork. He rolled it round the other way, then back again.

It was odd.

He'd spoken to her just now on the phone. She'd asked him straight out if he would mind returning her Chopin manuscript to the Pavilion, where she lived. It was a perfectly reasonable request, of course, but what bothered Monk was the way she made it. No, bother was too strong. Caught his attention.

She was curt. Polite, but curt. Her request was framed with such calm assurance and courtesy that Monk almost forgot that she was completely suiting herself. A well-disguised egoist, perhaps?

Never mind, Monk thought, squashing the pea into a splodge on his plate. *We'll kiss and make up later.*

He jerked to his feet, sending his chair crashing to the ground. He shoved his plate into the sink and went to the fridge to see if his mother had anything interesting in.

Yes! A white paper box. Monk removed it and opened the flap. Six beautiful meringues, bursting like breasts in cream. He poked a finger in one, then licked it. Dodgy? Hmm. Seemed okay. Probably just the added raspberry flavouring.

There was one way of finding out. Monk brought the box downstairs, out of the basement door. He placed a fat meringue in front of the recently returned filthy muck ball of a Jack Russell.

The meringue was gone in under a minute. The dog was doing so well that, in Monk's estimation, he deserved another. He placed a second on the ground and watched, fascinated, at the effect starvation had on a dog's manners. 'You've got ten minutes to digest,' he told the pig-dog. 'Then we're going for a walk on the pier. And remember – you do anything naughty on the premises and I'll drown you in the harbour. Got that?'

He went back up to his mother's kitchen, sat down at the heavy wooden table and started into a meringue himself. He crunched it up with the cream and shovelled it into his mouth. Not bad. He was nearing the end of his second meringue when he heard his mother coming in the front door. Monk jumped to his feet, stuffing the remainder into his mouth. He threw the white paper box back into the fridge and returned quickly to his seat with a glass of water, wiping the cream from his mouth.

119

She came in with some shopping. 'Phew!' she said, putting the groceries on the table. 'The humidity.' Her long sleeveless dress made her arms appear skeletal. A thick pearl necklace adorned her scrawny neck. She'd gone so haggard. She missed Monk's father and often talked about him, though he'd been dead for almost twenty years. Monk's much older sisters were often in touch with her, but one was in Stuttgart, married to a German, and the other had emigrated to Canada.

She picked up the butter and milk. She halted and cocked an ear. 'Was that a dog I heard barking just now?'

'Didn't hear anything.' Monk didn't want any fuss.

'I must be hearing things,' she said, shuffling to the fridge. 'I miss not having a dog, Myles, ever since our first Rufus died. I don't know why I never got another.' Passing the table, she stopped and stared at Monk's empty plate. 'Well? How was the dinner?'

He raised the plate from the table and offered a dramatic, humble bow. Unimpressed, his mother put the butter and milk in the fridge. 'I bought some meringues yesterday.'

'Oh, really, meringues, where?'

'Don't touch them,' she said, shutting the fridge door. 'They've gone off. The best-before date was the day before yesterday. I didn't see it till I brought them home. I'm taking them back for a refund.'

Monk brought his hand to his throat. 'Why didn't you tell me?'

'I'm telling you now,' she said, picking up a bag of carrots. 'Why, did you eat one?'

'No, I ate two.'

'What did you do that for? They were best-before Monday.'

'What did you leave them in the fridge for?' he retorted.

'That's where you're supposed to put meringues,' she replied.

'When they've gone off, you're supposed to put them in the bin.'

She returned to the fridge. 'I told you, I'm taking them back for a refund.' She removed the box and opened the flap. 'Or I was, at least.' She sighed. 'There are only two left. Don't tell me you ate *four* of them?'

Monk looked down at his plate and belched.

She crumpled up the paper box and stuffed it in the bin. 'Well, you're going to be sick now, for your gluttony.'

'Take more than a bit of sour cream to make me throw up,' he responded, patting his belly. 'Stomach of iron.'

'I know,' she replied, removing a bottle of lemonade from under the sink. 'Magnet for everything.' She moved out of the kitchen with her glass. Moments later, the living-room door banged shut. The house was now in silence again, except for the incessant buzzing of a fly against the window.

Monk finished his water and slammed the glass down on the table. Still he could not get the sound of Ellen's voice from his head. He got up and went to the window. He picked up a dishcloth, bunched it up and shoved it against the dratted fly, which had been pissing him off for the last half-hour. It fell dead against the sill. He folded the cloth neatly and replaced it in a drawer.

Again he heard her voice: poised and unbending; hard as granite; articulate. Good class, as Mother would have said.

Ha! His mother was forever at him to meet a girl of good class!

Monk snorted at the thought, then left the kitchen.

35

By six twenty she was on her third fingernail.

Ellen was perfectly well aware that biting her nails was not a very pleasant activity. But 'pleasant' was not a word she'd use to describe her mood right now.

For a start, she had a recital in two days' time, but she was unable to look at the Steinway on the far side of the room without feeling ill. The only thing that would help would be for Joel to return home and do what he was put on this world to do. Then, maybe, she'd feel like looking at the Steinway.

But he was late. Twenty minutes late, but still late. He'd called earlier, asking her out for a 'date' on the pier. She'd gladly accepted the romantic offer and he'd promised to be home by six. Ellen was tempted to go for a walk on the pier on her own, because she was afraid to rely on Joel. She had enough nervous energy inside her to power the lights and besides, if she left it much later, the beautiful warmth of afternoon would fade into the encroaching coolness of evening.

Ellen went to the telescope at the bay window. Panning to the extreme left, she trained it on the station and zoomed in. Soon she heard the faint rumbling of a southbound train. She watched the passengers mill out on to the pavement, magnified. Joel wasn't among them.

She stared out over the harbour. The centre of the bay was a playground of white, motion-free yachts, their masts piercing upwards like shark fins. The car ferry from Dublin port slid impassively across Howth Head. And way out in the Irish Sea was the catamaran, on its way to Holyhead. It was a small white box in the distance, suspended on the straight horizon line.

Dublin Baby whispered a voice in her head.

Ellen watched a pair of seagulls cackle as they traversed the sky above the catamaran terminal. They arched over to the People's Park on the extreme right. She stared at the Royal St George Yacht Club opposite. Her father used to take her there as a girl. He was an expert yachtsman and he took her sailing many times. She would always remember him sitting at the helm, stewarding the ropes, battling with determined jaw against wild wind and wave. It was exactly as if the billowing sails, the boat and the wind were his orchestra. And he conducted from his pedestal, flinging his whole being into the wild flow of the music.

Remembering her father, Ellen felt sad. She sat at the Steinway and lifted the lid. She ruffled her fingertips against the piano keys and breathed deep of its old wooden scent. It brought her back: far, far back to the sunny living room of their home where, as a young girl, he would teach her pieces by ear, sitting on his knee. They would play and sing together. Those early years were filled with the greatest happiness she had ever known.

And she would do him justice on Friday if it killed her.

Hearing the distant rumble of the next southbound train, Ellen got up again and returned to the telescope. Again the pavement became inundated with folk, fanning out in all directions.

Come on, Joel, where are you?

Unfortunately, he wasn't on this one, either.

The doorbell rang.

She darted into the hall and picked up the intercom. Damn, it wasn't him. It was that guy she'd given the piano lesson to that afternoon. He was standing in profile, frowning heavily.

Ellen watched him as he flicked a shoulder with a hand. He flicked his other shoulder with his other hand, then straightened. He narrowed his eyes, as if he was examining something in the distance. He slid a finger into his mouth, then ran it across his eyebrow. He repeated the procedure for the second eyebrow.

The bell rang again.

Ellen picked up the plastic bag containing his manuscript, drew a jacket over her bare shoulders and went down.

36

Monk stared at her through the glass door as she entered the lobby.

Long blonde hair, pegged back with a hairband. Long black dress. Perfect, slender figure under the tan jacket. Long legs. Mouth-watering cleavage. Fresh lipstick. Flushed face.

Christ, she was hot for him. After a mere five hours? Her cool tone on the phone had been a ploy.

She came out, but held on to the door. She nodded and smiled. Those eyes again. *Those eyes*. 'Very good of you to come down,' she said formally, making a big deal of glancing over his shoulder.

'Sorry about the mix-up again,' he said, staring with intensity into her eyes.

'Is that my . . .' She was pointing.

Monk handed over her Chopin manuscript. She returned his copy to him, inside a Waterstone's bag.

'Nice evening for a walk,' he began.

'Lovely evening,' she replied, 'I hope you get good use out of it, now.'

'What?'

'Your "Tristesse", good luck with it.'

'Oh, right.'

'Thanks for dropping it back. You're very kind.'

'You're looking well,' he shot out. 'Nice dress. Armani?'

'Chanel, actually.'

'Oh.' He raised his eyebrows to appear impressed but lowered them when he glanced at her feet. 'Shoes don't go, though. You probably know that already. No offence.'

She looked down only momentarily and, if she was mortified, she didn't let on. 'They're my walking shoes.'

'Oh?' Monk stuck his fingers in his mouth and blew a whistle. *'Here, boy! We're going for a walk!'*

There was barking from round the corner and all of a sudden Ellen's face lit up with anticipation, as she moved in that direction. Monk quickly undid the leash, which he'd tied to a rail beside the door, then followed her round. The Jack Russell, who had pulled Monk's extension lead to its full capacity, had strayed into the bike shed at the far end of the terrace. He was barking like mad.

Monk snapped out another command, but the mutt failed to obey. The way it was growling made it look to Monk as if there were someone else in that shed and he didn't want to hazard a guess as to who that might be. So he tugged the lead forcefully and dragged the dog back out in instalments of one metre at a time. Soon the Russell gave up and scampered over to Ellen's outstreched arms.

Ellen squatted down and began caressing the dirty mutt in the middle of the paving area, pressing her fingers into the soft crevices of its neck and jaw. 'It's a she!'

'So it is.'

'She's in terrible condition,' she remarked. 'Is she yours?'

'I think she got into a bit of a scrap today.'

'You poor thing.'

'I'll get over it.'

'I was talking to the dog,' she said, scrutinising the manky paws. 'She needs to see a vet. And she's filthy. Don't you ever wash her?' Ellen was holding up a clump of caked hair.

Monk knew there was probably a clever reply somewhere, but he couldn't for the life of him think what it was.

Now she was pulling back the dog's lips, exposing unhealthy teeth. 'Can develop all sorts of trouble, if you don't wash them.'

'Been meaning to do it for a while.'

She looked unimpressed. 'Does she eat much?'

'Like a horse.'

'You wouldn't think so.'

The Jack Russell was like putty in her hands, an affectionate cur at heart, despite all the bad press O'Leary had given it. In his enlightened world-view, if an animal happened to draw blood it was automatically the animal's fault. O'Leary was like a blind man who, when he walked into a tree, instantly blamed the tree. What he didn't realise was this: to control a dog you needed a lot of something he profoundly lacked. Charisma.

'Time for walkies! Here, girl!'

'You're going for a walk! Did you hear that?' The dog panted with excitement. 'Where are you going?'

Monk decided to assume she was addressing him. 'Down the east pier. I take her down every evening.'

'I'm surprised I've never seen you before. I walk there each evening myself.' She consulted her watch.

'Well, you're welcome to join us this evening,' said Monk, winding up the extension leash. 'Little girl seems to like you.'

She stood up and the dog jumped up against her knees. She took the two paws in her hands. 'You want me to come for a walk?'

The dog yelped eagerly and salivated all over her hand.

'I'm not so sure I can.' She peered absent-mindedly towards the steps leading down towards the train station.

'She likes to meet new people,' said Monk. 'Don't you . . . girl?'

'What's her name?'

'Sh . . .' He cursed under his breath.

'Pardon me?'

'Chopin,' came from somewhere inside him.

'Chopin? This is turning out to be a bit of a Chopin day!'

'Come on, Chops, let's go!' He tugged at the leash, jerking the dog's neck away from Ellen's lap. 'Well, fancy walking down with us for a bit?'

Ellen stood up. 'I wasn't going to go for a walk this evening but . . .' She glanced over to the steps, doubtful. 'You know, maybe I could do with some air. Why not? I'll just go a short distance.'

She gathered her thoughts. 'Let's see. I have my keys . . .' She patted her thighs. 'Okay, then, let's go, Chopin!'

The dog ran alongside her heel and they walked down the steps. Before he descended past the stone parapet, Monk looked back, just in time to see O'Leary sprint clumsily out of the bike shed towards the apartment. When he caught sight of Monk he gave him a frenzied thumbs-up. Monk just shook his head.

'May I?'

He almost walked into Ellen, who'd stopped on the steps just in front of him. She was pointing at his leash, smiling.

37

Joel rushed into the apartment, nursing leg scratches from the bike shed fiasco. It had been a close shave.

He ran to the bay window, breathless, and scanned the coast road. When he spotted Ellen and Monk ambling along the front together he threw a triumphant fist up in the air.

Twenty minutes to go, approximately, until his father arrived. Joel peered through the telescope, but because the window was grimy he decided to carry it out to the balcony and set it up on its tripod. When this task was completed, Joel stuck the telescope in his eye. The picture was much clearer, but that wasn't much use when all you got was a blur of vegetation. He panned the brass contraption up along the promenade to the right. Eventually he managed to spy Ellen's tan jacket, right up close. He pulled focus.

Reception was shaky. Joel was shaky himself and the two figures were now bouncing all over the place. He tried to keep the tube still, to ensure a steady picture. He zoomed in. He got the flowing hem of Ellen's black dress. What was she doing in her black dress? He jerked the telescope over and that god-awful dog came into view.

He tilted up. Yes! Their faces. The clarity was perfect. Ellen was speaking to Monk in a way that suggested they were having a mildly pleasant conversation. She was so close he could make out the small brown freckle just to the left of her mouth. He could also make out the sheen on Monk's black boots.

Joel sat down on the chaise longue, stretched his arms behind his head and waited for it all to unfold.

38

They turned into the pier.

Ellen was glad she'd agreed to take Chopin for a walk, even though she was dressed up to the nines. True, the Russell at the end of her leash was a bit of a handful, growling at just about every life form that passed by, be it human, animal or ant. But Ellen was far better off outside, walking on the pier, than moping around in the apartment alone.

Already she felt better in the fresh air. It was a lovely evening. The water in the harbour shimmered pinky blue, and you could hear the ropes from the boat masts tinkle and chime in the light wind. It would have been nice to get out with Joel on their 'pier date', instead of this strange Myles fellow beside her. Joel needed his exercise too. Knowing him, he'd spent the whole day cocooned away practising his sax, oblivious to the outside world.

Still, Myles was okay company. He was civil to a fault and had a reasonably good, if dry, sense of humour. The only things Ellen didn't fancy were all his questions, discreetly framed to dupe her into believing that he wasn't being inquisitive. So she'd steered the conversation towards classical music, the one interest they appeared to have in common.

Ellen established fairly quickly that, despite initial indications to the contrary, Myles hadn't a clue about classical music. But, like all skilful bullshitters, he did manage to scramble expertly out of each of his own holes. For example, when he proved unable to name even *one* of his Chopin favourites apart from the 'Tristesse', he deviated into Chopin's reputed sex life. Which was kind of beside the point.

Ellen tried to steer him on to the topic of Beethoven then, just to test out the theory that he was a total wind-up merchant. But he simply changed the subject to his mother, who had, apparently, 'bequeathed' to him his 'feel' for classical music. Supposedly, she could recite lines from any opera you cared to mention. He told Ellen that she was brought to Leipzig as a girl, where she saw Brahms conduct. Ellen decided against informing him that Brahms had in fact died in 1897, which would have meant that the great woman must have produced Myles in her eighties, an even greater achievement, surely, than learning libretti.

At one point during the walk, Myles bent down and patted Chopin fondly, speaking to her in the intimate way you'd address a child. Somehow, it didn't ring true. The man appeared to have as little regard for Chopin the dog as he had for Chopin the composer. He kept his Jack Russell in an utterly deplorable condition. The poor animal had been mauled by another dog, but the man hadn't even thought to bring her to a vet. It was cruel.

'How old is Chopin?' she asked, passing the National Yacht Club.

'Oh, we got her as a pup.'

'How old is she?' She cast him a direct smile.

'Two.'

'I would have pitched her at three myself.'

'Two or three, yes.'

She nodded. 'I assume she's had all the usual shots?'

'Yes. And you know what? She actually enjoyed them.'

Ellen shook her head and smiled. A charmer, through and through, although an admittedly good-looking charmer. So much so that Ellen was almost tempted to forgive him.

'Actually,' he said, as they strolled along the pier, 'Chopin belongs to my mother. I just take her out walking from time to time.'

A group of foreign students passed by, all licking ice-cream cones. The source of the delicious-looking whipped cream was a large white van, parked a small way down the pier: MISTER SOFTEE. Ellen hadn't eaten a thing since lunch with Ita, seven hours before. The ice cream looked enticing, but she'd left her purse in the apartment. She gazed ravenously at the chocolate-

128

finger-topped cones as they passed. Her stomach gave a low rumble.

'Would you be tempted by a sixty-nine?' he asked suddenly.

She glanced at him. '*What?*'

'Well, it's ferociously hot, isn't it?' he said, pointing at the ice-cream van. 'Wouldn't mind one myself. With chocolate on it.'

'A *ninety-nine*, you mean? Yes. I'd love a ninety-nine.'

He stopped and stared blankly at her, then his expression changed. 'My God,' he said, holding a hand up to his temples. 'My mind is going.' He moved swiftly to the van. He went to the top of the long queue and stuck his head in the window.

Ellen stood by the blue railing and observed her intriguing walking companion. He was at least six feet tall and had a slight stoop. Hand on hip, his stance was cool. The long fingers of his right hand tap-tapped against the aluminium above his head. It wasn't long before he managed to talk the ice-cream woman into giving him preferential treatment.

As well as being a chancer and a charmer, Ellen mused, the man had a dirty mind. That was okay. Most men had dirty minds. Dirty minds came in handy on occasion. With any luck, Joel would have a dirty mind tonight.

She turned towards the Pavilion and glanced up towards their apartment, shielding her eyes from the glare of the setting sun. She thought she could detect a dark shape on their lounge balcony. She narrowed her eyes into sharp focus to see what it was, but it was gone. Probably just the low sun's rays playing tricks with her eyes.

Ten to seven. Ellen would walk another ten minutes with Myles, then return home. She would put on some music to get Joel in the mood, something atmospheric from his jazz repertoire. She'd prepare pasta with his favourite pesto sauce, adding olives and sundried tomatoes. A glass of wine each. Joel needed to be well fed if he was to perform later – so long as he wasn't well drunk.

And then they'd go to bed. She was really going to enjoy it too. It would be an incredible release.

'Here you are!'

Ellen jumped round to face Myles, who was holding up an ice-cream cone, his arm extended dramatically in a pose reminiscent of the Statue of Liberty. She took it off him. 'I'm afraid I haven't any change to give you.'

'My pleasure, madame,' he said.

They moved on and she licked a sizeable blob off the top, to quench her hunger. Her teeth froze with the chill.

39

'You stupid clod!'

The reason that Joel, on this particular occasion, felt himself to be a stupid clod was that Ellen had almost certainly caught him spying on her just now, from in front of the ice-cream van. But he also felt himself to be a stupid clod because when he'd jumped backwards to hide, he'd brought the telescope crashing on to the floor of the balcony – and now he couldn't get the dratted tripod to stand up.

He decided to postpone the cumbersome task. He detached the telescope from the tripod, got on to his knees and crawled towards the metal barrier like a crab, safely concealed from the seafront. When it felt safe to do so, he rose a few inches and trained the telescope through the gap. He scanned the front section of the pier.

They were nowhere to be seen.

Joel panned left and right in the general vicinity of the ice-cream van, turning the Dun Laoghaire coastline into an infuriating succession of round peepholes. He still couldn't spot them.

They couldn't have got very far. That section of the pier was open plan. The toilets were too far down, unless they'd both sprinted there at full speed, which would be an unreasonably unlikely coincidence.

There they were!

The two of them, ambling towards the bandstand with the dog. They were eating ice creams. Excellent. And the way they were talking in between bites – they looked like a real couple. Very believable. From a distance, they could easily pass for intimates.

Sick! Joel checked his watch. Roughly ten minutes to go. His father should have left the house.

Joel stood up now, since it was safe to do so. He trained the telescope down the coast towards Sandycove, to see if he could spot his father walking up along the bend in the coastline.

But there was still no sign.

40

You *fool*, he thought, as he accompanied Ellen and the dog past the Victorian bandstand.

What bothered Monk wasn't so much that he'd offered Ellen a sixty-niner, but that he hadn't even been *aware* he'd offered her a sixty-niner. Having a porno brain wasn't the problem: it was forgetting you had a porno brain. It was imagining that if you relaxed your thoughts, you would effortlessly sprinkle the air around you with genteel poetry.

It was an unforgivable lapse.

Still, she'd handled his clanger admirably. She'd stared into his eyes and addressed him with confidence. 'A ninety-nine, you mean,' she'd said, without so much as flinching.

Monk had to hand it to her. She knew where she was at. Very much her own person. Let him get away with nothing. The flogging she dealt him over his dog care skills. The Beethoven near disaster. Her total disbelief when he proved unable to name even *one* other Chopin work. He was chancing his arm and she knew it.

But so what? She was loving every minute of it, you could see that from the way she was struggling not to smile at his outrageous quips and generalised statements, which amounted to little more than sundried bullshit. And why wouldn't she be loving it? She'd come out all tarted up. The whole time they were together she could not have dropped a heavier bucketload of hints if she'd tried. The rig-out. The cleavage, the hot face. Even the way she'd slid her slender tongue across the fat knob of her ice-cream cone. Freud would have had a field day.

As they walked along the pier, chatting and gently sparring,

Monk began to feel queasy. Watching Ellen eat her ice cream with such heightened eroticism had made him ravenous and he'd downed his own in seconds.

This he was now beginning to regret: the ice cream was not sitting well with the meringue gunge in his stomach. Perhaps his mother had been right and the meringues had gone off. The cream, certainly, had tasted fine, although he didn't discount the possibility that this was because it was sweetened. Ugh! The very thought of the sweet and sour creamy mess in his gut was making him feel even sicker.

Monk threw his head back and inhaled the blue sky above. He exhaled the sky into the choppy harbour water, then he focused on Chopin, to forget. Unfortunately, this only reminded him of his mother's meringues, which in turn increased the queasiness. He tried to concentrate on Ellen instead. She was bending down, feeding her chocolate flake to the dog, who exterminated it in seconds. 'You poor thing,' she sang, 'don't you ever get anything nice?'

She stood up then and gazed over the wall towards Sandycove. 'Beautiful,' she said.

Monk supposed that 'beautiful' was a word one might use to describe the rocky peninsula at Sandycove, delineated by its withdrawn foretide, its pubic seaweed and its prominent Martello tower nipple.

'I think that yacht is in trouble,' she remarked.

A small purple yacht was crossing the sound between the pier and the peninsula.

'Ever gone sailing?' he asked her, desperate to forget his nausea.

'My father used to take me.'

'Not any more?'

'He's dead.'

'I'm sorry to hear that, Ellen. So is mine.'

'Is he long dead?'

'Twenty-two years and three months, to be precise.'

She didn't reply.

'And your father?' he wondered.

'One year ago next Friday.'

The yacht was getting into some difficulties in the wind, which was now blowing Ellen's long hair into strands across her shoulders.

'And your husband?' Monk turned to her.

'He's still alive.'

'No, I mean, does he sail? I don't suppose so.'

'Joel was never into sports.'

'No.'

'Were you planning on walking much further?'

Monk shrugged. 'Just to the end of the pier and back.'

'I'll say goodbye, then: I'd better be getting back, I'm sure he's home by now.'

Monk was alarmed. He racked his brains to think of something that might change her mind. But his head was now engulfed with sickness, like a polluted sewer.

'I thank you for the lovely walk,' Ellen said. 'Because you're a good dog, aren't you? And when you get cleaned up you'll look so nice.' She fondled the dog's throat, then stood up to leave.

'Ellen, why don't we sit down on the bench for a while? Admire the boats, watch the seagulls . . .'

'Better go.' She smiled. 'Thanks anyway.' She handed Monk the leash and moved away, twiddling her fingers at the dog in a gesture of farewell. 'So long, Mrs Chopin.'

He watched Ellen descend the nearby steps to the lower level of the pier, stunned by the suddenness of her departure. The sole reason he'd let her go was that he was too queasy to think of a way to make her stay. Beholding the dog only made him feel worse – it reminded him of that soggy mush of sugar and sour cream festering in his stomach. He spotted a bench on the lower level. He had to sit down, fast.

Monk dragged Chopin to the steps and made her go down first. She refused. He levered his foot against her, but she struggled. He used threats and she submitted. Monk followed her down the stone steps. Halfway down, he stood still and stared at the bottom in horror.

Chopin.

She was squatting over the bottom step with intent. Monk shouted a warning, but it was too late: the deposit was laid and the cur was peering up at him in cowering innocence. Monk let go of the leash, his nostrils blazing with the dire stench. He backed up the steps again, but bumped into someone descending.

'Excuse me,' said the elderly gentleman. 'Are you coming up or down?'

'Up,' said Monk, feeling progressively iller.

'Too late, young man, my wife and I are coming down.'

'All right, all right.'

'Haven't got all day.' He chuckled.

Monk descended the steps, pinching his nose. He leapt over the foul-up to safety, but the sickness was coming full on him now. He cursed as he staggered to a bollard in the middle of the pier. He sat on it, hyperventilating the fresh sea air. He was on the verge of throwing up. He tried to focus on Ellen's diminishing form in the distance.

'Hey!' came a voice. 'Hey!'

Shakily, Monk turned. It was the old fogey.

'Is that your dog?'

Monk shook his head. 'Never seen her in my life.'

'That's his dog,' said a woman passing by. 'I saw him with it.'

'Of course it's his dog,' Monk heard the geriatric say. 'Would you think of cleaning up your mess?'

'Not my mess, not my dog' was all a trembling Monk could manage.

Seconds later, he felt the disgusting cur nuzzling against his boots. The old fogey made a smartass misquote about Nero sitting around while Rome shat. Monk was desperate to escape the fuss and be sick in private, but his legs were almost too weak to stand. He tried to focus on Ellen again, but her body was swaying from side to side. The pier walls were trembling and the sky was pulling strange shapes.

He fell to his knees on the hard concrete, the dog springing round and round, snapping loud barks into his ear. Monk rose heavily from the ground and stooped down to try to pick up his copy of the 'Tristesse'. He gave up. His stomach was heaving, urging vomit upwards. He staggered to the edge of the pier, leant over the edge, and released a slushy gobful into the sea, in full view of all these ogling assholes he wanted dead.

He monkey-walked to the nearest steps. Grasping the cold

railing with his trembling hand, he descended the slimy stepway, trying not to topple forward as he retched. He was on the bottom step now, just above the water, slipping around on the green seaweed. A second vomitation rose up from deep within him and his whole upper body heaved forward violently. He slithered on the seaweed and crashed on to the step. Before he knew where he was, he felt himself surrounded by freezing water, filling his mouth, nose and head. A strange thought occurred to him: *This is odd. What am I doing in the water when I can't swim?*

He roared and bellowed out loud, an animal madness he never knew was there. A surge of strength whipped inside him and he thrashed with his arms, but it was no use and he finally realised – with some shock – that he was drowning. He was sinking and gasping, twisting and curling, fighting with his arms and legs for a grip, but seeming all the faster to sink, and then suddenly rising again. It was working, he was rising and now he could see the pier again! He heard a dog barking. He gasped for air, but once more started to sink, his chest bursting for breath, his panic doubling. Making out the face of a beautiful woman on the edge of the pier, familiar to him and yet so different, a worried face, a pleading face. Then suddenly it was gone.

'*No!*' he bubbled into the water, one arm outstretched, then he swallowed a mouthful of sickening salt water, choking again. He was screaming into the foaming murk, filling up with it, then he was suddenly above again, gasping for air, pounding for all he was worth, roaring that he couldn't swim, and he was struggling just beyond the reach of the steps, struggling to keep himself afloat, but failing. No one on the pier above, just a dog. She was gone, disappeared, and the more he thrashed the quicker he went under, the worst was facing him, the very worst, oh God, Mother, where are you, Mother of Jesus . . .

A voice shouted out from above and suddenly he felt something knock hard and hollow against his head. A red object appeared beside him, he clung to it for dear life, stared up and tried to see who had shouted at him and it was her, it was Ellen, beautiful Ellen. She was calling out from above, and he was coughing and spluttering and staring up, and she was looking down at him, calling to him with the voice of an angel, and he

135

wanted to reach up into the skies and touch this angel, touch her hair, her pretty white face. And now there were others, one man holding the rope and pulling. He felt himself being pulled through the water, he clung fast to the ring, but he knew he was okay, he was saved, oh God, he was saved, he was being dragged to the steps, and now he was enmeshed in the thick drapes of black seaweed. Someone reached out a hand. Monk was hauled up, lifted out of the water, ice-cold, disorientated, brought up slippery steps, spluttering, one man behind him and one above. Near the top he saw her again, her face all kind concern. He reached out. She took his hand and helped him to the top, where he collapsed.

'Can you breathe properly?'

He stared at her and tried to nod. She knelt down and rolled up his trousers, saying something about a fracture. A handkerchief was provided, which she tore into strips, and she bandaged his knee and, when she spoke, it was with such softness, such kindness, such concern that all he could do was gaze at her in bewildered helplessness.

'We'd better get you home,' she said, tying the final knot on the bandage. She was so close to him that he could feel her breath on his face. She was staring at him, a look of desperate worry draining her face to the colour of chalk. She took his hand and stroked it. 'Are you all right?'

Monk was freezing and exhausted. His lungs were on fire and his mouth was poisoned with salt. His shirt stuck like cling film to his torso. Wet hair dripped icy droplets on to his face. His eyes burnt and his leg was beginning to pound.

'All right?' he repeated, incredulous, holding her hand tightly. 'I've never felt so wonderful.'

41

He managed it in the end, even if it did take him an age.

Joel stood the tripod upright in the middle of the lounge. It creaked, but it did not collapse. With an instinctive ingenuity of which he was justly proud, Joel had secured it with several pieces of sandwich-bag wire. He now fixed the telescope to the tripod. To his delight it still wasn't caving in, though it was more than a little shaky.

He carried the instrument back out on to the balcony and placed it at the edge. Resuming his surveillance of the pier, Joel was unable to locate Ellen or Monk in the viewfinder. Was it possible they might have reached the top of the pier in a mere ten minutes? Maybe it was, for people with long legs. Joel checked his watch.

Come on, Dad!

He panned along the coast road to see if he could spot his old man sauntering up. Suddenly he spied something which made his heart skip a beat. Plonk in the middle of the lens, sniffing at the blue railings along the coast road, was the dog formerly known as Killer. She was tethered to her leash. But there was nobody holding the other end.

Frantic, Joel pulled the telescope left and right, but he couldn't spot Monk or Ellen anywhere. '*Oh, God! Where are they? Where is she?*'

'Joel?'

He flashed round. Ellen was standing on the veranda behind him, clutching a glass of vodka to her chest with both hands. She seemed agitated.

'Ellen! I thought . . . hi there!'

She pointed at the telescope. 'Were you looking down at us?'

'What?' Joel glanced at the telescope.

'Did you see what happened?'

He shook his head. 'I didn't see anything, I don't know anything.'

Ellen smiled weakly, distracted. 'I thought you might have seen . . .' She went to the railing. '. . . down there, on the lower section of the pier.'

Joel moved closer to her, curious to know why she seemed so different. She was out of breath. Had Monk tried something on? 'What happened?'

'Fellow called Myles. I gave him a piano lesson today.'

'Oh yeah?'

'He went off with my music book by mistake, but he came

down an hour ago to return it. He had a Jack Russell with him –
like the one I used to have.'

Joel shrugged. 'Sure.'

'He invited me out for a walk on the pier, so I went with him
and Chopin.'

'Chopin?'

'That's his dog.' Ellen brought her hand to her mouth. '*Chopin!*
I forgot all about her! Myles let her go!' She peered through the
telescope and scanned the coastal area, but saw nothing. 'I
suppose she knows her own way home.' She turned to him. 'Joel,
you'll never believe what happened.'

'What happened?'

'The most incredible thing.' She shook her head. 'Over there,
on the lower section of the pier.'

Joel noticed her lips. They were redder than normal. Her face
was flushed and she was more than usually excited. It was Monk,
it had to be. Whenever women went near him they seemed to go
into heat. Bloody smooth bastard. How did he do it?

'*What* happened?' Joel was highly suspicious.

'It was awful.'

'What did he do? Tell me! Did he try something on? Did
he . . .?'

'He puked up.'

'*What?*' Joel eyeballed Ellen, disorientated.

'Over the edge of the pier, then he fell in.'

'He fell into the harbour?'

She nodded.

Joel darted his eyes back over to the pier. 'What the hell did he
go and do that for?'

'He said he'd eaten something that went off.' Her eyes were
wide open. 'He couldn't swim. He was drowning.'

'Did he . . .?'

'She shook her head. 'I threw him a life belt. Some men helped
to pull him out. He was okay, though his knee was gashed.'

'You didn't have to . . . resuscitate him in any way, did you?'

She shook her head. 'I bandaged his knee. It could be fractured
– he was limping badly on the way back.'

Joel closed his eyes in utter disbelief and ground his teeth in frustration. He began banging the back of his head against the plaster. Lavery had made a complete pig's ear of the whole operation. What the hell was he going to do now for money? What about the nest egg? The saxophone? Joel banged his head some more.

'The strangest thing was', Ellen went on, 'he seemed so elated afterwards. Euphoric. I suppose if you've just had your life saved . . .'

'Where is he now?'

'Went home. We hailed a passing taxi.' Ellen brought the drink to her mouth. The ice rattled off the glass. Her hands were trembling.

'Ellen, are you okay?'

'Not really.'

He came up behind her and enveloped her in his arms. Her whole body was tense. He rubbed up and down her back and kissed her on the back of the neck. She moved her neck from side to side and he wrapped his arms round her front. He was becoming aroused by the scent of her perfume and by the smooth feel of her bare skin against his lips. She turned round and kissed him on the mouth. Her lips were not hot, but they were moist. He kissed her gently, slowly, massaging her lower back. He trailed his lips down her throat and she held her head back. His hands clasped the curve of her behind and he lowered himself to his knees. He nestled his face into her belly and, as she breathed, it expanded and contracted against his cheek. Aroused, he began stroking her behind, while she ran her fingers through his hair. He put a hand through the slit in her black dress and slid right up her thigh. She did not object. He put up the other hand, although this was more awkward because there was no convenient slit that side.

'Do you want to go inside and lie down?' she moaned.

Holding her behind, Joel hugged his wife into his face. Her breath was quickening, to judge by the fact that her belly was now moving in and out more rapidly. Suddenly it tensed like a board against his cheek. 'Joel?'

'Huh?'

'I'm being stared at.'

139

Joel separated his face from her midriff and looked up. Her head was slanted downwards towards the terrace and her eyes were half closed.

'Bloody voyeurs. Don't mind them. They'll go away in a minute.' Joel returned his hands to her inner thighs and nestled his face into her belly once more. But it was still rock-hard.

'I don't think so,' she said.

He slipped his hand inside her panties and stroked her bare bum.

'Joel?'

'What?'

'It's your father.'

Joel lost balance and fell back against the wooden slats of the balcony floor. Ellen was speaking through the corner of her mouth. 'He's standing in the middle of the terrace. What am I supposed to do?'

'Wave,' said Joel, struggling to get up.

'He's glaring up at me.'

He stood up and looked over the railing. It was his father all right, in a navy pinstripe three-piece suit. His arms were folded high up on his chest, his feet spread out like a drill sergeant's. He was frowning and squinting up, the look of a thwarted lover on his face. Joel waved down. 'How's it going, Dad?'

After a brief staring silence, Joel saw his old man's face implode like a black hole. He waved again. Henry now offered an awkward smile, the pristine white dentures contrasting with his crimson face. He shook his head and strode off down the steps that led from the terrace.

'What was all that about?' said Ellen, leaning over the balcony. 'I had no idea your father was such a prude. Has he never seen people kissing before?'

'I think he's been drinking – bad news about Mother.' Joel darted into the lounge.

'Where are you going?'

'I'd better go down and see what's wrong. I'll be as quick as I can.'

42

'Dad! Wait up!'

While Joel was racing along the coast road towards his father, he brooded: they were wrong about jelly.

Oh, yes, they were very wrong. One day of forced marching around South County Dublin had convinced him that jelly was not just something you put in your mouth. It was something you tried to stand up with. Joel's legs felt so flabby with fatigue that it wouldn't have surprised him if they'd suddenly flopped out on to the pavement like something you ate for dessert. And he didn't even want to get started on his foot blisters.

He caught up with his father at the pier entrance. 'What's wrong, Dad?'

His old man ignored him completely.

'What are you so upset about, Dad?'

His father came to a sudden standstill. 'What am I so upset about? You've just made me experience the second greatest humiliation of my life and you ask me what I am so upset about.'

'What did I do?'

'You told me she was meeting this guy at seven o'clock sharp!' He said this through gritted teeth. 'You told me to come down to the apartment. I thought *you* were him. I thought she was with *him* on the balcony.'

'Hold on. I never said she was meeting him at seven.'

'You distinctly did.' His father resumed walking.

'No I didn't. I said *we* were meeting at seven, you and me. Ellen met him earlier.'

Henry halted on the pavement again. 'What did you say?'

It was too late to retract. 'I said we were meeting at seven.'

Henry was stony-faced. 'You said she met him earlier.'

'Exactly, yes. So you obviously picked me up wrong. Sorry about the mix-up. Would you like an ice cream?'

Henry was deathly. 'Where did she meet him?'

Joel kicked a pebble on the path. 'Well . . . on the pier, actually.

They met on the pier. They went for a walk together, with a Jack Russell.'

His father looked grave.

'They just got back now,' Joel added.

'My God, she did! It's true. I can see it in your eyes.' His old man stumbled back and grabbed on to the promenade railing. 'She *is* seeing someone else.'

Joel stared at his father, who looked devastated. He couldn't do it. After all this, he just couldn't do it to him. 'No, Dad, she isn't.'

'What?' He gripped Joel's arm.

'I got it wrong. I misunderstood.' As he said this, he looked as far away from his father as was optically possible.

'What are you saying? Look me in the eye, Son.'

'The guy she met on the pier . . . Just coincidence. She gave him a music lesson. He means nothing to her. In fact, she probably can't stand his guts.'

'She isn't having an affair?'

'No, and she's not even close. And to be honest, I don't feel too proud for having said it.' He noticed that his father's knuckles had gone bone-white from squeezing the railings.

'For God's sake, man, didn't I tell you? Didn't I tell you to ask her first, before assuming the worst? Why didn't you ask her first?'

'There's a very good reason for that.'

'Why?'

'Because I'm a bloody idiot, that's why.'

His father made no immediate effort to contradict this theory. They walked on for a while in silence, Joel staring down miserably at his cowboy boots.

'You've made a fool of me,' Henry said. 'I was staring up at her as if she was some sort of . . . *whore*.'

'She didn't see you. She had her eyes closed.'

'Do you think so?'

'Positive.'

'Well, then, I really am losing my marbles,' his father muttered.

'I'm sorry about everything, Dad, it's just that I've been under a lot of pressure lately. Stuff's being going on.'

'Oh, is that so?'

'Yes, it is.'

'Well, I don't want to hear another word about your stuff.'

They walked on in silence, along the curved coastline to Sandycove. Joel decided to accompany his father home, even if it meant his feet would face amputation on arrival. He was sorry for having put his father in such a position. God knows, his old man was suffering enough as it was.

'What stuff has been going on?' his father demanded to know suddenly.

'You don't want to know.'

'I suggest you tell me before I lose my patience with you.'

'It's about my saxophone.'

'Oh, dear God.'

'It was stolen, Dad.'

In some detail Joel recounted the tragic events of Monday to his father. He didn't want to push his luck, so he mentioned nothing about Ellen's nest egg. He concentrated on the saxophone heist and how it happened that Joel left all his valuables in the car of a total stranger he'd never seen before in his life.

Joel informed his father that he now had no way of earning a living. His father did not respond with sympathy, so Joel told him he was impoverished. This ploy fared no better. Joel told him he was totally unable to support Ellen. This time his father responded sympathetically, but he made no cash offers.

Joel decided that was it. At this stage he was resigned to his fate. He'd done with hoping. Hope was just a huge boomerang which, when you whirred it away, returned and smashed straight back into your face. His father wasn't going to help out and that was that. Monk wasn't going to help out and that was that. No one was going to help out and that was that. The only option – potentially – was for him to go home to Ellen and come clean.

But first he'd let her get a decent night's sleep.

As they walked, Joel took some time to mourn the passing of his Selmer. He wondered where it was at this precise moment. In England? France? Europe? In whose bedroom was it sleeping tonight? Whose coarse and filthy paws were manhandling it? Had that fake nun melted it down and sold it for cheap jewellery?

Soon they passed the yellow beach of Sandycove and, within a few minutes, arrived at the residence. His father stopped at the gate and stared at the mock-Tudor façade with loathing. 'I hate going back in there,' he said quietly.

'It's a nice house.'

'You don't have to live here!' he snapped.

'No. Sorry.'

'Tempted to sell the damn thing. Too big. Too cold. Besides, she tarnished it.'

Joel was unsure how to respond. 'How will you be spending the rest of the evening?'

'Festering, I suppose.' He opened the gate and trudged heavily up the short driveway. Joel watched him, as he paused to extract a key and open the front door. Stepping inside, he turned. 'Well? What are you standing out there for?'

'Maybe you'd like me to come in for a bit?'

'And why would you be bothered?'

It was several months since he'd visited his old man at home. 'Are you going to bed right away?'

'No, I think I'll get sloshed first.'

'Dad, you can't do that.'

'Oh, can I not?' He went inside, but left the front door open. Joel hurried up the driveway after him, went through the heavy oak door. He caught his father walking down the long hallway, removing a noggin of whiskey from his pocket. Joel heard the back door into the garden being unbolted. He went into the living room and collapsed on to the extraordinarily comfortable couch, which seemed to go on sinking for ever underneath him. Seconds later there was a sound of smashing glass outside. The back door was slammed and rebolted. His father joined him in the living room and put on the CD of Beethoven's *Archduke Trio*, which he'd bought in preparation for Ellen's recital. He poured them two glasses of lemonade, then stood at the window overlooking the back garden.

The familiar signature tune came on, and Joel's thoughts strayed to his wife and to what was likely to happen over the next few days of his life. Ellen was planning on buying the stroller on Saturday, from money she'd withdraw from their nest egg on Friday. Seeing the joint account empty, she would have a reaction. Such as going into a coma. There was no way out. Joel would have to tell her. He could break it gently. By phone, even, so that she'd have time to react in peace, before he got back.

His eyes began to close. He was dying where he sat, hunched like an exhausted sack of corn. Just another five minutes on this incredibly soft couch, no more. Then he'd ask his dad to run him home.

'Just look at the lawn,' his old man said, staring into the back garden. 'I can hardly see it for all the weeds.'

Joel tried to lever open his eyes.

'Hard to credit it,' his old man brooded. 'Seems like only yesterday when I used to carry you round that cherry tree on my shoulders. They were good times, Son, when you were a kid. Course they were. You, me, your mother.'

'What was it like?'

'What was what like?'

'Bringing up a child.'

'Why, are you thinking of having one?'

'God, no.'

'Well, maybe you should,' Henry said in melancholic tones. 'I won't be young for ever.'

Joel was unsure whether he was joking.

'What was it like . . .' mulled his father.

'I mean, was it a burden in any way?'

'No, Joseph.' His father turned and stared at him for a long time, with a look of dazed sympathy. Joel couldn't work out why; all he'd done was ask him a simple question. Henry shook his head and came over with the bottle of lemonade. 'Son,' he said, filling his glass, 'you were never a burden. You were a joy to both of us.'

'But I wasn't . . .'

'Yes, you were. You were always a good-natured boy, always keen to please.'

'Dad, I didn't mean that. I was asking you if . . .'

'The fact of the matter is,' Henry interrupted, returning to the window, 'when you were born, my life changed for the better.'

Joel stared at his father's back, curious.

'It stopped your mother gallivanting around the place, partying day and night.'

'Okay.'

'So I never want you to think you were a burden.'

Joel was simply too tired to explain himself.

'As a matter of fact, we both love you very much. Regardless of how ridiculously you sometimes behave.'

Joel closed his eyes and let his head fall back, feeling himself sinking further into the bottomless softness of the leather couch. His mind began swirling to the backing track of piano and strings, blossoming like gorgeous flowers around his ears. His father's words were now a blur, a dozen images and voices were penetrating his head – the voices of Ellen, Monk and his father. Of the dog and the dog man and the Alsatian. Of the waiter, the sweeper and the nun. Joel's dozing head was a chorus of confused dreams, impulses and voices, all talking at him, all demanding to be heard at once. 'Joseph,' whispered a familiar, benign voice from a place that seemed so distant and yet so close, 'you've fallen asleep.'

43

Ellen sat in her parked car outside Henry's house in Sandycove, her engine off. All the lights were off inside the house and there was no sign of waking life. Even the porch light was off. Ellen felt like an absolute idiot sitting there, knowing she could not and would not go in. But she could not and would not go home either.

Henry had phoned half an hour ago, sounding embarrassed, and told her that Joel had fallen fast asleep on the couch and he hadn't the heart to wake him up.

'Not to worry, Henry,' she'd replied, 'that'd be perfectly all right.' What she'd meant, of course, was that Henry should go ahead and wake him up, so that she could bring him home and jump on him. But he'd picked up the wrong meaning. 'Fine,' he'd said. 'I'll run him home in the morning, then. Goodnight, Ellen, and thank you.' And he'd hung up before Ellen knew what was happening.

She'd called him back at once, but the phone was off the hook.

'This is truely unbelievable,' hissed Ellen, restarting her engine. 'Maybe they know what I'm doing and they're trying to play a sick joke on me.' She put her foot down to the floor and sped up the coast road to Ita's place in Blackrock.

When she got there, Ita greeted her in flowing orange garments. Bangles dangled from her ears and black varnish marked her toenails. She led Ellen into the kitchen where, despite the summer heat, a fire was raging in the grate. She picked up a wooden spoon from the countertop and stirred a sweet-smelling liquid in a large black pot. 'You came down at the right time. I'm doing some cooking – specially for you.'

'Oh? What are you preparing?'

'Spring wine.'

'It's nearly autumn.'

'Not that kind of spring.' Ita eyed her mischieviously. 'I gave a few glasses of the stuff to Mark the other night, who is fifty. He said it was so good he's coming off Viagra. It's an ancient Chinese recipe. All you do is steep potent medicinal herbs in alcohol, to extract their essential active elements.' She raised the bowl to her nose and inhaled. 'These active elements, Ellen, will give you your baby.'

'Thanks, Ita, but I have a few active elements of my own, if I'm ever allowed to use them.'

'Here,' Ita sang, unperturbed. 'Want to help?' She took out a tin containing over a dozen small sachets. She tore one open and sniffed. 'Tortoiseshell resin,' she said, giving Ellen a sniff.

'Smells vaguely of sundried tomatoes.'

'As long as it does what it's supposed to, I don't care if it smells like farm manure.' She took a pinch, sprinkled it into the heating rum and stirred. Ellen read some of the labels: astragalus root; angelica root; dried human placenta; red-spotted lizard.

'Tell me, did that Myles chap bring you back your Chopin?'

'Yes, and you'll never believe what happened.'

'Oh, goodie!'

Ellen related the near-drowning incident, which sent Ita into a

147

bout of hooting laughter. 'It just proves it,' she said, when she'd recovered. 'Bad deeds come back at you threefold.'

'He's not that bad a person.' Ellen recalled Myles on the intercom, compressing his eyebrows with salivated fingers. 'Just a little vain, perhaps.'

'The man's got a bad aura. He needs to dominate, be in total control. Then he goes and falls into the sea.'

'He nearly drowned, Ita.'

'But he's alive, isn't he? A little wetting will do him the world of good.' She threw in some horny goatweed. 'It's great to see people so full of themselves brought down to earth like that! Or should I say to water? Chinese wolfberry!' Ita opened another sachet and sprinkled some into the rum. She reached out her wooden spoon and gently raised up Ellen's chin with it. 'I don't want you worrying about Joel. I'm getting positive vibes about you and him. I think it's going to work out exactly as planned. Here.' She gave Ellen the wooden spoon, then put in some Korean ginseng root. 'Why don't you stir?'

As she stirred, Ellen peered into the red vortex. Soon she became hypnotised by the tiny whirlpool motion of the red liquid in the pot. It was just so ridiculous. She was trying so hard, but was being thwarted at every turn. This evening, after the fiasco on the balcony, she'd done the test again. It had shown up bright red. She was ready. Everything was ready. Except that Joel got called away yet again. Was she destined to fail? Karma, it seemed, had decided to deal her a good kick in the teeth for her sins.

As she stirred, it occurred to Ellen that she should take a leaf out of Joel's book: he had a more carefree attitude to life. As a result, things always seemed to work out for him.

'Keep stirring,' Ita sang, putting on a *Forest Voices* CD on the countertop. She came over again and sprinkled raspberry seeds into the rum, then shoved in a bag which contained – supposedly – dried human placenta.

Ellen rotated the wooden spoon round and round, quicker and quicker, getting herself into an increasing panic as she went. She had only until tomorrow night. What if it didn't happen? *And what if it didn't happen next month, either?* No. She must not let herself think like that. She mustn't let herself become negative. She must believe.

Tomorrow, Ellen decided, *tomorrow it's going to happen.*

44

He was sitting on the wooden chair in the dim room, staring at the floor, sipping bourbon to ease his burning knee.

Outside was dark. The lone bulb over the basement door cast a miserly yellow light into Monk's quarters. Inside was quiet. Even Rufus had joined him in silent meditation. The night was deathly still and overhead there was not a sound. He was alone.

And yet not alone. Monk's mind was glued to the image of Ellen's face, shining like a bright halo in a bleak cavern. Everything about her. Everything.

On the pier. She was transformed. Holding out a hand, as he'd trudged up the steps from the freezing sea, rat-drowned. He clasping her hand, then collapsing on the concrete. The distress in her eyes as she'd taken off her jacket and bunched it under his head for a pillow. Gripping his hand as he lay there, recovering. Peering into him, that profound, inexpressible look in her eyes, Christ, the *way* she'd peered into him. Deep into him, with an intimacy he'd never before known, infinitely more deeply than all those countless, nameless, dead-eyed dozens who had prostrated themselves on his futon.

Sure, it all lasted only a few moments – she busied herself with his knee then. But Monk knew the signs. They were unmistakable. She was taken by him. And she'd communicated her desire in the most intimate way a woman knew, when he was at his most vulnerable. Her former act had vanished: the feigned censure, the sharp comments, the pretence of indifference. All this had disappeared and she was all over him, revealing a tenderness he never imagined her to possess. She was for once fully herself.

Monk gulped the bourbon from his glass and it deliciously crucified his throat. He poured another, emptied the glass down his throat and stood up. The pain had subsided again. He walked unsteadily to the birdcage, picked up Rufus and placed him on his

149

shoulder. He went to the barred window and stared out into the dark. Midgets danced joyfully around the luminous yellow bulb, which pushed the black night into temporary recess.

This strange, strange gloom . . .

He lit a cigarillo. The smoke buffeted against the glass and it came back at them both, discommoding Rufus, who stretched his head backwards to escape the nicotine cloud. Monk pulled down the window and the cool, perfumed aroma of night draped in. He offered Rufus a toke, but he jutted his neck back like a swan and gave Monk a look of blinking amazement. Monk stroked the bird under his chin, exhaling smoke out into the cool evening air.

Monk's knee rustled something on the windowsill. It was a piece of paper. Another of his mother's handwritten notes. What was it this time? He picked it up.

Myles,
A woman with red hair called over this evening. She wants to talk to you about something and said she'd call round tomorrow morning instead.
Your mother.

Monk tore up the note and flicked it into the basket underneath the window sill. He lifted up the piano lid and played the first two bars of the 'Tristesse' from memory. He tried to sit down on the stool, but groaned on account of his knee. He creaked up to his full height again and closed the lid. He limped across the room to his futon and laid his stiff body down, making sure not to graze his knee. He pulled the duvet over him, careful not to upset the parrot, and expelled a heavy lungful of air.

There wasn't a sound now, apart from the odd flutter on the pillow beside him or the occasional creak from his mother upstairs.

The darker the place got, the brighter Ellen's face.

'I almost died tonight, Rufus.' He closed his eyes and breathed deeply. 'She saved my life . . . now I'm going to save hers.'

thursday

45

Ellen rose at seven thirty and ran over the fast section of the 'Tristesse', playing silently on the keys. At eight, she began playing very softly and at eight thirty she moved on to the Shostakovich, at half-volume. The sonata went reasonably well, though you could never be absolutely certain playing on your own. The test would be her second-last rehearsal at ten thirty.

At nine she closed the piano lid, then drove to the nearby shopping centre to buy something special for their dinner. She was practically at the end of her tether and had decided that nothing short of a formal arrangement with Joel that evening would do. At a deli she purchased two fillets of beef with grilled Danish blue, tomato mash and a port jus, topped with French fried onions. A tomato, mozzarella and garlic salad. She bought wine in a wine boutique and a slab of rich chocolate gateau for Joel from a nearby patisserie.

Pressing home the chocolate theme – one of his principal addictions in life – Ellen bought a chocolate-flavoured aromatherapeutic candle for their bedroom and a box of Lir chocolates for his mouth. She drove home, then, practically broke. Back at the Pavilion, Ellen stuck her key in the lobby door, but her vexed train of thoughts was interrupted by a distinctively bad odour. She sniffed the air. Stale urine. She looked to see where it was coming from. To her disgust, she beheld a streak of damp on the wall two metres from the door and, below this, a small pool on the ground.

In the name of God, what was the *matter* with such people?

They were worse than animals. They should be fined. Whipped. Right beside the front entrance! They just couldn't wait. Probably too drunk to get the key in. What really worried her, though, was the thought that the pig who did this actually *lived* in this apartment block. Disgusted, Ellen twisted the key in the lock and entered the lobby. At that moment she heard an animal sound coming from outside.

She popped her head back out of the door. There, standing meekly beside the offending puddle, was Chopin. She was cold and hungry-looking. Her tail was up between her legs and she was whimpering. Ellen went over and caressed her coat. Oh, how awful; she was in a dreadful state. She was damp and there was evidence that she might have been in another minor scrap. She examined the dog closely and noticed that the red handle of her leash was indented with teeth marks.

'You poor thing. Could you not find your way home?' Seeing that the coast was clear, she lifted up the dog and smuggled her upstairs with her shopping. 'Don't you dare piddle, now.' Chopin sat on the kitchen floor and stared ruefully up at her.

Right, she resolved, food first, shower later. Ellen took a bowl of meatballs from the fridge and scooped several on to a saucer, which she put on the floor, along with a bowl of water. While she was eating a bowl of cornflakes, Chopin gobbled down the meatballs with such speed that Ellen felt obliged to give her several more. Afterwards she took the dog into the bathroom and gave her a good soaping and dousing in the bath. Chopin didn't object. In fact, she seemed to enjoy the attention. And she positively relished the warm blasts of air from Ellen's high-powered hairdryer.

When her coat was dry, Ellen took Chopin up on to her knees and patted her fondly. 'You're a much happier dog now, aren't you? All you need is someone to take care of you properly.'

Chopin barked happily and licked Ellen's face.

'I wish I could keep you for myself, but we're not allowed to have dogs up here, you know?' She checked the time.

Five to ten. The trio was rehearsing at the Conservatory from ten thirty onwards. She risked being late. 'I suppose I'm going to have to bring you back to your master, amn't I? I bet you don't want to go back to him, do you? I don't want to go back to him myself.'

She tried to remember Myles's full address. She knew that it was Crosthwaite Park, from his copy of the 'Tristesse'. But she couldn't for the life of her remember the number of his house. Never mind.

'You'll know where your home is, Chopin, won't you?'

46

Monk lay motionless on his futon in exactly the same position as when he'd fallen asleep. He'd slept soundly for the first night in weeks – probably a solid eight hours.

Had he checked the clock beside him, he could have found out. But Monk had no interest in doing this, for that would have meant opening his eyes. And he didn't want to open his eyes in case this blissful sensation disappeared. It was a new feeling, one of total and complete well-being. Monk had just been dreaming and he strove desperately to hold the dream in his head before it vanished.

He had been standing on an auctioneer's podium, holding a hammer. The room was full of sexy females throwing their hands in the air and clamouring to be chosen by him. As Monk cast his eyes around for a suitable lay, his attention was caught by a woman in the middle of the crowd, with long blonde hair. Her head was lowered and she stood quite still. 'You, over there,' he cried out, 'what's your name?' Everyone turned. The woman looked up calmly, but did not speak. There was the faint flicker of a smile on her lips. Monk beat his way through the throng of flesh towards her, but she disappeared into thin air.

Next, he saw her standing in the middle of a bright-orange cornfield. She wore a white dress and her blonde hair glowed in the hot sun. She was holding a bunch of flowers, lavender and yellow, and gazing into the distance. Monk was trying to get to her but an invisible force was preventing him. He called out. She raised her head and turned slightly, as if she'd heard something. She gazed through him, without appearing to notice that he was there. Then she moved off through the yellow corn stalks. He called to her again and she turned round. This time she saw him and gave him the most beautiful smile. She started walking towards him. She was saying something to him, he couldn't make out her words, she was coming closer and closer and . . .

Out of nowhere, the doorbell rang and Monk sat up in the futon. 'Jesus,' he groaned, 'who is that, at this hour?'

The bell buzzed again. A woman coughed, the redhead. 'Damn her!' he cursed. 'Why can't she accept what I told her?' Through the curtain, he spotted a forearm approaching the doorbell. 'GO AWAY!' he roared. 'Leave me alone!'

The hand stopped.

'Go back to your husband!'

The hand withdrew and the figure appeared to pull back. Monk rolled over on his side, hugging the pillow into his face to block out the interference.

The bell went yet again and Monk sprang out of the futon, livid. 'I said go away!' he bellowed, limping to the window. 'Do you hear me, you stupid woman? I don't want to see you again! Can't you understand English?'

A dog barked. Monk froze on the spot. He drew back the curtain an inch. To his horror, he saw Ellen ascending the steps, dragging the dog behind her. 'Oh, Jesus, no. This isn't happening. I didn't say that. *I didn't say that.*' He ran from the room and raced through the basement, flung open the basement door and hurried up after her. Ellen was at the top of the main steps to the house, just about to press the doorbell.

'Ellen, Ellen!'

She turned and looked down at him. He could not help it: his face was beaming. She wasn't smiling. He went up and stopped on the penultimate step. 'I'm sorry,' he said, 'was that you ringing the bell just now?'

She did not reply.

'I thought it was someone else. I'm sorry. I didn't . . .'

'That's okay. I was just bringing your friend back. She guided me here in the end, didn't you, Chopin?'

'So how are you? How are you this morning?'

'I'm well, thank you. And how are you, after last night?'

154

'Very good, very good.'

'How is your knee?'

'Can hardly feel it.'

She offered him the leash, but Monk looked down at Chopin. 'Where did you find him? Her?'

'Outside our apartment. She may have been out there all night. I gave her a good wash.'

Monk bent down and sniffed, from a safe distance. The dog had been transformed into a perfumed fuzzball. 'I appreciate you taking care of my mother's dog like that.'

'I figured someone had to. I gave her something to eat as well.'

He stood back up. 'Have you had breakfast yourself?'

She eyed him askance. 'Yes, I did, thank you.'

'Right, fair enough.'

'Didn't I, Chopin?' She glanced at her watch. 'Anyway, I'd better be . . .'

'So,' interrupted Monk, 'how are you anyway?'

She frowned at him. 'I'm well, thanks. As I said.'

'You're certainly looking . . . terrific.'

'Would you mind if I gave you the leash? I'm in a bit of a hurry.'

Monk took it off her and she moved down the steps. He quickly tied the dog to the railing, then followed Ellen down the front path.

'So,' he called after her, 'you've had breakfast, then?'

'That's right.'

'Did you have coffee? My mother has a great Javan roast.'

'I'm sorry, I'm actually in a terrible rush. I have a rehearsal at half-ten.'

Monk walked across the garden after her. 'All set for your concert tomorrow?'

She pulled open the gate, then closed it behind her, locking him into the garden. 'I hope it goes okay with your mother.'

'What?'

'For her birthday.'

'Oh, you mean the Chopin.'

Monk stared mutely after her as she strode up the pavement, powerless to stop her. The early morning cold, which was beginning to invade his bones, seemed to have chilled his brain cells to

155

a standstill and he could think of nothing to make her come back. She stopped at a battered black Nissan and stuck a key in the lock. Monk came out after her.

'Ellen, wait! I wanted to thank you, for yesterday, for what you did for me on the pier.'

She held the car door open.

'I'd like to get you something, give you something, lunch maybe? Would you be free lunchtime?'

'No, I'm sorry. I'm very busy at the moment. I'm completely tied up the whole day until six.'

'Six. That's completely fine.'

'Please don't go to any trouble, Myles. I'm just glad I was there to help.'

'I'm glad you were there too.' He slid her one of his best smiles.

Monk watched Ellen get into her car and drive off, brakes screeching at the main road. He was flooded with an unspeakable contentment.

Trouble! How could she imagine it was trouble? It was the very least he could do, to call up to her place at six o'clock this evening and give her a nice surprise.

Monk floated his way back to the gate and looked out across a sunny Crosthwaite Park. Everything about it looked beautiful. The grass and hedging glistened with early morning dew and tiny spiders' webs shone like miniature silver necklaces across the grass. Monk had never realised that his mother kept such a beautiful bed of flowers over by the front gate, that the doors of the houses across the park were painted in such vibrant reds, yellows and greens, that the place he'd inhabited all his life could manage to look quite so charming.

He tilted his head back and the early morning sun flooded his eyes, warming his face in a wash of gold.

47

'What's going on, up there?' bellowed his father from the bottom of the ladder.

Joel got such a fright that he nearly slipped through one of the rafters and put a foot through the ceiling of his father's bedroom below. He'd been searching inside suitcases and flinging them around the attic since seven in the morning.

'If you stay over in this house,' his father growled, 'you should know that at seven thirty in the morning I can't endure any sort of noise louder than a coffee percolator.' There were squeaky footsteps up the attic ladder. 'What are you doing up there, anyway?'

'Can't find my old clarinet,' Joel shouted. 'I think it's missing.'

'So why are you taking it out on my suitcases?' His father poked his head into the attic. 'They cost money, you know.' He climbed up into the cramped space in his navy dressing gown.

Joel realised it wasn't too polite ransacking your father's attic the one time you stayed over – even if it was on the couch. But he was desperate to locate his clarinet. 'I'm sure I left it here somewhere. Would it be in that trunk in the corner?'

'They're your mother's things. Don't go near it; you'll fall through the ceiling.'

'You didn't sell it, did you?'

'Your clarinet?' His father bent down and dusted off a suitcase. 'I should have, for all the use you got out of it.' He began medically examining several of his precious cases for signs of injury. 'I don't suppose you bothered looking in the obvious place?'

'Where's that?'

'In the music room?'

'It's not there; I checked.'

'Did you indeed? How well did you check?'

'I checked everywhere.'

'Well, you'd better go back down and check everywhere again.'

'But I looked . . .'

'On the floor behind the divan?'

'I didn't look there.' Joel immediately moved towards the ladder.

'Wait!' His father pointed to one remaining discarded suitcase on the floor. Joel picked it up dutifully and replaced it neatly alongside its matching neighbours.

'What do you want your clarinet for, anyway?'

157

'I thought I might try some busking in town.'

'*Busking?*'

'Dad, I've no way of earning a living without my saxophone.'

'*Busking?*'

Joel scuttled down the ladder before his father could stop him. In the music room he found his old clarinet behind the divan. He ran down the stairs and out through the front door into the sunny morning, but he got no further than halfway down the path.

His father was shouting down at him from the front bedroom window. 'Where are you running off to, Joseph? Will you come back and let me have a word with you, for goodness' sake?'

Joel shuffled back to the door and his father soon reappeared. 'You know I don't approve of the idea of you busking.'

'But I'm completely broke, Dad.'

'You won't earn a penny busking.'

'I've been told you can earn a fortune.'

'Well, I'm sure you can, by the standards of street beggars. But I won't have it! My only son reduced to upscale scrounging in broad daylight.'

'Come on, Dad, give me some credit. I wasn't going to stand in front of any of your clients' shops. Anyway, if I don't go now I won't get a pitch.' He moved off.

'Wait!' Henry grabbed Joel's arm. 'Would you for God's sake stand still?' He appeared to be softening. 'Now, look, I'm not going to make a habit of this.'

'Of what?'

Henry gave him a warning glare. 'I've already told you there would be no cash advances, because I wouldn't be doing you any favours. I don't take that back. But I wasn't to know you'd so stupidly lose the only means you had – decent or otherwise – to earn a living.'

Joel watched, frowning, as his father slid his hand into the pocket of his gown and withdrew a brown envelope.

'Now I don't want you to think I'm backtracking on what I told you, but in the circumstances, I might have to reconsider the moratorium.'

'You're actually going to . . .?'

'As long as you understand I'm not setting a precedent. Here.' His father licked the envelope and stuck it fast. He held it out. Joel had to pull it with some force to get it out from between his father's fingers. But when he felt it between his own, he realised it contained no more than a single slip of paper.

'Dad,' he said, his voice shaking, 'is this a cheque?'

'It is.'

'Is it, by any chance, made out to cash?'

'It is.'

'Oh, God.'

'I want you to know that this is absolutely just a one-off.'

'Absolutely.'

Joel didn't want to jump to conclusions, but he already had. Big conclusions. His father had slept on it. He'd ruminated on what Joel had told him about his saxophone. And this morning, after a good eight-hour sleep, he'd had a major change of heart. He'd decided not to reject Joel's appeals for help and let down his only flesh and blood. Deep down, his father was obviously a man of mercy and providence.

He did not dare ask how much was on that cheque. That would be blatantly rude. But the more he thought about it, the clearer the picture became. His father had already written him a cheque for ten grand earlier that week. *So what was to stop him writing another?*

Joel began to tremble. It would make everything possible. Everything! *Ten thousand Euros!* Oh, God, please, let it be!

'Well?'

Joel looked up, light-headed. 'Sorry?'

'Aren't you going to leave your clarinet behind?'

'Hmm? No, it's okay. I'll use it to practise with.'

'As long as you don't busk.'

'No way, Dad. I won't busk, I swear.'

'Do you want a lift home, on my way to town?'

'No, that's okay,' he replied. 'I'll float instead . . . I'll walk. Father, I don't know what to say.' He stepped out of the porch.

'Well, you could start by telling Ellen I was asking for her.'

'Sure, I'll do that.'

'And if she mentions anything about last night, just tell her . . .

159

I don't know . . . tell her I was drinking, tell her I was in bad form, or something, all right?'

'Will do!' Joel jaunted down the garden path with his clarinet case.

'Don't spend it all at once!' his father shouted.

'I won't,' he shouted back, waving. 'Thanks a million, Dad.'

Running out on to the footpath, Joel narrowly missed a black Labrador, tunnelling along the pavement. He apologised and hurried towards the small cove, where he would open the envelope in relative privacy and hopefully savour the wonderful experience of having all his grim expectations about life over-turned in the space of three seconds. As he walked, he gazed over the pale-blue sound opposite him. Across his line of vision stretched the east pier. Docked at the distant terminal was the bleached catamaran, hooked up to its white tubes. The coast looked astoundingly beautiful in the morning light.

Joel's heart palpitated with new hope. The sax! The nest egg! Ellen! The baby! Everything would be incredibly, totally fine!

He rushed over to the low wall just above the sandy beach at Sandycove. He sat down, took a deep breath and stared at the envelope, caressing the single piece of paper. He removed a steel comb from his back pocket, slipped it underneath the envelope flap and scythed it across. He hesitated some moments before pulling open the gap. He removed the cheque with extreme caution, as if it were about to break up into ashes. The envelope dropped to the concrete and he held the cheque before him like a holy offering, gripped between fingers and thumb. He was utterly transfixed by the words written on the line below his name: 'Pay *Joseph O'Leary* . . . the sum of *two hundred Euros only.*'

Joel reread the line: '*two hundred Euros only.*'

He bent down, grabbed the envelope up from the concrete and rooted manically inside it. On discovering what he already knew – namely, that it was empty – he scrunched it into a ball and stamped it several times on the ground, in a state of almost weeping disgust.

Two hundred Euros.

Joel picked up his clarinet and dragged himself to his feet. He

160

plodded along the seafront promenade towards Sandycove train station.

It was as if hope and good fortune had, for the previous twenty-six years of Joel's existence, vindictively placed themselves mere inches beyond his reach. And now they were jeering loudly at him for having been born short.

Ellen was going to see the account on Friday, he agonised. It was going to happen. She was going to try to withdraw money to buy the pram. Joel kicked a broken branch off the path, then stopped dead in his tracks.

Wait a second! He looked at the cheque again. *Two hundred Euros*. He put a hand to his forehead.

Maybe she wouldn't have to buy the pram after all . . .

48

Once upon a time, Joel did not swerve from the absolute conviction that street musicianship was a viable career alternative with excellent earning potential – at least in the short run.

He held that conviction approximately three hours earlier, when a busload of tourists disembarked and flung a massive sixteen Euros into his clarinet box, as they filed into the Gresham Hotel behind him. Since then, however, Joel had earned the monetary equivalent of three large bars of Toblerone. He concluded that those sixteen Euros represented the one-off generosity of a busload of tartan-trousered Americans who all went ape only because the loudest of them happened to hear him playing 'Danny Boy'.

Now it was nearly five o'clock and Joel was on his knees, packing up. Jaded after his marathon session, he was collecting the coins into a sock he'd borrowed from his left foot. As he did so, he wondered whether he should apply for substitute work in the army band.

He'd carried such high hopes! He'd heard stories of the fortunes buskers earned (though mostly told by themselves). But not just that. Things had started so well! The second he stuck the clarinet in his mouth, he burst into an astonishingly impressive frenzy of notes. People looked over as they passed. Some stopped to listen. Old men. Women with heavy shopping bags or lightweight children. Businessmen. Skinheads. Tourists. Africans. A priest. An unshaven and possibly inebriated old man with a skew-ways placard saying BRING JESUS BACK INTO YOUR LIFE. They all turned their heads in admiration and interest, although Joel feared that the standard-bearer was going to come over and hand him a miraculous medal.

After 'Danny Boy', Joel played a few Irish ballads. But they didn't bring in a lot, so he switched to standards. He played a succession of numbers off the top of his head. 'On the Sunny Side of the Street' (although the sun had momentarily disappeared behind a cloud), 'Let the Good Times Roll' . . . 'Killer Joe' . . . 'Make Someone Happy' . . . The music flowed freely, indeed – but less so the contributions from the passing public.

Even when these trickled out, Joel persevered, refusing to relinquish his dream of earning a vast fortune by five o'clock. He played some other numbers with more upbeat potential – the sort that would bring a smile to people's lips: 'Laugh, Clown, Laugh' . . . 'Un Poco Loco' . . . 'Nice Work if You Can Get It' . . .

But that was all these pieces brought: a smile. Joel was earning, on average, the price of a pack of M&Ms for every fifteen minutes of playing time. From here on in Joel's spirits began to slip, but he still refused to give up. The problem, he convinced himself, wasn't that busking didn't pay. It was that people didn't pay – at least for now.

So he dug into his vast repertoire of tunes. He tried 'Good Morning Heartache' in a syncopated, jazzy style. This got him no more than a Polo mint from a young heroin indulger with 'scrap' written all over his face. After this, things seemed to deteriorate. He played 'Cry Me a River', which went down well with a bunch of tourist scabs. He tried 'Singin' in the Rain', although a Japanese man with a smiling countenance came up to him and pointed out that the sun had just returned. Vexed at the criticism (or was it, perhaps, an Oriental version of a joke?), Joel played 'Rain Waltz'.

One thing led to another. Soon he was playing Stan Getz's excellent saxophone interpretation of 'A Day in the Life of a

Fool'. It got worse and worse. Shortly afterwards he was attempting an improvised rendition of 'Bass Blues' and 'I'll Never Smile Again'.

At about half-four, around the time he was getting desperate, Joel tried a version of Dizzy Gillespie's notable take on 'Salt Peanuts'. He finished the performance with 'Glad to Be Unhappy', after a header came along and flung a small coin into his clarinet box, as target practice.

It was now after five o'clock and Joel put the last few coins in his sock. He replaced his instrument in the case and closed the clasps. He pulled out his phone and was about to call Ellen, to enquire about the location of the baby shop, when it suddenly went off, making Joel jump. He hit the receive button.

'O'Leary!'

There was only one person in the world who addressed him in that way. It wasn't a voice he wanted to hear. 'Look, Monk, if you're calling about the two grand, you can forget it: the deal was that you walk on the pier with Ellen and the dog, not fall into the sea.'

There was a brief lull.

'Although', said Joel with added malice, 'I had to laugh when she told me.'

'She told you?'

'You ballsed up, Monk.'

'Forget about that. What are you up to, man?'

Monk sounded unusually friendly. Joel didn't trust him an inch. 'I'm in town. Busking. Making a fortune.'

'I promise – I won't tell a soul. Listen, the reason I'm calling is – I've got a letter for you, from Jan Fuks.'

Joel didn't trust himself to reply.

'He's offering you a job in Prague,' Monk said.

Joel halted on the pavement. 'You're taking the piss.'

'I am holding the letter in my hand.'

'*When does he want me? How long? How much?*'

'You want to find that out, you meet me in the Duke pub at seven thirty. I'll give you the letter then.'

Joel made some quick calculations. It was five o'clock. If he went and purchased the pram immediately, brought it home and

163

returned to town, he could meet Monk for seven thirty. *'I'll be there!'*

'If I'm late, wait for me. Do not leave until I get there, okay?'

'Absolutely, fine, yes, Monk. Cheers.'

'Because I may be very late.'

'Sure, Monk, sure. Listen, what I said about you on the pier just now . . .'

But the line went dead.

Joel picked up his clarinet box and his sock, then proceeded down O'Connell Street in a daze.

Jan? Offering him a job?

Could it be true?

Could things actually be looking up?

49

At four thirty they agreed to end rehearsals for the day.

Again, it had not gone well for Ellen. Errors had abounded, but there seemed nothing she could do to stop them except hope that concert nerves on the day would put her right. Ita, surprisingly, was blasé. She advised Ellen to go home, shag the brains out of her husband and get a great night's sleep. And the concert would go just fine.

Ellen didn't believe it.

They were both walking into Pearse Street station when Ita grabbed her.

'I forgot to tell you,' she said with conspiratorial hush, 'three glasses is the maximum you'll need for a man of his stature. Anything more and he might get pissed, which could scupper your chances.'

Ellen didn't reply immediately. 'I have to buy another train pass,' she said. 'My last one ran out yesterday.'

They queued up at the ticket counter.

'Did you put it in the fridge, like I said?' Ita asked.

'Put what in the fridge?' Ellen bowed her head and rooted for change in her purse.

'The spring wine.'

'Ita, I didn't take it home with me. I left it in your cloakroom.'

'What? But I gave it to you!'

Ellen softened her voice. 'He wouldn't drink that type of thing anyway, I know him. Joel is strictly a beer and whiskey . . . and vodka man.' The man gave her the train pass and her change, and she stepped aside and put the change in her purse. When she looked up, she saw Ita staring at her in dismay.

'You don't believe it works, Ellen, do you? That's why you didn't take it. Well, you're making a big mistake.'

A trio of businessmen in the queue appeared to be tuning in.

'The man's been limp for three days,' Ita said, broadcasting to the whole world. 'What makes you think he's going to be any better tonight?'

'Perhaps you could keep your voice down, Ita?' Ellen pulled her away from the group of tittering men and towards the turnstile. Her phone went off in her bag.

'You could still come back home with me now, Ellen, and I could give you the spring wine.'

'No, Ita. It's just not his thing.' She took out her phone. 'Hello?'

'How's my favourite mother-to-be?'

'Joel!'

'Listen, remember that pram you were talking about? Well, I'm in town and I thought I might have a look at it.'

'I'm in town as well. I'm up at Westland Row. Do you want to meet?'

'Nah, I have some stuff to do. I'll see you at home later.'

She told him where the baby shop was. 'When will you be back?'

'Should be home around six.'

'Good. I'm going to put on a special dinner for us both. Thought we might as well treat ourselves.'

'Sounds cool.'

'How's your back?'

'Not too bad. I'm walking around okay.'

'Good, that's a relief. I'll see you later, then.' She ended the call.

'Who was that?' Ita asked.

'Joel. You know the stroller I was telling you about? He wants to have a look at it. He's going there now.'

165

Ita was curious. 'He's going to the baby shop *now?*'

'Yeah.' Ellen was all smiles. She moved through the turnstiles with Ita. Joel was going to look at a pram. Who would have thought it?

'Flip!' cried Ita, as they were about to mount the escalators.

'What?' Ellen stepped aside.

'I've just remembered, I meant to get tights in town, for tomorrow.'

'I thought you bought tights at lunchtime.'

'Don't like them. Wrong colour. They make me look big. I want to get another pair.'

Ellen was puzzled by her friend. She was normally so *together*. They parted at the bottom of the escalator and confirmed their pre-recital rehearsal at the Gallery the following morning at ten thirty.

Ita gave her arm a squeeze. 'You'll be fine, love! Call me if you need to talk.'

Ellen went up the escalators. When she looked down, she saw Ita rushing back out of the station.

50

'Twelve chrysanthemums,' he told the woman over the phone. 'Beautiful Lady, if you have them.'

Monk figured that the least you could do when a woman saved your life was give her a decent bunch of flowers.

'Your name?'

'Myles Lavery.'

'Will I write down who they're from, on a note?'

'They're from me. She'll know who it is.'

'And the name of the person they're to be delivered to?'

'Bring them here. I'll give them to the person myself.' He gave his address, then his Mastercard number.

Afterwards he examined himself in his wardrobe mirror. 'Just look at that belly!' He pulled his belt as tight as it would go, but this only made the flab spill over like an abdominal tongue. The thought that Ellen had seen his belly that morning in the garden

166

considerably vexed him. He reined in his stomach muscles and strutted around the place in his new contracted state, surveying the effect in the mirror from various angles and distances.

Monk sat at the piano and slid his fingers lightly across the keys. As he did so, he thought of Ellen. Effortlessly, her image came to him in a perfect likeness. She was seated next to him, treating him to another lesson.

She was but inches away. Her smell: fragrant; a mild hint of soap. He could hear her too: that beautifully authoritative feminine voice. And he could see her: the haunted, almost forbidding way she was peering into him. Could he taste her? Not quite. But very soon he would be able to taste her. Her lips. Her cheeks. Her forehead. Her . . .

Monk closed his eyes.

'Try this,' she told him in a distant voice, raising her delicate fingers to the keyboard. And he obeyed. He brought his own hands over the keys. 'Very good. Now try taking my hand.' Monk took her white hand. 'Excellent . . . now try taking my other hand . . . Perfect! Now try . . . kissing me.' Monk pictured a rosy-red pair of lips with absolute precision. He pursed his own lips and turned to face her.

'Now tell me your story,' she whispered in his ear. 'Tell me your story and I'll give it a happy ending.' He could feel her breath waft against his earlobes. 'Who are you, Myles? What are you . . .?'

He attempted a reply: 'I'm . . . I'm a . . .'

'*Wanker!*' Rufus screeched, snapping Monk out of the reverie.

He shot a venomous look up at the parrot, who was tottering restlessly back and forth on the summit of the cage, craning his neck towards the window. Outside, the sound of furious barking. Monk leapt up. Chopin! He'd completely forgotten!

Monk ran out of his pad and limped up the steps. The dog was going bananas, barking and pirouetting at a passing ice-cream van. Monk untied the leash with some difficulty, then coaxed her down the steps. As they were descending to the basement, Rufus did his best impression of a killer vulture and Chopin responded by impersonating a raging leopard. Monk dumped the dog out into the back garden, where she wandered over to the flowerbeds, nestling finally beside his mother's neat row of potted azaleas.

He stared at the dog, impressed. How different she looked, compared with yesterday! A mangy cur transformed, by dint of some shampoo, into a born-again pup you could now look at without getting sick.

But what the hell was Monk going to do with her? Sure, Chopin had had a small hand in bringing him and Ellen together. But – and it was a big but – did this mean he had to look after her?

Not a hope.

Unless . . .?

Monk shut the door and went upstairs. He entered his mother's sitting room which, even after twenty years, still managed to stink of his dead father's stale cigarette smoke. She was reading Proust, her face encased in a large pair of glasses.

He coughed. Several moments elapsed before she raised her eyes from the page. 'Mother, I got you a birthday present.'

'Bit late, isn't it?'

'For your next birthday, I mean, not your last one.'

She frowned. 'It's not for another month, or are you trying to pass my time for me?'

'Do you want to see it or not?'

She lowered her eyes to his empty hands. 'Where is it?'

'In the back garden.'

His mother looked as though she'd prefer to stay put, but she dropped the book on the armrest and got up reluctantly. 'Do I have to wear a blindfold?' she asked, deadpan.

Monk led the way to the kitchen and opened the window overlooking the rear garden. 'Now, have a look down.'

She stuck out her head. She did not move or say anything for some time. No negative comment or reaction so far. Encouraging sign. His mother seemed pleased with her present. Of course, if she agreed to take the dog on, Monk would have to put his foot down as regards his level of participation in its future welfare. The most he'd do would be to purchase the dog food.

His mother pulled her head back in and slammed the window shut. She turned round and glared. 'What are you trying to prove?'

'What?'

168

'Is this supposed to be some sort of humorous joke? Because if it is, I'm sorry, but I'm not following it.'

Monk was dumbstruck by her reaction. 'What's wrong? I thought you'd like it.' He moved to the window.

'What are you trying to tell me?' she said. 'That I should get a gardener? Is that it?'

He opened the window again and peered down at the garden. To his horror, he saw that his mother's azaleas were lying about the lawn, torn up and in tatters.

An hour later the three of them were in the kitchen, drinking lemonade. Monk's mother was smiling at her new Jack Russell, who was lapping up his drink from a plastic container on the kitchen floor.

'Chopin has been drinking continually for the last fifteen minutes,' Miranda said, arching her eyebrows in amazement.

'I know,' replied Monk. 'And most of it will be coming back out too. A complete waste.'

'Is she house-trained?'

'She's not even street-trained.'

'Oh, well, I suppose if she needs a home. And you picked her out specially?'

'More or less.'

'I don't know what to say. You're a good boy, Myles. No, you *are*. Despite everything.'

The bell rang and she went out and opened the front door. 'Delivery for Lavery?' shouted an unfamiliar voice into the hall.

'Damn!' Monk shouted, suddenly remembering. He sprang up and ran out into the hall. 'Mother! It's probably for me! *Mother!*'

Too late.

She was closing the front door, holding a bouquet of flowers up to her nose. They were long-stalked, peachy-pink chrysanthemums. A youthful smile had transformed his mother's face and she was positively glowing with pleasure. She came up and kissed him on the cheek. 'They're absolutely *gorgeous*, Myles. Beautiful Lady! Who's the beautiful lady?' She chuckled. 'I don't see one. Dear, dear! First Chopin, now these. I don't know what to say . . .

I can hardly remember the last time someone bought flowers for me.'

She moved into the kitchen, inhaling the scent. 'Well, I'd sooner get them while I'm still alive, as they say.' She removed a vase from a cupboard, telling him about the first time she was given a bunch of chrysanthemums. She said it had all gone dreadfully wrong when she'd discovered, the very next day, a gap in her boyfriend's parents' shrubbery. 'But *these* are the real thing.'

Monk left the kitchen, almost as annoyed as he was pleased. He would pick up a bunch for Ellen in the florist's later on, on the way down to her place.

Back downstairs, he laid out his clothes. He pulled out his leopard-skin thong from his drawer of underwear, and put it on underneath a pair of black trousers. When he pulled these up, however, they felt uncomfortably tight. That stupid belly again. Monk tried on a new shirt, fresh from the packet. The cotton was crisp and clean against his skin.

Which aftershave? He picked up his two most expensive brands, the Armani in one hand and the Paco Rabane in the other. He smelt them in alternately. There was a knock on the door.

'Dear?'

'Yes?'

'I put them in a vase. Do you want to see them?'

'Sorry?'

'The chrysanthemums.'

'I'm in a bit of a rush right now, Mother.'

'Oh, are you heading somewhere?'

'Just out.'

'Oh.'

He levered open the door with his foot and held up both bottles of aftershave. 'Which smells better, this or this?'

She placed her spindly fingers over Monk's left hand, drew the bottle to her nose and sniffed, deep in concentration. She did the same for the bottle in his right hand, then returned to the first.

'Are you subtle?' she enquired, inscrutable.

'Often.'

'Then I'd suggest this one,' she said, pointing. 'It reminds me of your father.'

'I'll go for the other one, in that case.' He walked back in and busied himself at the mirror, dabbing aftershave on to his neck.

'Dear?' She was at the threshold.

'Yes?'

'Are you seeing a girl?'

'Mm.'

'Do I know her?'

'Ellen O'Leary.'

'Is she local?'

'Pavilion apartments.'

'The Pavilion? Isn't that where your friend Joel lives?'

Monk went to the wardrobe for his jacket. 'Mm.'

'His name is O'Leary too, isn't it?'

'Yes.' He put on the jacket in front of the mirror, whistling softly.

'Are they related?'

'She's his wife.'

'She's Joel's wife?'

'Mm.'

There was an awkward silence. He could see her reflection in the tarnished mirror over the old mantelpiece. She looked concerned. Monk checked through the tie rack.

'Will there be someone else there as well, with Joel's wife?'

'No.'

'Oh.'

'Blue or yellow?' He turned and held up two ties.

'Do you know her well?' she persisted.

He held both ties towards the daylight at the back of the room and stared at them, uncertain. 'Which one?'

'Joel's wife.'

'I mean, which colour?'

'Do you know her well?'

'All my life.' Monk removed a piece of fluff from the yellow tie. 'Or, at least, it seems that way.' He caught a flash glimpse of his rear in the mirror: his arse resembled an elephant's in these trousers, although a good deal less elegant. 'I think I'll put on the Lycra trousers, they've more stretch.' He undid the zip and was about to drop them, when he remembered his mother was there. With her permission, he suavely closed the door in her face.

Monk changed his trousers to a light-tan pair – Ellen's colour. He gave his boots a final aggressive rub, then put some finishing touches to his gelled hair. He grabbed his babe wad, his cigarillo case and two condoms from his other trousers. He left the room, sticking the condoms in his pocket, and almost walked into his mother.

She looked ill, all of a sudden.

'What's the matter, Mother?'

She did not reply, though she seemed tempted to. Disappointment was etched on a suddenly exhausted face.

Monk bade her farewell, breezed past and exited the house.

51

Joel stared through the glass into what seemed like an alien world. But it wasn't just alien. It was scary.

Not that he'd never before been inside a baby shop. He had, but that was roughly twenty-four years ago. Back then, he'd enjoyed the experience, wreaking havoc on every clothes rack, every mobile object and every child he could lay his plump hands on. But times had changed. He was now, incredibly, a grown-up. And the prospect of going in there was, to say the least, a bit freaky.

He peered nervously through the glass. Then he bit the bullet and entered.

Well.

It had certainly changed in twenty-four years. The first thing he noticed was all the colour. Not just on the clothes. On the *pillars*. The second thing he noticed was the surprising number of good-looking women around the place – presumably either entirely expectant mothers or entirely demystified mothers who had already endured childbirth. Then there was all the hi-tech stuff: swinging yokes for babies and appliances for hanging infants from doors, car seats and baby gyms, snuggly items and high-speed strollers.

Joel approached the main desk at the back of the shop. 'Hi,' he said, casual as can be despite his nervous state. 'I'm here to pick up a pram being kept for Ellen O'Leary. It had a missing tray.'

The woman disappeared into a room behind and re-emerged with a stroller. She left it beside the counter and fetched a cosy-toes blanket, which she said she'd throw in for free. Joel gave the woman a hundred and fifty Euros, from his dad's cheque, which he'd just cashed. Next he overturned a sock full of coins on to the counter: from these he'd make up the difference.

While the girl was sorting through all the coins, getting into a bit of a snot, Joel stared at his purchase with fear. The carriage was light blue, with pink stripes. The chassis was solid-looking and the hubcaps yellow. The thing was absolutely gigantic. How the hell was he supposed to carry it through town without being seen?

'Here's your change,' said the assistant, sliding a pile of coins across the counter at him. 'Next, please!'

'Hold on,' said Joel. 'You're not giving it to me like *that*!'

'How do you want it, freeze-dried?' Her colleague snuffled to herself.

'You don't expect me to wheel it out like *that*! I mean, this could have career implications.'

'It folds up,' returned the woman, unsmiling.

'Oh.' Lesson number one.

While she was folding up the pram for him, separating carriage from chassis, Joel collected his coins and returned them to the sock, vowing he would never busk again. But what if he didn't have to, ever again? What if Jan really *did* want him, as Monk had said? The thought was excruciating. Joel craved to know what was in the letter. Was it a permanent job? A six-month contract? A festival filler for a few days? He'd have to wait till seven thirty to find out. It was agonising. To play in Jan's first-rate jazz band even for a few months would represent an astonishing musical triumph.

'Here you are, sir.'

Joel looked up. The woman was holding out both parts of the

pram for him. He stared at them. 'Wait a minute, can't you wrap it up or something?'

'We've no bags that are big enough.'

'Couldn't you cut up a few bags and Sellotape them together?'

Five minutes and a lot of bad grace later, Joel left the counter holding his clarinet and two wrapped packages. Chest out and head erect, he walked down the centre aisle of the shop. When he reached the first break in shelving he stopped dead. He ducked and did a U-turn. He crept back up the the aisle and, when it was safe to do so, he peered down the length of the shop towards the exit.

He had just spotted some trouble at the main entrance which he wished to avoid at all costs. The trouble was about five foot ten and wore a long trench coat. It had a violin case on its back and weighed roughly two hundred pounds. It was, in other words, *big* trouble. And it had a name.

Ita Mulrooney.

She was parked in the doorway like a bus, blocking the exit. She was casually consulting a display of pop-up books on a rack.

Joel crouched as low as he could go without coming across as criminal. *Damn and blazes!* She was just about the last person in the world he wanted to meet at this time. Not only because he'd just purchased a pram. Not even because she might phone and tell Ellen, thus destroying the surprise.

No, it went deeper than that. Ita Mulrooney was the most overbearing human being he'd ever met – and it wasn't just a physical thing. The woman dominated every conversation she could get her teeth into. Travel, films, rugby. The weather. Ita even dominated the conversation whenever he tried to steer it in the direction of jazz.

Their last dinner party was the worst. She'd sat directly opposite him and spent half the evening – in front of everyone – recommending herbal cures for his baldness. Then, when she'd brought him to a fever pitch of embarrassment, she moved on to the subject of cures for excessive facial blushing. When they'd all left, Joel pleaded with Ellen to consider banning her from the apartment in future. She said to take no notice.

Joel kept his eyes riveted on the exit door. He was ready to make

174

a run for it the split second Ita moved off. But she was taking her time: she seemed to be reading every single pop-up book on the display.

He felt something against his foot and glanced down. A bright-green dummy had just struck his left shoe. The dull black leather was now splodged with saliva. A toddler lay on the ground beside his right shoe, gurgling. It had obviously crawled out of that open playpen near by. Feet away was its heavily pregnant mother, chatting obliviously to a saleswoman. Joel looked down again. The red-faced infant was now crawling and dribbling over his shoes, in an effort to get at the dummy on the far side.

Joel glanced at the mother, in case she might come to the rescue. But she hadn't noticed a thing and he felt too mortified to disturb her. He released his packages and bent down awkwardly to pick up the dummy, making sure not to dislodge the delicate baby from his feet. He was about to hand the dummy back to the baby, when he noticed it had fluff stuck to it.

Joel withheld the dummy from the baby and spent a few moments considering the current dilemma. He knew he should wipe the article clean before handing it back, because the toddler would put it in its mouth. But what would he use? His hand? Would his shirt be cleaner? Would that be hygienic? Joel was on the point of wiping the dummy on his jacket sleeve when, without warning, the little demon let out such an almighty ear-piercing shriek that everyone in the shop turned round and stared at him accusingly.

Joel stood, holding the dummy, crucified with guilt. Below him, the infant was screaming up at him, streaming tears. The mother picked up the baby and nestled it to her chest. Joel offered her the dummy and shrugged. 'He threw it at me,' he pleaded. 'It has fluff on it.'

The mother grabbed the dummy from him and wiped it on her sleeve. She stuck it in the infant's dribbling mouth and resumed her conversation, as if nothing had happened.

Joel picked up his luggage and scanned the exit for danger. It appeared to have disappeared. He could not see the Mulrooney woman anywhere in the shop. *Thank God for that.* Breathing a whooping sigh of relief, he bent over to pick up his packages. But just as he did he felt his backside press into something large and firm. When he turned round, he got the fright of his life.

She was standing right behind him. 'Well, hello there, Joel!' She smiled with bright mischievousness. 'Fancy meeting you here.'

52

'I think the Regaine's working,' said Ita, examining his head.

Joel glanced doubtfully up at her, puffing at the weight of his packages. In his own estimation he was losing the battle to save his hair. Sure, it was a gradual process, but it was happening with alarming determination. 'You think so?'

'I'm certain of it,' she replied. 'It's grown back at least a millimetre since we last met.'

'Whatever.'

'You should try a herbal remedy, though, to supplement. I have one at home. Why don't you drop in on your way back and I'll give it to you? I know someone it worked wonders for. Mark went to Peru bald. He came back after six months and I hardly recognised him: he had so much hair he could hardly see.'

'In that case I might give it a miss. My eyesight isn't up to much.'

'I'll lend it to you without charge.'

'Honestly, Ita, I'm grand.'

'Suit yourself.'

'Thanks all the same.'

'Anyway, you look terrific, despite the hair. You do!'

It struck Joel that either Ita was in an excellent mood today or Ellen had warned her off him. Or could it be that she was telling the truth?

After all, Joel knew he had good looks to burn, despite the nasty things certain people such as Monk said about them behind his back. On several occasions, for instance, Joel had been compared with Bruce Willis. Once, at a dinner party where Ellen had had a bit to drink, she'd told him she thought he looked like a handsome version of that famous actor. Two of the women present adamantly agreed, although three guys there violently disagreed. A fourth woman didn't want to commit herself either way, although she staunchly accused the three men of jealousy, which seriously pissed them off. Practically the only one of Ellen's friends who *hadn't* yet compared him with Bruce Willis was Ita.

Clearly, that was coming.

'Thanks, Ita,' he replied modestly.

'Very sharp in the outfit, too.'

'I like black. I try to stick to designer labels, though this one is five years old.'

'It's arty.'

'Ellen thinks it makes me look clumsy.'

'I wouldn't listen to her. There's nothing clumsy about you!'

'Cheers,' he replied, then figured he'd better return the compliment. 'You look well yourself.'

'Ha, ha, you don't have to say that.'

'I mean it,' replied Joel, slightly nervous at being caught out.

They crossed Nassau Street and walked in the general direction of Tara Street train station, where they were both heading. While walking past the Molly Malone statue, he tripped.

Joel was not the least gauche person in the world. He walked into things or tripped up on average once a week; twice in the previous three days alone. It wasn't that he was uncoordinated. Judging by his fingers alone, he'd surely be hailed as one of most co-ordinated people on the island. Problem was, Joel also had feet. And when they slipped so completely from underneath him, as they did on the College Green pavement, that they sent him to a ferociously powerful whack on his soft arse, he cursed foully at full volume, then raised his head and, seeing the noble Molly Malone loom vastly above him with her ample bronze cleavage, he immediately apologised.

Ita grabbed underneath his arm and swung him to his feet. 'Thanks,' he said, then groaned and clutched his back.

'Did you hurt yourself?' asked Ita, concerned.

'I'm fine,' he gasped.

'You're not one bit fine. Is it your back?'

'Just let me stand here a sec.'

'Your shoelace is undone.' Ita was pointing at his feet.

Joel raised his knee tentatively and placed his foot on the bronze ledge. He leaned forward to tie the lace, but his back wouldn't let him.

'Don't move!' she shouted. 'Let me tie it for you.'

'It was that baby in the shop,' he wheezed. 'It must have pulled the lace.'

'It didn't mean any harm,' Ita said, tying the laces extremely tightly.

'It was still unethical,' he gasped.

'There you are.' Ita stood up again and frowned at the packages on the ground. 'I can't carry those,' she declared.

'Neither can I,' Joel pointed out, lowering himself gingerly on to the pedestal.

Ita picked up the chassis and, to Joel's dismay, tore off the wrapping.

'*What are you doing?*'

She then tore the wrapping off the carriage. 'Neither of us is in any condition to carry this pram,' she said. 'We'll have to wheel it instead.' She stuffed the wrapping in a nearby bin and assembled the equipment with no-nonsense efficiency. She picked up the clarinet box and put it inside the pram. 'Are you okay to walk?'

'Walking is fine. It's standing up that's the problem.'

'Well, do you want me to put you into the pram and wheel you home like an infant?'

'Would you really do that for me?'

She hauled him to his feet. 'You can push the pram, it's good support for your back.'

He stared at the pram, outraged. 'I can't push that.'

'Why? Are you embarrassed?'

'Of course I'm not embarrassed. My back is sore.'

'I'll push it with you. You can lean on it. As I said, it's a good support.'

'Look,' Joel growled, 'there's no way I'm pushing that pram. And that's final.'

Four minutes later they were pushing the pram down College Green together. The first few minutes of the experience were problematic for Joel, from a purely psychological standpoint. It wasn't just the fact that he was pushing a pram through town for the first time in his life (albeit jointly), thus exposing himself to potential mockery if he were spotted by an acquaintance in this devastating gait. No. He was also worried that people might assume she was his wife because, let's face it, Ita wasn't really his type.

Still, Joel put up with the embarrassment. As they walked down the street, he gazed at the statues to distract himself. They were a bit intimidating. No, that was the wrong word. Overawing. Henry Grattan to his left wasn't too bad, because he already looked like a bit of a dork with his arm stuck in the air in front of the old Parliament, presently his old man's bank. But Joel was definitely overawed when they crossed the road and bypassed the contemptuously jeering and arrogantly stanced Edmund Burke, a politician who'd lived in Dublin hundreds of years ago and whom everyone was going to forget about pretty quickly, which was why, Joel reasoned, the guy had been turned into black marble in the first place.

As they walked towards the train station, the two of them discussed jazz, litter and herbal lip balms for wind instrumentalists with embouchure issues. Ita was gustily enthusiastic. She was far less domineering than before. Joel felt he should probably have given her more of a chance in the past, not been so fast to rush to judgement.

At the train station they queued up for tickets. Joel kept the pram to his left, disowning the embarrassing article as far as practicable. As the queue proceeded, he advanced it forward with a foot.

A man approached, wearing a tatty blue jacket. 'Where are you heading?'

Joel frowned. 'Why do you need to know?'

Ita nudged him. 'He's the ticket inspector.'

'Do you want to buy a ticket or not?'

'Dun Laoghaire, please.'

'Blackrock.'

'Three fifty,' said the inspector, scribbling on his green pad. 'You can bring the baby up on the lift, over there.'

'It's not a baby.'

179

Ita nudged him.

'How old is it?' wondered the man.

'Ancient.' Joel reached into the pram and removed the sock of coins, concealed beneath the cosy-toes. He dipped a hand into the sock and removed a handful of coins. He counted out the correct amount.

'Ah, now,' said the man, tearing out a ticket. 'Taking the poor infant's pocket money like that.'

'Don't worry,' said Joel, handing him the money, 'he's loaded.'

Ita cackled out loud and the inspector gave them their tickets. Then the man leant over the stroller and addressed the contents. 'You'd better wise up, little fella; your father is ripping you off, did you . . .?' He stopped abruptly, as if he'd just seen a bomb inside the pram. 'That's not a baby,' he shouted. 'It's a bleedin' box!'

'It's a clarinet,' corrected Joel.

'And I thought I'd seen it all. Go on through, anyway. You look like a nice couple.'

'We're not a couple,' corrected Joel again.

'Believe nothin' you see these days, eh?' He chuckled as he led them through the gate to the elevator.

By the time the packed train reached Booterstown, the thick mesh of passengers began to thin out. Joel was relieved, because he'd spent the previous ten minutes squished against Ita's very ample bosom, while she was holding the vertical bar and staring out of the window. It wasn't that Joel had a problem being squished up against a woman's ample bosom (aside from the fact that he was married and he was very happy with Ellen's) – but certainly not in public.

Joel now observed Ita from a more discreet distance of one foot. She possessed an abundant mane of shiny dark curls. Joel was attracted to impressive heads of hair, for obvious reasons. Hers was absolutely terrific. The market for floor mops could go through the ceiling with hair like that.

He noticed other things about her too. She was, he guessed, the sort of woman who'd give a man a run for his money in bed: big, sensual, red-lipsticked lips; large, man-eating eyes; big, commandeering hands; tennis-racket-size tongue; vast cleavage. Apart from all this, she also had an impressive nose, with a hump halfway down. Quite unlike Ellen's perfect aquiline nose, which, among other attributes, lent her face a quality called class.

'*The brochures!*'

The whole train stared at her, Joel included.

'*What?*'

'Ellen's brochures. I forgot to give them to her.' She moved to the door, because the train was now entering Blackrock station.

'What brochures?'

'The ones advertising the recital tomorrow. I left them at home. I have to get them to her.'

'Why don't you drop them over later on?'

'My car's not working.'

'Then why doesn't Ellen pick them up herself?'

The train halted and the doors swished open.

'Joel, I'm going to ask you to come home with me and I'll give you the brochures to take home to Ellen.'

Agonising, he explained that he had a rendezvous in town and he had no time.

'It'll only take five minutes. Literally.'

'Is that all? Still, I dunno.'

'Brilliant! Thanks a million, Joel! You're a star.' Without further ado, Ita pushed the pram out of the door and wheeled it on to the platform. Joel stood inside the train, gaping out at her.

'Aren't you coming with me?' She was frowning.

'I . . .' Joel stared at his pram, in a bind.

'Joel O'Leary, I am asking you to get off that train!'

He glanced around, only to see that the whole train was looking on in amusement.

'I will leave this stroller on the platform,' Ita threatened, 'if I have to.'

The doors began closing. Joel squeezed out through the rubber just in time, leaving his jacket pinned behind him. He wriggled out of the jacket and started pulling. It wasn't coming. Ita joined him and they pulled together. There was a tearing sound. She grabbed the collar and pulled again. There was another tearing sound. The doors opened. The contents of the train were now splitting their sides laughing.

Ita ignored them and waved at the driver. 'That was a close shave,' she breathed.

'Just five minutes, no more,' replied Joel, putting on his jacket, despite the noticeable tear down the side.

'You're a star!'

'And you'd better not ask me to help you up with the pram.'

'No need.' At the footbridge, Ita single-handedly lifted it up into the air, then ascended the steps. Joel trooped up after her, disgusted with himself for a lot of reasons, including the exasperating tendency to have his jackets either ripped off or ripped to pieces.

Ita wheeled the pram along the bridge and carried it down the far steps.

'Where is your house?' asked Joel, once outside the station.

'Avoca Avenue.'

'But that's fifteen minutes away!'

'You're a good man, Joel. Offer it up.'

53

Myles was walking down Marine Road towards the Pavilion, holding a bunch of flowers and whistling Thelonious's own 'Ruby, My Dear'.

He'd spent some time in the florist's and purchased another bunch of Beautiful Lady chrysanthemums, even more lush than the ones delivered to his home, and at five Euros a whack they'd want to be. These ones were more peach than pink, and the stamens in the centre were pure gold.

As he walked, Monk could not help musing over his balding friend, who was due to turn up at the Duke pub in town shortly. It could not be denied that O'Leary was an okay bloke, for all his faults. He had a great comic outlook on life – just as well, when you considered how much he needed it. But he was also generous. This had to be conceded. The guy had compassion. He had the sensitivity of a man with *don't hurt me* oozing from every pore. He had feelings in abundance. And soon those feelings were going to get squashed like a slug.

It was sad, but that's the way it was.

In a relatively short stretch of time, Monk predicated, Ellen would lose interest in the man. Then she would lose the man. This was the usual outcome where a woman permitted Monk into her fantasy life. And he did not feel the slightest tug of guilt. It was entirely the woman's choice what she wished to do with her husband. Nothing to do with him. Any other conclusion would have been presumptuous.

Monk walked up the steps that led to the Pavilion terrace, reasoning that it would be wrong for him to lose sleep over O'Leary, considering the inevitable. Nature was inevitable. It happened and you didn't mess with it. Sad or happy didn't come into it. The little man would get along just fine. After all, he had one quality Monk was delighted to be able to say he lacked: a neurotic craving to prove himself, coupled with the obsessive compulsion to make it to the top of the jazz ladder. And, as a rule, neurotic people survived remarkably well without their spouses. As did their spouses without them.

O'Leary now had the chance of a lifetime. The moment he saw the letter, he would go dizzy and promptly faint. Once recovered, he would vanish into the hovels of eastern Europe for six weeks, leaving Ellen behind, unhindered.

And six weeks was all the time Monk needed.

As he was approaching the front entrance to the Pavilion, Monk overheard the melodious tinkle of a piano wafting through the air. He looked up. It was coming from above. He rounded the corner, peered up and stopped to listen. Instantly he recognised Ellen's style. She was playing the chordal arrangement from the intensely romantic third movement of Beethoven's *Archduke*. Monk tilted his head upwards, the better to hear the music, which seemed to appear and disappear, depending on the chance direction of the breeze. He stopped at the parapet and sighed with pleasure.

Monk gazed out at the thin blue line of the horizon, starkly separating sea from sky. He looked left and peered at the heavenly sun of early evening, shining its warming spell over an enchanted port. Soon it would be low in the sky and turn orange, like a fire glowing among cinders, surrounded by a fungus of dark clouds. To this handsome evening, Ellen's backing track would provide the sublime accompaniment . . .

Ah yes, it would be easy to live here. Just the two of them.

Monk did not delay long listening to the music from above. It was, after all, time. So he went to the lobby entrance and stood at the square pillar. While he was waiting for someone to come and open the door, he examined the tapered petals of his flowers for imperfections.

Monk was not long waiting. He was alerted by the clickety sound of a latch. The glass door swung open and a stocky woman stalked out. The second she passed him, he dived towards the lobby door to catch it before it shut. Too slow: it slammed in his face. Monk roared out loud in dismay. His chrysanthemums were clenched in the jaws of the metal frame. He glowered at the peach-coloured heads in disgust, trapped on the inside of the glass.

Chrysanthemums had, it seemed, brought him nothing but woefully bad luck.

'Oh dear,' said a voice behind him.

Monk turned to the woman and pointed at the door. 'Perhaps you could open the door for me, please, so I can retrieve my flowers.'

'Do you live here?'

'What's that got to do with it?'

'We're not supposed to open the door to strangers.'

'Of course I live here.'

She eyed him suspiciously. 'I don't remember seeing you. What's your name?'

'Joel O'Leary.'

'You're not Joel O'Leary! I know Joel – he changed a light bulb for me two weeks ago. I'm very sorry, but you'll have to ring the intercom.'

'If I stand over there, will you get my chrysanthemums for me?'

The woman came over to the lobby door, looked in and inspected his crushed, wilting bouquet. She glanced up at him, fearless. 'I'm awfully sorry, but I think your flowers are well and truly done for.'

'Thank you.'

'You're welcome.' She stalked off again.

Furious, Monk paced along the edge of the terrace. He could

not go back to the florist's, because it was now closed. But neither could he approach Ellen empty-handed.

So where to find some decent flowers that wouldn't turn on him like a cobra?

54

'More?'

'I don't want to be greedy,' Joel said, eagerly holding out his glass.

'Nonsense! You must be thirsty after all that walking.' Ita picked up the bottle, which had '*Vin*' written on the label. She poured out some more of the crimson, home-made herbal juice.

'What's it called, anyway?'

'Midnight Erection.'

'Never had one.'

'Well, now's your chance.' She replaced the jug on the table and returned to her woman's magazine, humming something so peculiar that Joel guessed it might have come from Shostakovich.

It was a nice, bright room and they were seated on two exceedingly blue armchairs, on either side of a Kenyan coffee table. The only thing Joel didn't like about the place was the incense. It wasn't that he resented incense per se; he merely resented it when it trailed directly up his nostrils. He'd tried to blow it away several times but it kept coming back at him.

'Did you add much alcohol?' he asked. 'I don't want to be on my ear when I get home.'

'Just a smidgen of rum.'

'A smidgen, is that all?'

'So you can have plenty more. Drink up!'

He brought the glass carefully to his mouth, because she'd poured it right up to the brim. As he did so, he noticed that Ita was staring strangely at him. He'd already made a bad impression by polishing off the first glass in five seconds, totally forgetting his table manners. 'Aren't you having some yourself?'

'Now that you mention it, I think I'll get myself some lemon tea.' She clambered to her feet and left the room.

Joel really needed to get going, but the more he drank of this delicious cocktail, the harder it became to shun the comfort of the exceedingly blue armchair beneath him. It was an unexpected treat, it really was, and Joel was going to relish it. Only thing was, it needed something extra.

He stood up and went to the shelving in the corner, where he'd noticed Ita's alcohol collection earlier. To his delight, he spied a flask of Armenian gin. He brought it over and poured a double portion into his glass. He debated whether to pour some into the jug as well. After all, Ita was on lemon tea, for chrissakes.

Before he knew it, Joel must have poured the equivalent of five measures of gin into the jug. He heard a door open. He ran back, corking the bottle, and replaced it on the shelf. He was racing back to his armchair when Ita re-entered and caught him halting in the middle of the room.

'Your back's better, I see.'

'Much better, thanks.' He pointed at the diagram pinned to the wall. 'I was admiring your coloured foot.'

'That's a reflexology chart. Were you interested?'

'Sure, seems interesting enough.'

'Put your foot up on the table, then.'

'What?'

'I'll give you a foot massage.'

'Oh, a massage. Well, I dunno.'

'Go on! Give it a try!'

Ten minutes later the sole of Joel's bare left foot was being manipulated across the coffee table, but he was so stocious he didn't care. He'd just finished his third glass of Ita's fruit juice, now deliciously laced with gin. 'Any chance of some more?'

'Three glasses is enough.'

'Grand.'

In the midst of this warm, relaxed feeling, Joel allowed himself once more to dream. This time he dreamt of Prague, that city of unsurpassed beauties – not to mention its architecture and its history, its music and its beer. How wonderful it would be if it only worked out! Playing jazz in the capital of the Czech Republic! Bringing up their baby! Imagine! Pushing it across the

Charles Bridge in their pram – though the cobbles might cause a little squawking pandemonium. And if his father got lonely, why, he could always fly out and set up a peanut subsidiary.

But why hope?

Yes, why hope? In the past week alone, hope had behaved like a fleet of ships in a high wind, amid sharp rocks. Hope was like the Irish weather: always changing and normally pissing on you. The point was this: he knew nothing about what Jan was offering, so it was a little unrealistic to be counting his saxophones. And even if he was being offered a permanent place in Jan's band, why be so naïve as to suppose that Ellen would just drop everything and come with him?

Basking in the misery of this realisation, Joel took another sip of his Midnight Erection.

'Joel, there's something I wanted to talk to you about.'

He looked up.

'I'm going to be blunt about it, now that we've the chance to be alone.'

Instinctively, Joel tried to withdraw his foot, but she held it in a vice grip.

'What is it you want me to do?' he asked, nervous.

'First, I want you to promise you won't tell Ellen what I'm about to tell you. All right?'

'But what are you going to tell me?' He swallowed.

'Promise me first.' She was staring at him with diabolical meaningfulness.

He reached for the jug, but Ita confiscated it and put it on the floor. 'Promise!'

'Can I just say something first?' Joel glanced over at the window to see if it was wide enough for him to escape through, in case he had to make a dash for it. 'I just want to put on record that I think you're . . .'

'What?'

Joel went for it. 'I think you're a very attractive woman too . . . but I've always been faithful to my wife. We have an agreement, you see; it's called marriage. And I'm sorry if I gave you the wrong impression on the train, it was just a bit squashed. But I didn't ask to come here, you're the one who . . .'

187

'Would you stop talking codswallop, man!' Ita shouted. 'I'm not talking about that. I'm talking about me not playing properly because your wife isn't playing properly, and do you know why your wife can't play properly? It's because there's a problem.'

Joel frowned, confused. 'What's the problem? I didn't know there was a problem.'

'It's because something's wrong in the bedroom, Joel.'

'*What?*'

'Come on, now. Don't deny it. This is what happens when there's neglect within the marriage.'

'Neglect?'

'It's obvious you don't fancy her any more.'

'What? That's bullshit!'

'Don't be so defensive.' She shrugged. 'Happens to lots of couples.'

'Of course I fancy her!'

'Well, you've a funny way of showing it.'

'I'll always fancy her.'

'Well, then, why can't you satisfy her in bed, like any normal man would?'

'She said I didn't satisfy her in bed?'

'She didn't have to. It's obvious.'

'How is it obvious? Ita, what the hell are you talking about?'

'What I'm talking about, you thick eejit, is that your wife . . .' She bit her lip and whispered across the table. '. . . *your wife may be falling in love with another man!*'

Joel withdrew his foot so fast that he knocked his heel into her cup of lemon tea, sending it crashing into the incense, which immediately went out. Ita clutched on to his right foot before Joel had a chance to remove it. She ordered him to calm down, but he demanded to know who this other man was.

'His name is Myles.'

'*Myles?*' Joel stared at her, dumbfounded.

'And he's a very good-looking fella.'

Joel struggled wildly to release his foot, but she would not let go. She told him he needed to relax. Joel shouted that he'd be extremely relaxed if she weren't clinging on to his goddam foot.

She let go, then. He demanded to know what was going on between Ellen and this Myles guy.

'Don't get me wrong. I don't think they've done it yet.'

'Done it? What do you mean *done it?* Done *what?*'

'But she's *this* close to crossing the threshold.' Ita measured out how close they were with her thumb and index finger. '*This close.*'

'Ellen would never do that.'

'I'm just telling you, Joel. Ellen's my best friend and believe me, I want to protect her.'

'So, you're saying . . . so you think . . .'

She stood up and left the room. 'I'll get the brochures.'

Joel stared after her. *The evil bastard. He was going to kill Monk. He was going to murder him. Hang, draw and quarter him. The scum-sucking cad!*

As he was standing up, he spotted the jug on the floor. He picked it up and filled his glass. Furious, he knocked back the gin-infested fruit juice and slammed down the glass so hard on the coffee table that it made a dent on the bamboo. He went to the door, lurching across the room.

'What in the name of . . .' Ita had just appeared at the doorway.

'Take me to him!'

'God!'

'I know where he lives. He's a complete and utter . . . *bastard* and I'm going to make him pay for it. I want you to take me to him. Oh no, isn't your car broken?'

'Jesus, man, you're completely drunk!'

'I'm going to make him eat his brain. Like in *Hannibal*. Remember that? I'm gone.' He went out to the hall and grabbed the pram, opened the front door and wheeled it outside. He scraped past her car and started trundling the pram down the narrow driveway.

'Come back, will you, for God's sake!'

Joel stopped and turned. 'Why?'

'I'll run you over in the car.'

'You want to run me over?' He was frowning.

'No, you idiot, I'll give you a lift home.'

'I thought your car was banjaxed.'

'Whatever gave you that idea? Bring back the pram and I'll put it in the boot for you.'

55

She stepped out of the shower and returned to the bedroom, draped in a towel.

The room was scented nicely of chocolate from the aromatherapy candle. Joel would love it. Ellen moved the candle to the edge of the dressing table and opened up the hinge mirror. She stared with grim foreboding at her reflection. As usual, she was not fully happy with what she saw. But as long as Joel was, she didn't mind.

She took out her hairdryer and blow-dried her hair.

Tonight is the night, gorgeous.

She left her hair damp. Joel preferred the sexy, sultry look. And because this evening was probably the last chance she had, Joel was going to get precisely the look he wanted.

Ellen ran a knob of dark-red lipstick across tightened lips, then smudged them together into a luxurious kiss. She added blusher, then carefully insinuated mascara into her lashes. She turned to view her profile, right and left.

Perfect.

She stepped out of her towel and put on the black lace lingerie she'd bought that lunchtime in the alternative lingerie boutique. Nothing, according to the woman, focused a man's mind like black lace. Ellen had specifically sought a pair of panties that would not require to be removed during sex and was surprised when the woman produced two different brands. Not wanting to get into the gory details of each brand in front of the customers, she'd quickly purchased the less expensive.

Ellen started in to the fingernails of her right hand, daubing them a deep red. She went slowly, to ensure even and precise application. When her first hand was done, she held it up in the air and dispassionately examined the result. She was quite the vamp. Tart, temptress, cock-teaser – Ellen didn't care. Tonight she was not going to fail.

She started in to her left hand, now, and paused only when she

190

got to the ring finger. Three years married, she brooded, and still nothing to show for it.

She went inside when she was finished, careful not to smudge her varnish. Ellen had turned the apartment into a temple – though not necessarily a holy one. Pleasant scents and light jazz music, delicious cuisine and rich wine. The silver candlestick in the middle of the dinner table was crowned by a yellow candle, its solitary flame burning pale in the bright summer evening.

She went out to the balcony to cool off. She inhaled deep intakes of fresh air, admiring the light-blue sea in the harbour below. The clock of the Town Hall said nearly seven. She looked down. There was some commotion in the garden strip below. Two men were standing in front of a flowerbed, shouting and gesticulating over a rose bush. It did not take her long to work out what was going on. A large section of the rose bushes below had been shorn of their beautiful red flowers.

Ellen glared down in utter disbelief that anyone could do such a thing. Disgusted, she went back inside and sat down on the three-seater, letting her shoes slip to the floor. She lay back against the couch and closed her eyes, listening to 'Embraceable You', which had just come on. Her left leg felt smooth as silk, after the treatment. She caressed it slowly. She imagined Joel was caressing her, delicately, wanderingly, teasingly, up her thighs. Her pulse picked up and as she ran her fingertips, featherlike, up and down her leg, she imagined it was Joel's lips, and now he was kissing her inner thigh, up as far as he dared go, and now that quiet, creeping craving for him was beginning to surge upwards and he came up to kiss her and she could hear her breath quicken and he was unbuttoning her blouse and removing her bra by its front clasp, and now he was licking her, he was stroking her beautifully with his moist tongue and now . . .

The bell went.

Ellen sprang open her eyes. Had he forgotten his keys again? She stood up and walked out into the hall. She picked up the intercom. 'Joel?'

When the screen lit up, it was full of red roses.

56

Monk lowered the bunch of ripped-off flowers and stared pen-
etratingly into the camera, as if he were looking straight into her
eyes. 'Hello, Ellen.'

There was no reply.

He smiled. 'Are you looking at me?'

'Hello,' she said, after a brief pause.

'I brought you something, as I said I would. To show my
gratitude. For saving me.' He raised the roses to the camera once
more. 'Can I give them to you?'

'I can't come down,' she said, not sounding over-friendly. 'I'm
in the shower.'

'That's all right, someone's just opened the lobby door. You
stay where you are. I'm coming up.' He moved into the building,
picked up the destroyed chrysanthemums from the floor and
shoved them into someone's letter box. He took the lift up to the
sixth floor, sucking at a finger he'd ripped open while breaking off
the damn roses out back. At Ellen's front door Monk knocked and
waited, staring humbly at the doormat in case she was at the
peephole.

Eventually the door opened, sending a cloud of fresh perfume
pulsating into the corridor. Monk stared at Ellen through the
narrow gap in the door, amazed by her appearance. Her eyes were
fiery, her face flushed. Damp strands of hair clung sexily to her
face. Although he could not see the rest of her body – Ellen's
shoulders were wrapped in a white towel – a powerful sexual
shiver snaked down Monk's spine and sent him into immediate
arousal. He stared at her with urgency.

'Where did you get those?' she asked, as if hostile.

Monk held them up, bowing gently. 'Flowers for the fairest.'

'I can't take those.'

'Are you allergic?'

'I just can't take them.'

'But they're for you. For what you did.'

She stared at them with mistrust.

'I asked the girl not to wrap them up,' he spoofed. 'I prefer them au naturel, as it were. More spontaneous that way.'

'Very spontaneous,' she replied, reaching out a bare arm and clutching the base of the stems. She pulled the flowers through the gap so briskly that several of the red petals dislodged and fell to the ground. 'Thank you,' she said. 'Thanks for coming down.'

'Is there any chance that . . .'

'Look, I'm really in a bit of a rush at the moment. So I can't invite you in. Perhaps we'll meet again some time, on the pier.'

Monk hungered for her. She was ripe, scented and hot. She was available, at least for the next two hours. Sure, she was in a bad mood, for a reason probably connected with her useless husband. But that was okay; he would change all that. Monk now slid her the deepest and most meaningful gaze he could muster, pressuring his fingertips against the wood, but she recoiled, said goodbye and closed the door quietly in his face.

Monk took a deep breath.

It was silent on the landing. Apart from the faint buzz from the open lift behind him, he could hear no movement from behind the front door. As he waited, he fixed his eyes unwaveringly on the peephole in the middle of the door.

Thirty seconds later, the peephole went dark and light again. Monk knocked on the door. 'Ellen!'

There was no reply, so he knocked again.

'What is it?'

'I need to go to the toilet.' He placed all ten fingertips against the wood. 'I'm very embarrassed to have to ask you, but I really need to go. I have a medical problem and if I don't get some relief I may have to humiliate myself on the flowerbeds below. Please.'

There was a period of silence, after which she told him to wait. One minute later the door opened.

Ellen was now in a revealing white silk bathrobe. She was holding the bunch of roses against her cleavage. Her beautiful face was framed by her hair, falling long and damp down past her elbows. The expression on her face was vulnerable, otherwise indescribable. 'Come in, then.'

'Thank you, Ellen,' Monk said humbly. 'I won't be long. I'm sorry for disturbing you. It's hanging around that dog all the time

– gives you bad habits.' He entered the apartment, glancing at the outline of her hips and thighs through her skimpy bathrobe as she closed the door behind him.

'It's at the far end of the corridor, to the right.' She nodded in the direction of the bathroom.

'Thank you.'

Monk walked up the passageway, switched on the bathroom light, went in and closed the door. This had to be the Gents' – O'Leary's toiletries were arranged messily on the sink. In fact, one could have been forgiven for thinking that women never strayed in here – but for a multicoloured display of underwear, laid out on a drying rack over the bath. Black, white and pink panties predominated, although there were also a few pairs of boxer shorts, one with Mutant Ninja Turtle imprints.

Ignoring the boxers, Monk picked up a damp pair of pink panties, with a strawberry design. He brought it to his face and closed his eyes. *Ellen.* He inhaled the fresh scent, while fondling the silk between his fingers. He inhaled again, more deeply this time, and passed the smooth material gently over his cheeks, nose and lips then replaced the panties in precisely their original location.

Monk spotted the bloodstains from his finger with a shock. He grabbed the panties again and shoved them in the sink. He raided a wall-cabinet for a plaster and, incredibly, located one. He washed and dried his bloody finger and applied the plaster. Then he thoroughly rinsed out Ellen's panties in the sink. He wrung them tightly, then replaced them on the rack.

Relieved, he examined O'Leary's toiletries. He made sure not to touch any of the tubes or bottles, lest he become infected. Shaving cream, razors and an underarm deodorant which had been discontinued at least a year previously. That's when he saw the anti-balding ointment: REGAINE, EXTRA STRENGTH. Monk picked up the bottle and read the small print: '5% minocidil cutaneous solution. To be used twice daily. Should notice a hair change within eight weeks.'

At the rate that O'Leary was losing his hair, Monk mused, he would notice a change in eight weeks all right. The change would in all likelihood be total, but it would have nothing to do with the

Regaine. It was a pity, he considered, that instead of pouring it on to his scalp, O'Leary didn't decide to pour it down his throat: the effects would have been more noticeable in the short run and far more positive. Shame indeed to waste the stuff.

Monk opened the bottle and held it over the toilet bowl. He squirted it noisily into the water below, a trickling urination which continued until the bottle was completely empty. He re-screwed the cap, flushed the toilet and returned the bottle to its perch on the sink. He washed his hands, contaminated by O'Leary's fingerprints, and dried them on a towel, which he folded and repositioned neatly on the bar. He readjusted his tackle and left the bathroom.

Outside, Monk delayed in the hall. He sniffed the air, which was perfumed with Ellen's delicious after-shower bouquet. But where was she? It was reasonable for the average male guest to assume that his hostess was in the lounge at the far end of the passageway – the door was ajar, allowing a beam of evening sunlight to filter on to the polished wooden floor.

But Monk wasn't, strictly speaking, a reasonable guest. He had to consider possibilities. And one of those possibilities was that the room opposite the bathroom door was Ellen's bedroom. Monk had an instinctive feel for women's bedrooms, almost as unerring as his feel for women's bodies. The possibility that she was lying inside on her bed, waiting for him, swelled up in his mind, but not just in his mind. He went for the bedroom door, his leather boots squeaking in the silent passageway, and pushed down the handle.

'Excuse me.'

Monk swivelled round. 'Ah, there you are.'

She was standing at the other end of the corridor, at the door into the lounge. 'The front door is up here,' she said, pointing.

'I'm sure it is.' Monk let go of the handle and walked slowly up the passageway towards her, refusing to take his eyes off her for a second. She had combed her hair back off her face, hooking it behind perfect ears. She was still holding the roses, barefoot and in her skimpy bathrobe.

As he came close, he noticed a single wet strand of hair falling forward over her cheek. 'Oh dear,' he said, pointing. 'You missed a hair.' He brought his hand slowly to her face. 'May I take the liberty?' Gently, he pushed the strand of hair off her face with his index finger and curled it over her ear. 'That's better,' he said, bathing in her heightened sexual aura. 'Shame to spoil so perfect a picture.'

A dangerously erotic vibe now passed from her body to his. Ellen's eyes were moist with anticipation and her face was glowing with sensuality. If she was apprehensive, Monk reasoned, that was quite fine. The nervousness would dissolve the moment their lips melted into one another, along with all the unfocused ideas she had of right or wrong.

He could almost feel the heat from her slightly parted lips as they pouted towards him, inviting him to make the first move. He tilted his head down slowly towards her. He could feel her knee rising up, caressing the inside of his thigh, moving inexorably towards his groin. Ahh, thought Monk, his eyes narrowing in gratification. This was the precious moment he'd been waiting for, the moment he'd spent every waking and sleeping second dreaming of. It had come sooner than expected. And for her too. He reached a hand down to caress her behind and . . .

Bang!

He twisted towards the front door and Ellen jumped back to the wall. Something large and heavy had just whacked against the outside of the door. A groaning voice could now be heard from the other side. 'What the hell happened?' It was a thick, horribly drunken voice.

'You fell over,' replied a woman. 'Come on, get up. Put your arm round my shoulder, or you'll fall back down.'

Monk stared at the door in disbelief, his heart sinking into his stomach. *It can't be him, it can't be.*

57

Ellen brushed by Monk and swung open the door.

Bollocks. It is him.

Why the hell isn't the balding turd in town?

'Ellen,' said a large matron in a trench coat, holding up the sack of potatoes beside her. 'I'll just bring him in for you. He's not walking right.'

Monk stared at the appalling scene in disbelief, as the fat matron dragged O'Leary through the hall, his head hanging forward and his sock of coins crunching against door frames as he clumped past. She dumped the gobshite on to the couch and put him sitting up straight. She started slapping his cheeks and now O'Leary began a drunken protest.

Monk could not believe his luck. The moment had been utterly destroyed. Another minute was all it would have taken. Another twenty seconds, even. A single kiss and the threshold would have been crossed for ever. Instead, it was crossed by a carcass hauler with a drunk in tow.

Ellen, too, was furious. She was staring at the pair of them with a mixture of staggering disbelief and extreme annoyance. *To have been so close!*

Big Mama returned to the hall and curled up her nose at Ellen's bathrobe. She eyeballed Monk directly. 'I thought you'd be alone.'

'Are you addressing me?' He could smell a man-hater a mile off and this one's odour was triple-X.

'No,' returned the culchie, glaring.

'Excuse me,' said Ellen.

Monk looked down at her, standing so close beside him.

'I'm sorry, Myles,' she said, 'but I may have to ask you, would you mind leaving?'

He frowned.

'I need to talk to Ita,' she added.

'Of course.' He bowed his head respectfully, then moved into the living room and closed the door.

Once inside, Monk pressed his ear up against the wooden panels, his fist flexed in frustration. Ellen was speaking to Big Mama in a frantic whisper. But he couldn't make out the words, so he turned round. O'Leary was flopped back on the couch. His hair was straggly and his nose a deep shade of red, possibly from having smacked it against the door. His glazed eyes were fixed sourly on Monk, who put his hands in his pockets and started ambling around the room. He stopped at a painting over the

197

mantelpiece, featuring a dead and bloody bird. 'I don't know if you've heard,' he said, examining the gory art. 'But your wife saved my life last night.'

As he moved around the room, Monk became aware of O'Leary's bloodshot eyeballs as they slid across their sockets, following his every step like a spiteful reptile.

'So I came down to thank her,' he concluded, admiring the dinner arrangement. Two crystal wineglasses and a bottle of red wine. Silver cutlery. A candle, burning away. A small bunch of flowers in a tiny vase in the middle of the table. Pity the dinner had to go to waste, like the marriage. Monk crossed to the piano and helped himself to a chocolate from the box on top.

'You don't mind, do you?' said Monk, popping a second in his mouth. Very succulent, indeed. 'It's only right to share with one another the things we love.'

He wandered around the room and reflected. It would not be hard to settle into an abode such as this. Not hard at all. Once O'Leary was debugged.

It was certainly a well-appointed apartment. The Steinway and the pine drinks cabinet, the teak bookshelves and the crystal chandelier, the brass coal scuttle and the Regency music stand. Monk had to admit he was impressed by such elegant furnishings. Such tasteful decor! Such refinement, for a woman who'd unwittingly chosen a chimpanzee for a husband.

Then again, in the heat of the moment we all made alarming character misjudgements.

'I brought her some roses as a token,' he told O'Leary. 'Because of what she did. And because I respect your wife enormously.'

Monk removed Fuks's letter from his inside jacket pocket and went to the couch. 'I might as well give you this – saves us the bother of having to meet in town later on.' He handed it to O'Leary, who refused to take it, so Monk removed the crumpled letter from the envelope himself, opened it out and held it down in front of the man's stony face. 'Here, read it.'

But O'Leary simply glared up at him, his nostrils so flared they looked as though they were about to catch fire.

'Have it your way.' Monk shrugged, returning the letter to the envelope. 'But he wants you over there as soon as possible. If not sooner. He's offering a six-week stint, with possible permanency. They're offering you a hundred thousand crowns for the period, lodgings included.'

There wasn't a flicker from O'Leary, so Monk stuffed the letter into the inside pocket of his jacket. 'Consider yourself lucky,' Monk added. 'It wasn't talent that got it for you.'

Monk continued on his pleasant perambulation around the room. He caught sight of a silver-framed picture on the mantelpiece. 'Ah, so this is the wedding photo? How many years ago is it? Three?' He picked it up and laughed. 'You know, you looked even funnier when you had hair.'

And he did. He looked hilarious. In fact, in the oversized tuxedo, the man resembled a circus clown. Monk smudged his thumb on the glass to block out the offending half. Ellen looked only a little younger in her wedding dress.

'You know, Joel . . . I can call you Joel, can't I? You mustn't worry about Ellen, when you're in Prague. She'll be perfectly safe. After she saved my life in the harbour yesterday, I feel obliged to look out for her.' He replaced the picture on the mantelpiece, but was unable to take his eyes from her image. 'We got on well together. She's an excellent piano teacher. I feel I'll learn a lot from her.' He straightened the frame. 'So when you're in Prague, I wouldn't want you to lose sleep over her.'

When he turned round he recoiled. O'Leary was standing right behind him, his red face an inch away from his chin.

Monk quit the posing sham at once, sensing he was perilously close to that nose job he'd been contemplating for the past year. O'Leary was wielding that sock of coins at him like some balding Visigoth and, if you knew your history, you knew that the Visigoths were notoriously unpredictable.

Monk spoke calmly, appealing to whatever rational instincts the leprechaun had left. 'What's the matter, Joel? You told me Ellen would never do it with another man, so what are you worried about?'

'You bastard.'

If O'Leary was hyperventilating like a bull before the charge, then he was doing a bad job of hiding it.

'If you don't go to Prague, Joel, that's as good as saying you don't trust her. Now, that's not very nice, is it?'

'You're the one I don't trust, Lavery,' O'Leary hissed. 'And I've no idea why I ever trusted you. Now, I want you to get the hell out of this apartment.'

Monk held his ground. 'And do you think *she* trusts you?'

'Of course she trusts me.'

'And how do you think Ellen would feel if I told her you set her up as an adulteress?'

'*What?*' O'Leary eyed him, suddenly rabbit-scared.

Monk sauntered across the room, smirking. 'Would she trust you *then?*'

'You leave Ellen out of this, Lavery. She wouldn't believe anything you told her.'

'All I'm saying, Joel, is go to Prague. Your residency with the Leading Frights has been terminated. McCoy is coming back. In Prague, you'll earn good money and you'll get some decent experience.'

'You're a shit, you know that?'

'Fine.'

'A complete shit.'

'Great.'

'Ellen thinks so too.'

'Oh, she does.'

'Yes, she does.'

'And did she discuss this with you?'

'Yes,' Joel replied, after a moment's brief hesitation.

'When?'

'Last night.'

'You try too hard, O'Leary.' Monk sniggered at the man's desperation.

'She thinks you're vain and arrogant. She told me all about you falling into the harbour. She had a good laugh.'

'I don't believe you.'

'She thought it was hilarious. I didn't think so. I was upset. Very upset you didn't drown.'

Monk pulled the most disappointed face he could convincingly fake. 'You've just hurt my feelings, Joel.'

'Piss off away from my wife, Lavery. She wants nothing to do with you. She barely even knows you and you hardly know her.'

'I know some things about her.'

'What would *you* know about her? Well? What?'

'I know she wears strawberry panties.'

There was a dangerous silence in the room. O'Leary was advancing slowly towards him, brandishing the sock of coins.

'What did you say?'

'Your wife is outside the door, O'Leary. You do anything stupid and you'll have some explaining to do.'

'*What did you say?*'

'I said I know she wears strawberry panties.'

58

'You've ruined it all!' Ellen was furious.

'All I did was give him two glasses!' protested Ita.

'What on earth did you put in it?'

'Just a smidgen of rum!' Ita pointed adamantly towards the lounge. 'Definitely not enough to explain *that*.'

'A smidgen? Ita, he's not able to walk!' Ellen opened the garbage chute and stuffed down the roses. 'I just can't believe this is happening,' she raged. 'It's my last night! I hope you know, Ita, that I am going to make a total hames of the recital.'

'Stop talking nonsense. Joel still has plenty of action in him yet, I promise you.'

'You just dragged him in the door, Ita. He looks half dead.'

'He's full of pent-up energy. Sure, he was threatening to kill him all the way down here in the car.'

'Kill who?'

Ita pointed towards the lounge.

'*Myles?*' Ellen frowned. 'What's he got against Myles? He doesn't even know him.'

'No, but I took the liberty of telling him that Myles had a crush on you, which may be partly true anyway.'

'You did *what?*'

'Just to get him to cop himself on, because frankly, we have a concert tomorrow at lunchtime and . . .'

'Ita, that was none of your business! That was . . .'

Ellen shut up. She'd just heard a sound of clashing metal coming from the lounge. She ran past Ita out of the kitchen and burst through the lounge door.

Joel was lying on top of Myles next to the fireplace, in a tangle of arms and legs. He was calling him a filthy bastard, through teeth clenched against his sock of coins. He thrashed out a foot, kicking the coal scuttle into the middle of the floor. Ellen screamed at them to stop, but Joel was too busy wrestling to release his wrists from Myles's tight grip. He tried head-butting Myles, but his neck wasn't long enough. Again, Joel called him a filthy bastard and the next moment the coins were smashing noisily all over the mantelpiece.

'Get off him, Joel,' shouted Ellen, pulling at Joel's torn jacket. 'You're making a mistake! Get off him!'

Joel began gnawing Myles's hand. Now Ita came over and grabbed him by the shoulders. In a matter of seconds she had him on his feet, head-locked between her arm and her hip. With no difficulty she dragged him out of the lounge, Joel bawling blue murder. Myles struggled to his feet, just as Ita pulled shut the door.

'What did I say?' Myles protested.

'Myles, I'm awfully sorry about this.'

'If I only knew what I said!'

'It's not your fault,' Ellen insisted.

'I was just admiring the view and he came at me out of nowhere.'

She shrugged, embarrassed and helpless. 'He had drink on him, I'm so sorry. I had no idea he'd . . .'

'That he'd interrupt us like that, neither did I.' Myles clapped the carpet dust off his clothes and limped over to a loose scattering of photographs that had been swept off the mantelpiece to the floor. He picked them up and placed them on the table.

'*Oh, no!*'

Myles started. 'What's wrong?'

Ellen pointed at the dark stain showing through his tan trousers. 'You've got blood on your trousers. Don't move!' Ellen ran into the kitchen and returned with a bottle of Dettol and a pad of cotton wool. She knelt down and pulled up the bottom of his trousers. Blood was trickling down through the thick hairs of his lower leg. She mopped it up.

'I'd better have a look. It's seeping.'

'I'd be honoured.'

'I'll just pull the trousers up over it, is that okay?'

'I don't think they'll make it.'

'Don't worry, I think they're wide enough.' She rolled up the trouser leg, but when she got as far as the knee, Myles grabbed her hands.

'It's too painful,' he groaned. 'Better if I pull the trousers down.'

She looked up at him. He seemed sincere. 'All right, so.'

He unfastened his belt, unzipped and dropped the pants before her. Ellen did a double take when she observed his leopard-skin thong hanging out in front of her face like a spotted reptile. 'Did you disinfect it last night?' she asked, returning her eyes to the wound.

'I did.'

'It's a bit of a mess. I'll have to clean it again.'

'Would you mind if I lie down on the couch? I feel a bit weak, after the assault.'

'Of course,' she replied uneasily.

Myles stood out of his trousers and shuffled to the couch, practically bare-buttocked. He sat down and arranged cushions behind his back. He lay back in a comfortable position, separating his legs, for her benefit.

Ellen sat on the coffee table next to him and spun the cap off the Dettol bottle. It slipped from her fingers, bounced on the floor and rolled just under the couch. She leant over to pick it up, spreading her feet apart to steady herself. She sat up again and caught Myles peering up her legs. She snapped them together again but too late . . .

Damn!

He'd seen her crotchless panties. She quickly drew across her bathrobe and took hold of the cotton-wool pad.

203

'You have beautiful taste in underwear,' he remarked smoothly, 'if you don't mind me saying.'

Ellen crossed her legs and tilted the bottle over the pad.

'I hope you'll forgive my natural reaction,' he said, squirming his buttocks on the leather sofa.

She didn't quite grasp his meaning but when she shifted her eyes up along his long hairy legs, she got the full picture. His 'natural reaction' was impossible to miss: it was stretching out the leopard-skin material like a tent pole.

'Do you mind if I say something very honest to you?' Myles continued, lowering his voice to a bass pitch.

Ellen felt the cotton pad getting soggy in her hand. She looked down and realised she'd just poured half the bottle over the cotton wool. It was saturated and was beginning to sting her skin.

'You may well be one of the most beautiful women I've ever met.' He shifted himself forward. 'I say that from a purely objective point of view.'

Ignoring him, Ellen wondered what she was going to do with the sodden pad. Suddenly a hand appeared on her thigh. It was hairy and bony and it had a plaster on one of the fingers. Ellen neither said anything nor looked at him. Instead she brought the soaked swab to the open wound and pressed down hard on top of his knee.

Myles groaned and jerked violently, as if he'd just stuck his hand into a mains socket. His fingers squeezed momentarily into her thigh, then fell away. His whole body was now rigid but Ellen continued to press and dab and wipe and pat until she was happy everything was clear.

When she'd finished cleaning the wound, Ellen looked up and saw that he had a confused half smile on his face. His eyes were watery red and his hand was now safely gripping the cushion underneath. The central tent pole had been lowered.

59

'. . . my whole life . . . one big disaster after another . . .'

Joel's head was spinning. He tried to focus on the light shade above him, but it kept jumping backwards up the ceiling. So he closed his eyes. However, even behind the cosy comfort of his eyelids there was swirling.

'My whole . . .'

'Here,' came a woman's voice above him, 'don't fall asleep on me now. You've still got business to do tonight, sonny.'

He felt something prod his cheek and he opened his eyes. Oh yes, her again. Let's see, now . . . her name . . . Iti? Ati? Yeti? Joel couldn't rightly remember. What was she doing here? What was she doing with her hand on his inner leg? Why was she stroking the hairs on his chest? Why was she now patting his cheeks?

'Hey!'

'Wake up,' said the woman. 'I want to show you something.'

Joel felt thick hands on either side of his face, straightening his head. She patted his cheeks harder. 'Wake up!'

'What's going . . .?'

He struggled to open his eyes. Either it was the fault of the room, or of his eyeballs. Whichever way, the dimensions were all wrong.

'Didn't I tell you about that fellow inside?' she demanded. '*Didn't I?*'

'. . . bastard!'

'Do you want to lose your wife to *him?* Is that what you want?'

Joel tried to sit up, but couldn't.

'Of course you don't,' she said. 'So you know what you have to do, don't you? What I told you in the car.'

Joel didn't even have the strength to pull a fist. '*The swine!*' he shouted, shaking his hand loosely in the air.

'Of course he's a swine, but don't worry – he'll be gone soon. Wake up!'

'I'm awake.'

There was a sharp snapping sensation against his waist.

'*Hey!*' Joel suddenly realised two things: one, he was naked apart from the boxer shorts; and two, this very familiar woman had just snapped the elastic of his boxers against his bare skin. He felt disconcerted in a fuzzy kind of way.

'Your wife will be coming in to you in a minute and you better show her some affection, do you hear me? Whatever it is that's been bothering you, you're to put it out of your head.'

'Sure, sure . . . I'll do anything, as long as you let me . . . sleep.'

'Because I know you love her, don't you?'

'Yes. Yes . . . love her, I'll always love her . . .'

'Well, you've a funny way of showing it.'

'. . . and I did it for her . . .'

'Did what?'

'My saxophone . . . in real trouble, never told you, Eti, but it's my saxophone. Our egg nest . . . Totally gone, out of eggs, I'm completely out . . .'

'That's perfectly obvious.'

'. . . She'll kill me . . .'

'It's not just you she'll kill.'

'. . . when she finds out and I can't go back to Dad . . .'

'Wake up, you're rambling.'

'I just can't, Yeti, don't know what's going to happen . . . in Hollywood, Holyhead, the shyster nun, can't trust anyone . . . know what I mean?'

He felt warm breath on his cheek. 'No, sweetheart, I haven't a bloody clue what you mean.'

Joel struggled to open his eyes, but he could not. He had no idea what time of day or night it was. He felt his lips being kissed. It was reasonably agreeable, except that he wasn't sure Ellen would agree. The kissing stopped.

'*Wake up!*'

'I'm awake, I'm awake.'

'Ellen is coming in to you, do you hear? You have to make her happy.'

'Ellen? That's my wife! It's all I want to do, Jesus, all I want . . .'

'Then you'll make love to her, like a good man.'

There was the distant sound of a doorbell. Joel opened his eyes and realised that he was in his own bedroom. The woman above him, he remembered with a shock, was Ita. Yes, Ita, with that crooked nose and those great tits.

'What are you looking at?' the woman enquired.

'Nothing.'

'Oh yes, you are.'

'No, I'm not.' Joel closed his eyes again. Immediately he felt himself being kissed by those moist lips once more. 'Hey!' He was gasping for breath. 'Did you just kiss me?'

'I did. Did you like it?'

'Are you going to tell Ellen?'

'I tell her everything.'

'Then I didn't like it.' Joel closed his eyes.

'Liar!' she accused. 'I can see you're getting excited.'

Again he felt his lips being kissed. He felt too weak to resist, although he sensed that something was seriously wrong. Now her large lips closed firmly, lingeringly over his. He felt a burst of arousal from down below.

'Wow, careful! I might just want to do something I'll regret in a minute . . .'

'I think you could be right there.'

There was the sound of a door opening and Joel heard someone whispering the word 'taxi'.

'All right, darling,' Ita said, in a more detached voice.

'Are you going already?' he asked.

'Yes, Joel,' she replied, patting his hand. 'I'm going now.'

'What? Hey, no, don't go! It was getting good!' He felt her mass lean over his chest. Her mouth was against his ear.

'Don't forget about the pram down in the lobby, sure you won't?' she whispered. 'Behind the flower pot.' She got up. 'See you round, cowboy,' she said in a more normal voice.

Joel turned his head on the pillow and was surprised to see Ellen standing in the doorway.

'He's all yours,' Ita told her.

The door closed and so did Joel's lids.

60

'What's he doing in his boxer shorts?'

'I thought I'd save you some time, Ellen. Get him undressed.'

'Well, thank you, Ita, that was very considerate.' She wasn't too impressed.

'Go on in, Ellen! I'll get rid of Mr Smoothie for you.'

'I don't think he wants to go home.'

'But you called a taxi for him, didn't you?' Ita went up the passageway to the lounge. 'You go in – I'll get him out of here.'

But Ellen needed them both gone first. She followed Ita into the lounge. Myles was sitting back on the couch, thankfully with his trousers on.

'So!' announced Ita. 'Are you ready for discharge?'

'I thought *you* went home,' he said, raising a sarcastic eyebrow.

'I'm going home now.'

'Good.'

'And you're going too. The taxi's outside.'

'Oh, that's all right, thanks. I er . . .' He glanced at Ellen.

'*What?*' demanded Ita, hands on her hips.

'I want to speak to Ellen,' he said. 'Alone, if that's okay.'

'Ah, for goodness' sake, man, can't you let the woman get to her bed? We've got a concert in the morning.'

'She's right, Myles,' said Ellen as sweetly as she dared. She glanced at her watch. 'It's getting a bit late, with that recital. I'll see you around some time.'

Myles fought to stand, then he patted his pockets.

'Don't worry about money,' said Ita. 'I'll take care of the taxi fare, if you come now.'

'I was looking for a pen.'

'What do you want a pen for?' asked Ita.

He addressed Ellen. 'I want to write down my number for you.'

'I already have it. I rang you yesterday, remember?'

'Come on,' called Ita. 'Can you walk?' She went over to him, but he brushed her away.

'Suit yourself.'

Myles hobbled towards Ellen who now retreated into the hall to evade any farewell kiss she might otherwise have to field. She opened the door.

Ita clasped her in an urgent embrace and whispered into her ear, 'Better get in to your man inside, before he loses conscious-ness completely. I'll see you at half-ten in the morning. You'll play brilliantly, I know you will.'

She stepped out on to the landing. Myles moved in swiftly and

208

embraced Ellen, kissing her on the cheek. 'What time is the concert starting?' he asked.

'Two thirty,' Ita said sharply.

'Two thirty?'

'See you tomorrow, then,' Ellen said to her friend.

'Yeah,' said Myles, 'I'll see you tomorrow.'

Ellen watched the two of them move to the lift. She closed the door with quiet and stupendous relief, then took a deep breath.

Crazy.

This was the most crazy, lunatic day she'd had in her entire life.

Ellen rushed down to the bedroom. Inside, she pulled the curtains across, shutting out the bright evening. In the solitary light provided by the flame of the chocolate candle, she watched Joel for signs of life.

There weren't too many: he looked asleep, though there was no evidence of deep breathing. She sat on the bed and ran her hand down his chest. Joel responded with a faint smile, although his eyes remained closed.

She slipped off her silk bathrobe and straddled him on the bed. She leant down and kissed him on the mouth. But his lips were like jelly – no grip. Ellen examined his inscrutable face. '*Joel!*'

'You're back,' he slurred, his eyes still closed.

She removed her lace bra and pulled his hands to her breasts.

'Wow! Quick mover!' he grunted, still not opening his eyes.

Ellen held his hands to herself for some time, then let go. They flopped back down on the bed. She kissed him once more.

'Hey,' he slurred. 'What will Ellen say . . .?'

Ignoring this confusing question, she kissed him some more, but he wasn't responding; his mouth was like warm, lifeless rubber. She began squirming and moving and thrusting up against him. It seemed to be having little effect.

Ellen tried a massage where it usually worked.

'Hey! What's going on down there? . . . She'll never forgive me . . . what are you . . .'

She kissed him yet again but she could not continue, for he had begun giggling uncontrollably. 'Stop laughing.'

'What's your name again?'

'Joel,' she said sternly.

209

'*Joel?*' He started giggling again, then stopped. 'That's my name, too.'

'Oh, come on, will you?' she shouted. '*Get it up!*'

'But what will Ellen say?'

She forced open an eyelid. 'Honey, wake up. Put your hands on my back,' she told him.

He didn't respond, so Ellen lifted up one of his hands and curled it awkwardly over her back. She did the same with the other. The first one slid off, then the second. '*Darling, wake up!*' she shouted, patting his face. '*Wake up!*'

'Why is everybody slapping me?'

'Wake up, honey!'

'Have to sleep.'

'And I have to make love, now, come on. I'm in the right mood tonight. It doesn't happen that often. You can do your special thing if you like.'

'Special?'

'You know, the thing you like to do.'

'Fall asleep.'

'Open your eyes!' With her thumbs, she forced open both eyelids this time. His pupils rolled to the corner of the ceiling above the door. 'Please, baby.' She kissed him tenderly on the mouth, but the rubber sensation was still there. Ellen sat there for several minutes, forlorn.

Never did she imagine this would be such a trial. The *one* night he was available, he had to go and get drunk. What had Ita put in the spring wine? She was going to kill her!

She sat up again and peered at the motionless mass below her, feeling angry, inadequate and helpless in equal measure. Joel's breathing was so calm and rhythmical that he looked as if he were about to fall permanently asleep.

No way, Ellen resolved. Absolutely no way. She had come this far. No way was she going to let Ita ruin it for her when she was this close. Ellen reached across to her bedside table and grabbed her brooch. She undid the clasp and pulled out the pin. It was long and sharp, but at least it was clean. She straightened herself over him and fortified herself for what she was going to do.

No. She couldn't.

She dropped the brooch on to the duvet beside her and sighed. It wasn't his fault. She leant both hands against his chest and massaged the muscle with her fingers. She stared at the cute, sleeping face. She stroked his forehead with a thumb, then lowered her mouth to kiss him again. There wasn't so much as a twitch. She broke off angrily and grabbed the brooch again.

It just wasn't fair.

It was always women. Always women who had to suffer the pain and the agony when it came to babies. And what did men have to do? Ejaculate. That's all they had to do. *And they actually enjoyed it.*

It was so unfair.

She pricked the pin into the top of her finger. It was sharp, but not too sharp. She brought the pin to her husband's upper hindquarter. She poked a finger into the soft flesh. On impulse, she kissed the tip of the pin, apologised out loud, closed her eyes and jabbed hard.

She opened her eyes.

A full two seconds later Joel's nose twitched.

But his face soon returned to its state of restful repose.

61

'Stupid wench,' Monk muttered, as the taxi drove off.

Big Mama had done her best to humiliate him just now at the Pavilion, but he'd simply ignored her to save himself the effort. She'd asked him how his lungs were holding up after yesterday's little dip in Dun Laoghaire harbour. She'd then proceeded to tell the taxi driver the whole story through the window, and they'd both had a good laugh at his expense. Monk wasn't too worried, though, because he knew it wasn't Ellen's take on events.

At Crosthwaite Park, he'd paid the driver and limped up the garden path. There was no doubt about it: that woman was like a twisted thorn in his arse. If it hadn't been for her, he'd be in bed now with Ellen. And as for that overnourished loogan, O'Leary . . .

There and then, Monk made a vow. He was going to get that puppet-head to Prague, even if he had to pay the plane fare.

Monk gingerly descended the staircase, grimacing at each step. At the bottom he searched his pockets for the keys, but all he could find were two condoms, his babe wad and his cigarillo case. He frantically patted his shirt pockets, then it dawned on him. He'd left them in his other pair of trousers.

'*Asshole*,' he spat, glaring with dread at the steps he'd just descended, now looming above him. He gripped the rail and hopped up the first two steps on his good leg. Then he rested. Then hopped, then rested again. The only consolation in the midst of all this discomfort was that each new step upwards brought with it a fresh perspective on how to cause the maximum physical pain to O'Leary's cranium.

He shuffled round to his mother's front steps. He repeated the hopping process, his good leg now almost bunched. When he finally reached the top he checked his watch. It was only eight, but his mother was probably in bed, watching TV.

Too bad.

He rang the bell once, then pushed open the letter box. 'Mother!' he shouted in. 'It's me!'

There was no reply. 'Mother?' He heard a movement in the hall. 'I forgot my keys.'

'*Rrrrrough.*' Something fierce snapped at Monk's lips and he darted backwards in fright, tumbling on to the rail behind him. He got to his feet and attacked the front door with a thump. 'You stupid bitch!' he roared at the barking cur. 'I'll have you put down! Do you hear me? I'll have them stick the needle in you!'

The door opened. His mother was standing there in her dressing gown, eyeing him with suspicion. Monk straightened and groaned in pain.

'I was talking to the dog,' he explained. 'She tried to bite me.'

'You make it sound like it's my fault, dear.' She restrained the mutt.

'Well,' he said, surprised at her tone, 'she's your dog.'

'For all of five hours?' She spoke cordially. 'I'll need a little longer than that to put some manners on her. I've been trying for twenty-six years with you and I still haven't succeeded.'

212

'I'm not in the mood for lectures,' Monk panted, hobbling inside.

'What's wrong with your leg?'

He moved towards the stairs. 'Nothing. It's fine. I feel fine. In fact, I haven't felt this wonderful in ages.'

'You don't sound wonderful.'

'My leg hurts.'

'Do you want me to have a look at it?'

'It's okay, Ellen did.' He went downstairs and poured himself a glass of Southern Comfort. He flicked out the photo of Ellen that he'd stolen. She was staring straight at him with a relaxed and appealing, though guarded, smile. They'd been so close, *so close* . . .

Monk knocked the Southern Comfort back in one and poured himself another glass. No sooner had he put this to his lips than there was a rat-tat on his door. He hadn't heard her come down the stairs. He hobbled over and slid the narrow bolt silently across. 'Yes?'

'Can I come in?'

'The door's locked.'

'Could you unlock it?'

'I'm getting undressed.'

'You said you saw Joel's wife this evening?'

Monk did not respond.

'How was she?'

'She was wonderful. I'd recommend her to anyone.' He was getting tense again.

'Was Joel there?'

'Joel came back late. Drunk, with a whore.'

'Myles, I don't want to be telling you what to do with your life . . .'

'Right, so, I'll say goodnight.' He moved away from the door.

'Do you really think you can have any woman you want, even when she's married? Is that what you think, Myles?'

Monk shook his head. Mothers. In just one day he'd given her a dog and twelve beautiful chrysanthemums. This was how she repaid him. 'I know I can have any woman I want,' he replied.

'But does she want you?

'I have to go to bed.'

213

'Joel doesn't deserve this.'

'He had his chance.'

'Myles, you're going to hurt him.'

'Good.'

There was silence, but Monk heard no footsteps.

'I don't know where I went wrong,' came a weaker, sadder voice from outside. 'I tried to show you love. Your father too. And I expected better.'

'Well, I'm sorry I've had to shatter your illusions.'

'Oh, don't worry about that. I'm well used to having my illusions shattered.' Her voice faded away.

Monk put his ear to the door. All he could hear were quiet creaking noises up the basement stairs.

62

'*Stop!*'

Ellen was seated on the piano stool in the candlelit room, her right arm outstretched in front of her. She was concentrating furiously on her heavily trembling fingertips.

'*I said stop!*' she ordered. She gathered together her mental forces and focused on the shaking hand. Unless it stopped, she would not be able to go to sleep. She'd tried sleeping in the guest room for the last two hours, but in vain.

Mind control! It's all about mind control. Will-power. You have an abundance of will-power.

The trembling did not stop.

Ellen ground her teeth. *You are calm and you are in command. Your hands, fingers and arms are controlled by your muscles. Your muscles are controlled by the median, radial, ulnar and musculospiral nerves. These nerves, in turn, are governed by the cortex. The cortex is in your brain. From the cortex, orders are dispatched setting these nerves in motion.*

You are giving these orders.

You are in control. It is three in the morning. You have a recital in exactly ten hours' time. You will stop shaking. You will then go to bed and sleep for a solid seven hours.

I said, stop shaking!

But the fingers wouldn't stop shaking.

She lowered her arm in disgust and walked to their bedroom, where Joel was still snoring away to his heart's content. In the en suite, she ran the fertility test for the fourth time that evening. It was still showing up red.

In fury, Ellen slammed the appliance down into the bathtub, making a loud racket. In the bedroom, Joel was still snoring away, oblivious. She went over, grabbed his arm and started pulling him towards the edge of the bed. She was only able to move him a foot, he was that heavy. She shook him and ordered him to wake up. But he just turned over in the bed, groaning to himself.

Ellen stormed into the kitchen. She stood on top of a chair, reached a hand over the top of the presses and located the bottle of vodka she'd hidden from Joel a month ago. She poured herself a glass and drank it down. She was not tippling, no. She was merely ensuring that she got a decent night's sleep.

She poured herself a second glass: two glasses was her limit. She drank back the second glass and filled a third to half. She stared at it and judged that she would not sleep properly unless she downed this one too. So she did. She rinsed the glass, then remembered the fertility book.

You're not supposed to drink! You're supposed to be pregnant! Yes, you are! You are pathetic! Deeply pathetic. And you are going to make a hames of the recital. Ita will never speak to you again.

Your name will be muck in this city! You will have to emigrate.

She got a brainwave. She went into the lounge and picked up her collection of baby magazines from the coffee table. She brought them into the kitchen and started tearing off the front covers. When that was done, she began tearing off the back covers. Then she started on individual magazines. Soon loose pages lay scattered all over the kitchen table and floor. In a fury, she gathered them up and jammed the lot down the garbage chute.

That felt better. It was a case of spring cleaning your life all over again. She went back inside and snuffed out the yellow candle flame, shining mournfully over the elaborately set dinner table. She went outside to the balcony, clutching against anything that would prevent her from toppling over. Out here, she would soon cool down. Out here, she would not have to listen to her inept husband snoring like some underground animal. The only sound out here was the swish of distant waves.

She gripped the bar, distraught and pissed. An easterly breeze swept off the bay, cooling her hot skin. She would stay out here until her body froze. Then she would be able to sleep. She lay back on the chaise longue, relishing the cool breeze.

Ellen stared up at the bright stars, forlorn, and started wishing. She wished that a mysterious force of nature or heaven could rise up and influence events in this world. Because if there was such a mysterious force, perhaps it would listen to her. And Ellen had two fervent wishes. Above all else, she wished for a child.

But she had another wish. She also wished, with all the drunken passion she was able to muster from within her, that tomorrow's recital would be called off.

But what was the point, Ellen brooded, wishing upon a star? In the end, you just had to wake up and smell the coffee.

friday

63

Ellen was breathing deeply when she heard the Town Hall clock strike two dongs. She jerked on the chaise longue and unstuck her eyes. The sunlight made her squint. Bright already. She must have fallen asleep. She remembered being awake for the dawn so she'd probably only nodded off for an hour. But it was better than nothing.

She stretched and blinked across to the Town Hall to check the time. When she saw the clock face she stopped blinking. *Half past eleven? Half past eleven?* Ellen felt the blood drain from her head. *How can it be half past eleven?*

Horrified, she jumped off the chaise longue and tore through the French doors. She raced into the kitchen. The cooker-clock said eleven thirty-two. She checked for messages. Ita had left five.

She'd already missed the rehearsal. The recital was at one. An hour and a half to go . . . Oh, no – *she'd left her music at the Conservatory!*

She sprinted into the shower and stood under the hot water for less than one minute, quickly soaping herself down. No time for hair. She jumped out, wrapped in a bath towel. 'Joel!' she shrieked, dashing into the dark bedroom, dripping on the carpet. She turned on the light. He was fast asleep. He'd slept through her seven thirty wake-up call!

'My dress, my dress!' She slammed back the wardrobe door and ripped through the hangers. 'Joel, wake up, it's half-eleven!'

There was no movement from the bulky mass underneath the blanket.

'My shoes, where are my shoes?' She rooted through the

217

bottom of the wardrobe, causing mayhem among the neat rows of footwear, and eventually found her good pair.

'Time! Time!' She rushed to the bedside locker. 'Twenty-five to twelve – oh, no!' She shook Joel's shoulder violently. 'Joel! Wake up, wake up, for God's sake!'

He moaned, but did not move. Dead, for all the use he was. 'Joel, I have to go! I can't wait for you. You'll have to get the train. Do you hear me?' She shook him again. '*Do you hear me?*'

She put on her underwear, pulled up her concert tights; she put on her concert dress then arranged herself in the mirror. She ran into the kitchen, her head throbbing. She grabbed the vodka bottle from the countertop and flung it under the sink, cursing again. Her dull black shoes . . . no time to polish.

'Keys, keys!' She was frantic until she found her car keys, concealed on the kitchen table underneath a newspaper. Her bag, her raincoat and she fled the apartment, into the lift, sprinting through the rain to her car, dived inside and slammed the door shut.

The rear-view mirror told her she could not have looked worse: hair scraggy, skin pale as a ghost's; circles under her eyes; make-up patchy. Dehydrated, sore-throated and stiff. How could she show up like this? Her father's memorial recital! The one time! All his friends and associates. Her own friends, colleagues and relatives. All had been invited. What a disaster! What had she been doing last night, sleeping outside? *What was she thinking?*

She started the ignition, but it chugged. 'Take it easy, take it easy.' She tried to calm down. She checked her watch. Nearly a quarter to twelve. If traffic was busy on the Merrion Road then her life was over. The car sprang into action and she went into reverse. If she made a hash of the concert she would leave Ireland, go abroad with Joel and her Steinway, and never be seen or heard of ever again. She jammed her foot down and the car shot backwards. A horn honked, she slammed on the brakes and turned round.

She'd narrowly missed colliding with a large silver car. She crept back a few more feet, then put the car into first and accelerated. The silver car honked again. She braked. What was his bloody problem? She turned again. The Mercedes pulled up alongside.

218

She didn't have time for this. The tinted passenger window scrolled down and, to Ellen's dismay, Henry's sharp and clean face appeared.

'Are you on your way in?' His worn façade was softened with good humour.

'Henry, I can't stop, I'm going to be late for the recital. I've got to drop in to the Conservatory first to collect my music.'

'Is he at home?'

Ellen was unsure whether he'd heard her. She raised her voice. 'I'm going to be late, Henry, I slept in. I haven't got time to . . .'

'I wanted to drop something up to him.'

'He's asleep. He won't answer the door for you.'

'Oh, would you have time to . . .?'

'No, sorry, I'm already late. I slept it out. I have to go in.'

Henry paused for thought. 'You wouldn't have a spare key on you, then? I could give it back to you after the concert.'

Ellen wanted to scream. Instead, she smiled. *Just give him the key and get rid of him.* She turned off the ignition and snatched out the keys, removed the car key and was about to fling the others through his car window when she hesitated; it was a heavy bunch of keys. Furious, she jammed her thumbnail into the ring and removed the apartment key from the bunch. She also removed part of her nail. She fought against her seat belt to get out of the car. Frantically she pulled it away, jumped out and ran over to Henry's side. He was getting out of his car. This meant a conversation. Ellen slapped the key down on the bonnet of the Mercedes, shouted an apology and ran back to her car.

'Thank you.' Henry nodded. 'I'll give it back to you after . . .'

'Okay!' She turned over the engine and slipped the car into first.

He raised a hand in the air 'Oh, and, eh . . .'

Oh, for goodness' sake . . .

'I . . . eh, I wanted to, by the way, apologise for last Tuesday. I hope I didn't seem too . . .'

He looked embarrassed. 'Henry, it doesn't matter. I haven't time to . . .'

'Just received some bad news, wasn't in great form.'

Ellen gripped the steering wheel so tightly she wanted to pull it out and hit him with it. 'I forgive you, Henry. I forgive you a

219

thousand times.' She smiled desperately, then revved up the engine.

'To do with Joel's mother. Maybe Joseph mentioned it?'

'See you later, Henry.'

She didn't even look at him as she slammed her foot on to the accelerator. With the rear wheels spinning, she tore out of the car park.

64

He lay in the lukewarm bath and wallowed, sicker than a dog in a pool of puke.

And even that didn't quite capture it. Without doubt, Joel's awful nausea was the fault of the Midnight Erection Ita had given him last evening. *What the hell had she put in it?*

He raised a hand. Hanging from his fingers was Jan's letter, now a soggy, blue-stained mess which resembled a facecloth more than a letter. And might as well be a facecloth, for all the use it was to Joel.

He slapped his arm back down into the water. What a sickener. All his life he'd waited for an opportunity like this to come along. All his life. And now, the very time it did . . . Joel couldn't bear even to think about it. He bunched up the letter into a sodden pulp and flung it into the toilet.

Amid all this misery, there was just one thing that prevented Joel's life from being worse than total dung: it was the thought that they were going to have a baby. But apart from this, dung didn't even come close to equating to how he felt. Not even total dung managed that. Not even total dung with sewage added came close. No, the writing was on the wall.

Inevitably, Ellen would go to the bank very soon and discover their nest egg gone. She would come home and demand an explanation. Joel would supply the explanation, adding that he'd done it for them both. Then she would kill him. But moments before she succeeded in killing him, she would make him promise to apply to McDonald's.

McDonald's?

Joel wondered how many years it would take him to earn the cost of a decent saxophone – after his family was fully catered for – turning burgers and shovelling French fries in a customer-friendly environment while his armpits frazzled beneath him and his head erupted over the hotplates like a Mount Etna fireball. Five years? And what if she had twins? A decade? Triplets?

Oh, why did reality have to be so cruel?

Joel hoisted himself out of the bath. While he was drying himself, he brooded that maybe he deserved his punishment. He'd been a shit all week. He'd had Ellen's precious nest egg stolen. He'd spent the last five days deceiving her, covering up, lying to his father about her. And Monk, the rat-turd, was right: what Joel had done was set her up as an adulteress. Then he'd come home last night, drunk, and fallen asleep without even saying goodnight. He'd been so drunk that he'd practically given Ita the green light to kiss and seduce him like she had, and then sit on top of him like that, ordering him to get it up. It was shameful what he'd let her get away with, right behind Ellen's back.

Then, this morning, to cap it all, he hadn't even had the decency to grin and bear his nausea and trudge in to her recital. What sort of person was he, after all?

Joel knew what sort of person: he was a horrible excuse for a human being.

When he had finished drying himself, he got into Ellen's white nightgown, which hung on the back of the door, because he was too unwell to bother getting his own. He stepped into her fluffy blue slippers, then plodded down the hall corridor towards the kitchen to drown himself in black coffee.

On his way into the kitchen, Joel cast a lamentable glance into the lounge, where he fancied he could smell Monk's sickening aftershave from the previous evening. The couch was empty except for a few cushions and a cream saxophone case leaning against the armrest.

Joel continued into the kitchen in a daze and slid the arm off the espresso maker. He took out a packet of Rombouts coffee, spooned two generous helpings into the coffee filter and slid the filter back into the machine. He took an espresso cup from another press and

221

filled it three-quarters with water. He poured the water into the espresso maker, replaced the lid and pressed the button. It lit up red and he placed the espresso cup under the filter.

While he waited for his coffee to percolate, Joel recalled certain details of the previous night, which brought a rush of blood to his face. That bastard. Joel was glad he'd attacked him for making that snide strawberry panties remark, which he'd refused to withdraw. The sly creep had deserved every punch. He was only sorry he hadn't stuffed the sock of coins down his throat and made him bloody pay.

When the coffee had stopped percolating into the cup, Joel picked it up and brought it to his mouth. It got no further than his lips.

Hold on.

Had he or had he not just seen . . .

Joel spent some time frowning at the wall opposite, wondering if Ita had added acid to his Midnight Erection yesterday. Because, unless he was grievously mistaken, Joel had spotted a saxophone case in the lounge just now, leaning against the sofa.

He left the kitchen, cup in hand, and went into the hallway, still frowning. He stopped outside the lounge door and peeped inside.

His mouth dropped. So did the cup, landing with a crack on the wooden threshold below him. There was indeed a large cream saxophone case leaning against the armrest.

Oh my dear sweet . . .

Joel rubbed his eyes, in case they were playing tricks. No, the mirage was still there, a golden oasis in the middle of an arid desert. He trod warily into the room and stopped in front of the mirage. He put out a hand. He touched the mirage. It was not a mirage. It was real. This was his saxophone case.

Joel withdrew his hand, because a thought had just occurred to him. What if it was empty?

Oh, what cruelty, what savage cruelty!

He touched it again, his hand shaking. The box slid slowly away from the armrest and tumbled on to the floor, landing with a weighty clump. He dropped to his knees and in a split second he'd opened the four clasps and there, yes, unbelievably, astonishingly gleaming before his eyes was his beloved Selmer, untouched, as he'd left it five days ago.

As Joel knelt there, he ogled his golden saxophone, zombified.

He dared to touch it. It was cold to his fingertips. He lifted it up by the bell and took it into his arms. He raised it to his mouth and pressed his lips into the cold keys, kissing them repeatedly. They responded by gradually warming up. Then he started hugging and kissing the golden bell. He cuddled his precious Selmer like a baby and tweaked its keys as you'd tweak an infant's nose. He stroked and caressed the bell as you would a baby's soft face and showered it with so much care and affection that he wanted to weep.

He licked a reed and fixed it to the mouthpiece, assembled the instrument and attached the neck strap, put it into his mouth and blew a short scale. *It played like a dream! It was the old sound! It was!* Within moments he forgot his nausea and was lost in a random waveform of chords, a rush of notes that soaked him in a joy and relief so indescribable that he wanted to levitate. Eyes closed, Joel swayed in formless circles, as if in a wonderful dream, playing an onslaught of beautiful improvised patterns. Then he stumbled, lost balance on Ellen's high slippers and plunged into the armchair.

He was giggling hilariously until he spotted something underneath him, six inches from his nose. He knelt in joyful disbelief over the article, holding his hands together like a priest. 'It's too much to hope for,' he whispered. 'I'm never that lucky.'

Joel struck up the courage to unzip the inside pocket of his stolen jacket. He pulled out a thick wad of banknotes – sterling. Frenetically, he began counting. It was all there. He counted the lot again. There was no doubt. It was all there.

Joel thrust up his arms into the air and roared for joy. He jumped to his feet and hurled the banknotes into the air, from where they returned in their dozens like a swirling heaven of confetti.

But how?

Joel blew another few notes, but they ended in a breathy mess because he was too bewildered and stunned to continue. He removed the strap from his neck and placed his Golden Goddess on the couch. He paced up and down in front of the couch, frowning and grimacing at his saxophone, and scratching his head. What had happened? What was going on? Was he dreaming? Had Monday not happened?

He kept pacing, trying to work out what the hell his saxophone was doing in his apartment.

At one point Joel looked up.

He stopped pacing.

There was someone outside on the balcony, leaning against the rail and staring in at him. His arms were folded and he had a broad grin on his face.

It was his father.

65

He pushed through the French windows and stepped into the lounge, pointing at all the banknotes on the floor. 'Nice to see you having a good time for a change.'

Joel stared at his old man, dumbfounded.

'I believe congratulations are in order, Son.'

'Father, did you bring home my . . .'

'When is she due?'

'What?'

'When is Ellen due?'

'On stage? Five past one. But I don't think I can make it.'

His father frowned at him. 'No, Joseph, when is your *baby* due?'

Joel walked up to his father, stopping just two feet away. 'Father?'

'Joseph.'

'How did you know Ellen was pregnant?'

'Aha! That's the question.' He was smiling now.

'I never told you.'

'Nor did Ellen.'

Henry went over to the piano and poked at Joel's sock of coins lying on top. He began tinkling the upper keys. 'Can't you guess?'

'No, I can't.'

'It's connected with your saxophone.'

Joel couldn't, for the life of him, work out how Ellen's pregnancy might be connected with his saxophone and he said so. 'Dad, how did you get hold of my sax?'

'I'll give you three guesses.' He was attempting to play 'My Way' with a single index finger, in an inappropriately low register.

'Okay.' Joel sighed, not really in the mood for his father's party games. 'It was found by a Welsh policeman.'

'It was not.'

'An English policeman.'

'It wasn't found by a policeman.'

'A policewoman, then?'

'No. She's not a policewoman either.'

'It's a she? So she's an ordinary citizen?'

'No, she's not that either.'

'What is she, then? An alien?'

'All I'm asking you, Joseph, is to use your head for a change. Start again.' He moved up an octave and continued his attempted reconstruction of the Sinatra hit.

Joel was bewildered. 'Don't say you met her.'

'You met her yourself,' his father replied, blasé.

'Pardon?'

'On the catamaran.'

'Dad, the only person I met on the catamaran was the sham nun I told you about on Wednesday.'

'Sham nun. I see.' His father was nodding as he ambled around the room, ignoring the scattered banknotes underfoot.

'For chrissakes, she ripped off my saxophone and my money.'

'Is that so?'

'Yes, it is so.'

'You're quite sure she did that?'

'What do you mean, am I sure? I was *there*. I witnessed it with my own eyes. I left all my stuff in the back seat of her car and when I came back out of the supermarket she'd driven away.'

His father stopped to squint at a still life over the mantelpiece. 'That's a very interesting interpretation, Joseph.'

'It's a bit gory, but Ellen likes hunting scenes.'

'I'm talking about your interpretation of what happened,'

225

Henry replied, still admiring the still life. 'Very interesting indeed.'

'I can tell you, it didn't feel very interesting at the time.'

'Because I heard something different.'

'From who?'

'From a woman called Sister Boniface.'

Joel gawped at his father, dumbfounded. '*You met the thief?*'

'She's not a thief, Joseph. She's a very kind and thoughtful human being, as I discovered. With a very busy schedule.' He rubbed a light fingertip across the name at the base of the canvas. 'And you put her to extreme inconvenience.'

Puzzled, Joel watched his father walk to the window and put both hands in his trouser pockets. He stared out, balancing back and forward on his heels. 'She called me from her convent last night,' he began, back to his normal voice. 'Said she found an old business card of mine in your jacket pocket. She told me the whole story. The *correct* interpretation. She told me she met you on the catamaran and offered you a lift. She told me you went into a shop in Holyhead to buy provisions, but while you were gone she was waved on by a traffic warden and she got lost in the surrounding streets. She found her way back, a mere twelve minutes later, and went straight to the supermarket to look for you and drive you to London.'

'I . . . I . . .'

'Guess how long she waited there for you?'

'I, eh . . .'

'Two hours!' His father flipped round from the window and glared at him. '*Two whole, goddam hours!*'

'Okay.'

'And she was simply wondering, Joseph, why the hell you never showed up.'

Joel stared at his father for quite some time, unable to respond. Then an extraordinary thing happened. His father's face, which up till then had been sombre and morose, turned very wrinkled and very red. He bent over double, gripping his chest as if he were asphyxiating. Joel rushed over to him. 'Dad, are you okay?'

His father waved him away, still bent down, still grasping his chest. He gasped out a semi-sentence containing the words *unique* and *priceless*. It came as a shock for Joel to realise that his father was in the middle of a convulsive laughing episode. He appeared to be finding the whole thing utterly hilarious.

Joel studied his old man, choking and chuckling away at his expense. It struck him that the last time he'd creased him up this much was when he'd sleepwalked, as an adolescent on holiday in Spain, straight into a swimming pool.

'In future, Son,' Henry wheezed, recovering slightly and mopping his eyes with a handkerchief, 'will you please try to be less reckless where your money and your possessions are concerned?'

'Sure, Dad.'

'Will you try to do that for me?'

And he was off again. Joel made to go to the balcony, but his father grabbed him. He became serious, then. 'But that's not what's important,' he said. 'She also told me you were going to be a father.'

'She told you that?'

'I think she let it slip out. Well? What's the secret, Son? It's *wonderful* news!' Laughing, he grabbed both Joel's arms and shook him till his jaws rattled.

'Thanks, Dad, that'll do.'

'Wonderful for you, wonderful for Ellen. Wonderful for me. For your mother, even. Oh! Now that I think of it – I must get down that train set from the attic.'

'Sure, Dad, but we don't yet know if it'll be a boy or a girl.'

'Haven't you thought of a name yet?'

'Not really.'

'Permit me to make a suggestion.'

'Absolutely, go ahead.'

'Cecil, if it's a boy. It was your grandfather's middle name.'

'Sure.' Joel nodded, severely hesitant. 'You never know. I'll say it to Ellen, see what she thinks.'

'Will you do that? It's always nice to keep the memory of one's ancestors alive. My God, look at the time! Better get going. Are you coming or not?'

Joel explained that he didn't want to end up barfing on the floor of the concert hall, metres away from his performing wife.

Fully apprised of the situation, his father stepped out into the stairwell.

'Dad?'

'Yes, Son?'

'You needn't tell Ellen anything about this, will you?'

His father reached over and ruffled Joel's hair like a dog's. 'I wouldn't dream of putting her through it, Joseph. Living with you must bewilder her enough as it is.'

'Sorry?'

'Well, look at you! What will she think when she comes home and sees you wearing her bathrobe and slippers?'

'Thanks, Dad,' Joel replied, faintly embarrassed.

'Oh, by the way. That cheque I wrote you last Monday. I was too busy to have it cancelled, so it's probably cleared by now.'

His father's expression had taken on that playfully cryptic, pre-punchline expression again. Then he smiled. 'You'd better hold on to it, son.'

'You mean I can . . . I can actually . . .'

'What with Cecil on the way, et cetera.'

'I don't know . . . I don't know what to . . .'

'Don't look so guilty. I'll be selling the Galway flats to stop your mother hounding me – so I can afford it. And remember: it's for the baby, so I don't want you spending it on whatever.'

'For the baby. Absolutely. For the baby.'

'Have to dash.'

Joel gaped after his father, who rushed downstairs in a frenetic pitter-patter of feet. He went out to the stairwell and watched his father's white head, dark shoulders and flying red tie spiral all the way down the stairs to the ground floor.

Then, without warning, the whole stairwell turned into a giant cavern, reverberating to the sound of belly laughter.

That's when Joel remembered the pram in the lobby.

66

As Monk limped through the concert hall, his footsteps squeaked on the polished woodblock floor and the echo spiralled up to the high, ornate ceiling. The large hall, with its giant columns, its paintings and its huge pear-shaped chandeliers, was lined with rows of still-empty seating. On a marble platform at the top of the hall stood a polished grand piano. There were two chairs, two music stands and several microphones. Flanking the stage were two majestic flights of steps, sweeping upwards in a vast curve and arching together at the top.

Monk had on a smart black leather jacket and dark, blood-proof slacks. He wore a black shirt and cravat, and he could almost see himself in the sheen of his own shoes. He was perfumed and squeaky clean. He strode up on to the platform and sat down on the leather stool. He opened the piano lid and caressed the rows of Colgate-white piano keys. He put his fingers into the E position and closed his eyes. Very quietly, he played the first few bars of the Chopin.

That afternoon the two of them were going to communicate. Properly. Monk would get rid of O'Leary after the concert, approach his wife and whisper in her ear: lunch in the Unicorn? They would take a discreet table in the corner and talk, over a bottle of red. He would cut the double meanings, the fake charm and the bullshit. Soften the hard edge, because there would be no need for it. He would be his sincere, unaffected self. Whatever that was. He would be without motive, without artifice. And she would relax, content to be herself.

During the main course she would open up to him, as she would to her roast duck. Talk about herself, confess her plans, her secret fears and dreams. And he would be the responsive listener. He would emit supportive comments and shoot appropriate one-liners when she was least expecting them. He would make her laugh. Like she hadn't in years. And eventually, in that quiet, discreet corner of the Unicorn, their lips would join together and . . .

Monk's eyes shot open. He'd just heard something. A violin twang, coming from somewhere above him. He cocked an ear. Looked to be coming from the top of the staircase behind him. There was a lower string sound, too. *They're warming up: she must be here.* Monk jumped to his feet, straightened his cravat and took to the left stairway, holding the thin brass rail. He limped with some difficulty up the twenty-eight marble steps. At the top were two doors, one ajar. Inside, the strings were tuning up. He tapped on the door and the squeaky strings fell silent.

'Who's that?' shouted out a thick, Midland accent. 'Come on in, will you?'

He went in and glanced around. Only big boobs and this geek with triple-glazed glasses were present. 'Where's Ellen?' he asked.

'Good question,' said the geek.

'She isn't here yet,' said Ita. 'You'll have to wait outside.'

Monk scoffed at the woman and turned to go. Then he remembered what she had told him. 'You told me last night the concert was at two thirty.'

'Did I, indeed?'

'Yes, you did, indeed.'

'And what time is it now?'

'Almost one o'clock.'

'Well, I must've known you'd be early, so, mustn't I?'

Monk grimaced sarcastically, then left the room without a word. On this epochal afternoon, what was the point of getting sore about it? Monk descended the flight of steps again, clutching the rail and clenching his teeth in pain. The first well-dressed arrivals were now entering the hall, which looked rather grand from this altitude. The front rows were slowly filling up. His brochure had not been touched: it lay on the seat which he'd reserved earlier, two rows back from the stage.

Monk left the hall and stood at the colonnade outside, keeping watch over the narrow pedestrian entrance at the far end of the tarmac drive. People were filing through the gate, but Ellen was not among them. Where was she? Had something happened? Monk glanced at his watch. It was after one. Had General O'Leary offered to drive her in, to spare her nerves, then promptly collided into the back of a bus? Monk sincerely hoped not. Ellen would be devastated if she missed the recital. Devastated. And she would definitely not be in the mood for lunch in the Unicorn.

As he waited he continued to survey Dublin 4, now milling through the gate in droves. They were well dressed to a person, crouched underneath umbrellas. They passed him by, parading their self-esteem, their affluent aromas and their pompous east-coast accents around themselves like articulate turkeys. Some, even, it pleased to sprinkle water spray at him, as they ignorantly shook out their umbrellas from just two feet away.

One distinguished gentleman walked up the tarmac drive, accompanied by an older couple. He looked somewhat familiar. Wasn't that O'Leary's old man? Yes, it was him all right. Henry – that was his name. He hadn't changed much from the days when he used to bring O'Leary to school. He looked impressive, in direct contrast with his son, if a little sanctimonious and stiff. He was tall, white and handsome. Well decked-out and sporting a full head of hair that looked like he treated it daily with bleach. As he watched Henry move into the foyer, it occurred to Monk that his wife must have been the most hideously balding dwarf imaginable.

A clap of thunder tore through the sky above. Monk turned. Still no sign of Ellen. Ten past one. Rain was now spattering hard on the steps of the Gallery. He turned back to the foyer. The father had disappeared. He shot another look towards the gate and was again disappointed. He broke off and followed Henry into the hall, now nearly full. Mr Peanut Incorporated was sitting in the front row, just below the stage.

Monk returned to his seat to the left of the centre aisle. He observed the well-heeled guests around him with disdain. Sure, the recital was ten minutes overdue, but most of them were consulting their watches and shaking their heads. Some, even, were muttering complaints, tutting a beautiful, talented artist simply because she happened to be a few minutes late.

Monk raised up his brochure and read:

Hugh Butler Memorial Recital

Shaw Room
National Gallery of Ireland
Friday, 25 August
1.05 p.m.

Beethoven	Piano Trio No. 7 in B♭, op. 97 (Archduke)
	1 Allegro moderato
	2 Scherzo (Allegro) & Coda
	3 Andante cantabile
	4 Allegro moderato

| Shostakovich | Sonata for Violin and Piano |

| Chopin | Etude No. 3 in E major – Tristesse (piano) |

Ellen O'Leary (Butler), piano
Ita Mulrooney, violin
Sean Knowles, cello

The crowd was making noises behind him now. The loud murmur fell to a hush. Descending the curved staircase to the right was the skinny wuss, his cello a massive boat in front of him. Descending the staircase to the left was a large figure in a swishy, flowing garment. It was the Bulgarian yeti, flaunting her violin like a carpet beater. She sported a serious expression on her face, as she gracelessly plodded down the steps, one hip at a time. Monk checked the chandeliers above to see if they were shaking. Surprisingly they weren't.

When she reached the bottom, she walked to the centre of the stage and stared solemnly down the centre aisle. She cleared her throat. 'Ladies and gentlemen, I have an announcement to make.'

The audience rumbled with disappointment behind Monk and everyone seemed to be consulting their watch. Big Mama did not continue with her announcement, however. She had stopped short in anticipation. A door at the back of the hall had just clattered shut. Monk turned round.

Ellen was at the rear of the hall, removing a raincoat.

'The concert is now about to begin,' Monk heard the woman announce, to the eruption of applause from the audience.

Monk beheld the beautiful sight of Ellen, walking up the side aisle in her blue velvet dress, her heels clicking against the floor. She was gripping sheet music to her chest and staring at the ground. She progressed quickly to the stage, went swiftly past Ita and moved to the piano like a ray of light. She sat down, dragged forward her piano stool and lifted the piano lid Monk had just closed.

Something was not right. Ellen's hair was wet and dishevelled, and she had a ladder in her tights. She looked pale and gaunt. Had she rowed with her husband? He was nowhere around – the insensitive cad hadn't even bothered his arse to come.

She placed her music on the rack in front of her, opened the first page and said something to Ita. She did not seem her usual confident self. She looked harassed. Her eyes were moist, her forehead troubled. But there was something else. She was vulnerable. Indescribably so. Fearful. Her fragility was enhanced by her thin shoulders and her pale bare arms. *Look at her . . . look at her . . .* he whispered to himself.

It was astonishing. She was utterly beautiful.

Monk stared at her, as if in a dream, until his concentration was broken by a note she hammered down. The cello and the violin drew their bows across the strings to tune up, then they adopted the position, clutching their instruments in the air. The silence was pin-drop and the three musicians became concentrated and still. Ellen was eyeing both of them intently, then returning their attention. They looked back at her. Ita raised her bow, turned to Ellen and suddenly jerked.

A beat later they sprang into the race.

67

Ellen hit the final triumphant chord of the Shostakovich and the hall broke into loud applause.

Ita had on a wide grin. She took Ellen's hand and they both faced the crowd. Ellen was puzzled by the audience reaction. The applause was resounding. How could they possibly have missed the errors? Were they completely deaf? The Shostakovich was a disaster. The *Archduke* was shaky, although she'd found her form in the slower *Andante cantabile*, where she'd been carried by its quietly creeping intensity. But the scale passages in the first movement? Her fingers had tripped at least five times. Surely they'd noticed? Were they being nice?

233

As she bowed, Ellen scanned the crowd for Joel, but couldn't see him. There were a lot of familiar faces. The first person she saw was Joel's father, standing tall in the front row, nodding and clapping passionately. She nodded and smiled back, proud and delighted that he'd come. She spotted her old teacher Ivan Beausang and his wife, then that Myles chap who was staring up intensely at her, clapping high.

Scanning the hall, she spotted colleagues of hers from the Conservatory and friends from Trinity College. One well-known music critic. Retired colleagues of her father from the Conservatory or the orchestra and other walks of life. All had come along to pay their respects to her father. Most knew her or knew of her. Yes, Ellen decided, they were being nice.

She addressed the audience and the hall filtered down to a hush. She thanked all concerned for attending this special occasion to commemorate her late father, Hugh Butler. She spoke briefly of his achievements as a conductor and of his legacy as a teacher and father. She told the audience that she was going to play a piece that used to be one of his favourites, a piece he'd taught her himself as a girl, the one piece which kept alive his memory whenever she played it.

As she spoke, she noticed Henry nodding intently. Filled with emotion, she walked to the piano, past a seated Ita. Quietly she played a chord, then closed her eyes, her hands hovering over the keyboard.

And she started playing the 'Tristesse'.

Softly and beautifully she played, slowly, slower than usual. She played with feeling, with loving motion, responding, restraining. She delayed on the C♯ of the third bar. The *poco crescendo*, reaching upwards in intensity . . . *con forza* . . . culminating in the high G♯, peaking like a mountain of emotion, then falling away sweetly and sadly, dropping down the other side. She believed she was in their Glenageary home, the sun pouring in through the shutters of their living room, while she watched her father playing the Chopin, smiling down at her, telling her that one day she too would play like this, even more beautifully. And when she played it he would be there to hear her.

She believed in her heart that he was there, listening. *My sweet pet*, she heard him whisper, *don't try so hard. Let go – you want for nothing . . .*

And Ellen played through the turbulent middle section of the piece without error and descended into the soft repose of the melody once again, and reached the last quiet chord. She stood up, walked past Ita and Sean and bowed to the applause. Soon people were rising from their seats, exchanging enthusiastic words and picking up their belongings.

'Ellen?'

Henry took her hand warmly in his. He was filled with emotion. 'Ellen, you were terrific. Magnificent. You've done your father proud! Yes, you have. You absolutely have! I'm only sorry Joel didn't make it: he said he was sick and couldn't come in. Here, this is yours.' He pressed the apartment key into her palm.

'You'll come to the reception, won't you?'

'I wouldn't miss it.'

'I'm really glad you came, Henry.'

'Ellen, I'm so happy for you.' His expression had become kindly. 'Joel told me. I know you don't want any fuss, but it's *super* news.'

Ellen felt herself swallow.

'When is it due?'

'Keep it down, Henry!' she whispered, dismayed. 'Someone will hear!'

He apologised and lowered his voice, flushed and eager. 'Will it be next May?'

'I'm not sure,' she lamented, glancing around her, alarmed. 'I haven't really thought about it . . .'

'Of course you haven't.' He laughed, hugging her to himself. 'It's early days yet! But you'll be happy with a baby, I know you will.'

Henry continued speaking, saying something about Joel taking responsibility for his life at long last, but Ellen wasn't listening. While he was tapping her on the back and rocking her over his shoulder, she was gaping in increasing horror at a small group of people who were standing no more than three feet behind Henry's back. They had heard every word. She knew them and they knew her. Two of the women were colleagues from the

235

Conservatory: one was that nosy Imelda and one was an acquaintance from the symphony orchestra. Another was a rival pianist she'd faced through years of piano competitions, defeating her every time but one. She was a noted gossip who thrived on scandal like a dumpsite vulture. Ita stood a little further away, talking to her mother and watching Ellen with grim foreboding.

'Oh, God,' she said, separating herself from Henry, her hands joined over her mouth.

'Is something wrong Ellen?'

'I didn't want anybody knowing. I didn't want anybody knowing.'

'Oh, dear,' said Henry, visibly embarrassed. 'My big mouth.'

'Would you mind . . . excusing me for a minute?' She grabbed her sheet music, stepped off the stage and rushed down the aisle, with as much decorum as her upset would allow. She retrieved her coat from a chair at the back of the hall and left the National Gallery. She stepped into the hard rain and ran across the road to Merrion Park.

68

'You stupid bitch!'

With clenched teeth, Ellen stormed down the tree-lined pathway, getting soaked under the light but drenching rain.

You have just cocked up. You didn't just try and fail. No; you tried pathetically, then followed it up by failing miserably. It has just been announced to the whole wide world that you are about to give birth to a baby.

Only there's one slight problem. Here goes.

You never got cocked-up in the first place.

'Holy *Jesus!*' Ellen steamed, sending a shower of starlings shattering from a nearby bush. She tried to analyse by what spontaneous bout of craziness she'd so completely lost her faculty for judgement last Monday when she'd told him.

She would now become the object of universal gossip. Her fertility would become the object of universal speculation. Her insides would turn into a public gambling house. It would be hell.

236

Even at this precise moment they were probably all inside, prattling on about her. And when they went home they'd tell their families and friends, and by Monday everyone would have heard the great news. In the Conservatory, everyone would come up to her. All her colleagues, all her pupils. Associates of her father. Tom at reception. Word would spread outside. What would she tell them?

Pardon me, there's been a misunderstanding. I'm not actually pregnant, even though I said I was. I'm not actually the nice, polite, honest young woman you think I am. I'm actually a barefaced liar. I stood before my husband and I lied to his face through my teeth. I watched him go into shock, nearly choking, and I did nothing. Oh God.

She felt a lump in her throat. What was she going to tell Joel? How could she tell him the truth?

As she walked, Ellen stared around the wet pathway, feeling raindrops trickle down her face. The fact of the matter was that she *couldn't* tell him the truth. It would be too great a blow for him. How could she shatter his beautiful naïveté? No, Joel must never know. Ellen would have to go back home, this minute, and lie to him again. Straight to his face like she did last Monday.

But hell, she was used to it, so why stop now?

Why did she do it to him? Why did she treat him like that? Acting superior to him. Joel wasn't perfect, but at least he wasn't low and devious. He didn't stoop to secret schemes behind her back. And she used to think *she* was the one with the high moral ideals, with the integrity! What a stupid joke.

Ellen completed yet another revolution of the park, passing by an enclosed playground area for kids, its metal gates painted red, yellow and blue. Oscar Wilde came next, seated up on the rock, wet but cordial-looking in the rain. Scowling at him, she turned the corner, disdaining the shelter of overhanging trees.

She wanted out. Not just out of the deceit. Out of everything. The routine of it all. The slaving away to put a few extra Euros in the bank each week, instead of going out and spending it on a Saturday evening with her husband. There were no comforts, no luxuries. No evenings at the theatre or the opera. They couldn't even have sex without Joel's back rupturing. What was the point of it all? She couldn't see one. Where was the fun in bringing up a child on the breadline, in one of the most expensive cities in Europe? It struck Ellen that she would probably be childless. And so what? There were worse things that could happen in life.

Ellen was striding swiftly towards the exit gate when a man's voice called out her name. She looked across the grass verge and saw a familiar figure at the intersection, standing underneath an umbrella. *Oh please, no, not him, not now.*

'Ellen!'

'I'm sorry, I can't stop.'

'Wait.'

She bit her lip, then turned and smiled as he approached. *Always the perfect girl. I'm sick and tired of being so perfect. It's time to be honest.* She stopped smiling.

'You're wet.'

'I like the rain,' she replied.

'Here . . .' He held the umbrella over her.

She pushed it away. 'Thanks, anyway.' Her hair was already soaked and she wanted this slimy person out of it.

'Is everything okay, Ellen?'

'I was on my way home. What are you doing here?'

'I just came out of the concert.' He nodded towards the Gallery across the road. 'You were astonishing.'

'You were at the recital?'

'Yeah.' He grinned, puzzled. 'I'm the guy you were staring down at from the stage.'

'I don't think so.' Ellen walked up the pathway, her eyes fixed on the approaching park gate. He limped alongside.

'Listen,' he said, 'we need to talk.'

'What about?'

'About us.'

'Us?'

'Don't laugh.'

'There's nothing to talk about. I'm sorry. I'm in a rush. I have to get home.'

'Ellen, would you stop and listen to me?' His voice had an edge to it now.

'I can't stop.' She went out through the gate and strode along beside the railings. 'I have to get back to my husband.'

'I'm not able to walk properly.'

'Then go back in and take a seat, and stop following me.' She increased her pace but he managed to keep hobbling alongside.

'Ellen we need to talk.'

She halted. 'Look, Myles, isn't that your name?' She did not look him in the eye. 'What do you want me to say to you? I'm sorry if I've given you a false impression, I really am. It wasn't my intention.'

'You could never give me a false impression, Ellen.' He touched her arm. 'I can see right through you.'

'Don't touch me.'

'I don't forget the way you were with me last night in your apartment. I could read your mind.'

'I didn't want you in my apartment last night. I didn't ask you to come down. I didn't ask you to bring me flowers. Now take your hand off my arm.' She resumed walking next to the railings and he hobbled abreast.

'Come on, Ellen, what are you putting on the performance for? You're not on stage now. Why aren't you like you were last night? When we were alone. You were going to kiss me.'

Ellen felt her stomach turn. She looked at him with disgust. 'My God, you really are deluded.'

He laughed. 'No, no. You're the one who's deluded. You don't want to face the truth. You won't even admit that you're attracted to me.'

'I'm not attracted to you.'

'See?'

'Oh, for goodness' sake.'

'Almost everything you did since I met you. First, the music lesson. You didn't know me from Adam. You offered it to me for a reason.'

'Because you asked me for it.'

'That Wednesday evening I came down to return your "Tristesse" and you came down, looking like a movie star on Oscars night.'

'I happened to be . . .'

'And yesterday morning, when you called over with the dog. Why didn't you pick up your phone and call me instead? I don't want to hear it! Yesterday evening, in the hallway, what's that you were doing with your knee between my legs?'

'Do you want me to show you?'

Monk grabbed her arm roughly and hauled her to a halt. 'Would you listen to me?'

'Let go of my arm!'

'I just want you to come clean,' he said, trembling.

'*I said, let go of my arm.*'

He pulled her to him and held her fast, his grip a nasty parasite on her back. The umbrella fell on to the pavement and he began stroking her hair.

'*I said, let go, let go!*' She shoved hard against his chest, broke away and ran.

'DAMMIT, ELLEN, I LOVE YOU!'

She halted before she'd got ten feet. She turned back and stared at him, astonished. He stood there, his hands outstretched towards her, his lips trembling. The rain was glistening on his forehead, collecting in his thick dark eyebrows.

She backed away, turned and took off next to the railings, down towards the traffic lights at the corner of Merrion Park, where her car was. He shouted after her. Only when she reached the lights did she look back. He was still some distance behind her, struggling towards her, hauling himself along the railings. She begged the pedestrian light to go green. She looked back again. He was waving at her, shouting something at her. The rain was pouring mercilessly down on top of her, crawling down her cheeks.

The green light blinked and she ran diagonally across the road to her car. Fumbling with her keys, she got in, feeling her sodden dress cling to her legs, and started the ignition. He was at the corner, now, across the road. She checked for oncoming traffic, swerved out on to the road and rammed the accelerator to the floor. Racing down the street, she consulted the rear-view mirror and was startled by what she saw. There, on the roadside, that was him, it was definitely him in the black leather jacket, there was no doubt.

He was lying on top of a bicycle, flailing his arms out, struggling to stand up.

69

Ellen got home, saturated and shivering.

She poked her head in the door and listened, but could hear no sound. There was a strong smell of percolated coffee. She came in, kicked off her heels and hung up her wet coat. The hall mirror reflected back a sorry, bedraggled sight: dark patches of wet splotched her blue velvet dress, soaked through from the knees down. Her hair was wet and lank. Her face was in a mess and she noticed a ladder in her tights.

'Joel?'

There was no response. The living-room door was ajar. Ellen went over and pushed. The door swung open. She peered into the living room to see if he was inside. He wasn't, but something else was. Her heart sank. *Oh God, no.*

There in the middle of the room, standing like a grand monument to her fraud, was the stroller from the baby shop. Ellen approached it with dismay. A big, shiny red ribbon was wrapped round the raised hood and tied in a bow at the top. Inside the pram, where the baby's head normally lay, was a handwritten note. The words 'To Ellen' were visible at the top of the note. She pulled back the cosy-toes and picked up the page.

Sorry I couldn't get to the concert. Hope this makes up for it a little. Nine months and counting.
Love Joel

A lump entered her throat. Ellen left the lounge, picking up a stray twenty-Euro note from the floor and putting it on the hall table. She plodded to their bedroom, exhausted, her dress sodden to her skin. The room was in darkness and the air was heavy. She went into the en suite and flicked on the light. She couldn't bear to look at herself in the mirror. She rolled down and removed her moist tights, then unzipped her dress at the back, letting the wet garment slide heavily to the floor.

'Hello, sexy!'

'Jesus!' She spun round. Joel was sitting halfway up in the bed, partially covered by the duvet. His arm was wrapped round his saxophone, bathed golden in the reflected light of the bathroom. The swanlike neck of the instrument was curved over his shoulder like a wilting lover and its body was nestled close to his, protected by the bedding.

'Don't stop there,' he said, half sleepy. 'I was enjoying it.'

Ellen folded her arms, hunching her shoulders forward. 'I didn't see you there.'

'How did the concert go?'

She shivered, but did not reply. She wanted to tell him she'd make a mistake, but not yet. Not in her present state.

'I'm really sorry I couldn't make it,' he said.

'Joel, you've nothing to be sorry about, believe me.'

'Felt a bit sick after Ita's Midnight Erection yesterday. God knows what she put in it. Did you get wet?'

'Soaked.' Ellen retreated to the en suite and stayed behind the door, concealed. She simply stood there, staring down at the white tiles, unable to move.

'Ellen?'

She did not come out. 'Yes?'

'Could you come here a moment? There's something I want to show you.'

Ellen cringed. What was it now? Another item for the baby? Jesus, woman, tell him! Get it over with! She returned to the bedroom, barely able to look him in the eye, and trooped over to the bed.

He smiled approvingly at her damp underwear.

'Have a look down there,' he said, pulling the duvet away from his legs.

Ellen had a look to see what he had hidden.

'Mount Vesuvius is no longer dormant,' he said proudly. 'It's back to normal. Just after coming up.'

'Well done,' she whispered, feeling more wretched than ever.

'Please, I insist you take all the credit.' He lowered the saxophone to the floor beside him. He leant forward and took her arm, pulling her down to him. She sat across the bed and he pressed his warm face into her bare tummy. 'Oh, I've missed it, baby.'

Now Ellen felt his lips hot against her skin.

'You're cold,' he observed.

Tell him!

'Joel . . .'

'But delicious . . .'

Tell him now, for God's sake!

'Joel, I have to tell you something . . .'

'You know, it's going to be funny when you start growing, getting your bulge.' He was smooching her lovingly, all the way across her belly. 'You've always been so skinny. I can barely imagine you with a belly.'

He licked her belly button, sending a tingle up her spine.

'You'll never be able to slag me again,' he added. He hoisted himself up and ran his hands up her back, kissing his way up her front, until his face was buried between her breasts. 'Oh, by the way, I was just thinking, this morning, when I was in the middle of my cornflakes.'

'Joel?'

'Will you be breastfeeding?'

Ellen shook her head, grieving. She stared up at the ceiling and without warning her eyes started to water.

'Hmm?'

'Don't think so,' she lamented, stroking his hair. Her voice was beginning to crack.

'Hey, it's all right. No one's going to force you.' Joel made a circle of kisses around her nipple. 'If you're nervous about it, we could always try a few dry runs together, know what I mean?'

She felt his lips close in around her nipple. She threw her head back up to the ceiling and moaned, 'Oh God.'

Joel now guided her gently on to the bed and put his body over hers. She tried to wipe away her tears before he noticed, but it was too late.

'What's wrong, baby? Did the concert upset you?'

'Joel . . .'

'Well, you can relax now. I know it's been a hard week for you. Just relax. It's all over now.'

He wrapped his arms round her and gave her a massive bear hug. He massaged her back, squeezing her shoulders and drawing his hand right down her spine. It was good to feel his touch on her body, but Ellen felt unable to respond, not with all this going on. Now Joel was massaging her outer thighs, planting his warm lips over her face.

She turned her head so that she could see him to speak. 'Joel, there's something I have to tell you.'

'Can't it wait?' he said, removing her panties.

Ellen felt hot breath over her breasts, while he got to work on her bra. 'It really can't wait, love.'

'It's just that I've got a lot on my plate right now.'

'Joel, I wanted to tell you that I'm . . .'

'Oh, this feels good,' he cut in, licking her all over. 'Been denied it all week, because of my damn back, know what I mean?'

'I do know,' she whispered, 'but Joel, I have to tell you, I'm not . . .'

'Shush! Later, baby.' He kissed her mouth into silence. 'Let's just make love.'

early november

70

It was one of those quiet evenings.

And not only quiet, but extremely cold.

Winter was on its way, and the damp was spreading across the ceiling and down the walls. Soon his mother, who was making distant creaking movements in the room above, would insist he come up from the cold basement and inhabit one of the spare rooms upstairs. Up to now, Monk had refused. But this winter he might reconsider. It could get depressing down here.

He stood at the window and stared through the bars. A woman would not go amiss. He hadn't had one in over two months. Monk continued flicking through the names from his address book: Alison Fennell, Rosaline Fogarty, Karen Galvin, Bridget Geraghty, Susan Guilfoyle, Kate Hegarty, Martha Lowe, Christina Matthews, Mona Mulholland. Monk couldn't think who she was – hardly surprising with a name like that.

When he got to the Ps, it struck him that the only missing entry so far was Ellen O'Leary.

Monk dropped the address book on to the piano stool, where it landed on top of his copy of Chopin's 'Tristesse'. He stared through the bars again.

He hadn't been out today; he simply hadn't been inclined. Normally there was a gig on Fridays, but everything had changed when O'Leary departed for Prague. A day later the bass player pulled out. A week later the band fell apart. A fortnight after that Monk stopped playing jazz.

He picked up the 'Tristesse' from the stool and sat down. He placed the folio on the rack and opened it. Her photo fell out of the manuscript on to the piano keys. Monk straightened it. Her smile seemed more distant than before. He drew his thumb over her hair. Untouchable. Mind and heart set like stone, chiselled with the initials of the man she loved. And clearly he was not that man.

Monk slapped the photo down on the piano top, shaking his head. Extraordinary lapse of judgement. Was it something he'd drunk in the sea? Some pollutant chemical that bollocksed up your faculty for spotting sure-fire disasters?

He eyed the first bar of the 'Tristesse' and the rhythm played at once in his head. *Lento, ma non troppo*, he could hear Ellen say.

He began playing. Slow as a hearse, he pressed into the keys. The plain, solitary notes reminded Monk of Ellen, of everything about Ellen. They filled the room with a desolateness he'd forgotten was present, lurking behind the cold and the damp like a contagion.

Since Merrion Square, they'd barely exchanged a word. He had tried to contact her the following Monday, to afford her a dignified apology, but she said she was unable to see him. Unable. That was the word. Impersonal. Non-committal. He'd tried to contact her the following Wednesday also. He'd invited her for a coffee and chat. Can't. That was another word.

So he'd bidden his time. A fortnight following O'Leary's exuberant vanishment to the Czech Republic, Monk went down to the Pavilion with Chopin. He did not bring flowers. Ellen was at home – he heard her playing the piano six floors up. He pressed the intercom several times, but she did not answer, although he was standing off-camera. He rang her phone number, which he'd located in the directory, but there was no reply.

He repeated this procedure each day for a further fortnight, at different times and intervals. But he met with no success. She was avoiding him.

Monk did nothing for a solid week. Then he went down, one grey, wet evening. The apartment was in darkness. He came down the next evening and the next, but it was the same thing: no lights on, no window open, no sounds of piano music from above. He called in to the Conservatory and spoke with the secretary with the giant earlobes. She told him Ellen had taken leave of absence.

That was when he stopped playing jazz.

There was a noise. Monk cocked an ear.

Nothing. Only a distant bark. Chopin in the back garden.

Monk returned to the main theme of the 'Tristesse', playing it out till the last chord, sustained until the sound died down.

'That was beautiful.'

He jumped. 'Jesus, Mother, you gave me a fright.'

'Play it again, Myles! I had no idea you could play classical music like that!' She walked in, holding a tray with an afternoon snack and a pile of junk mail.

Monk played one or two jazz chords.

'Did you know, somebody used to sing that tune back in the fifties?'

'I wasn't aware.'

'It was a love song.'

Monk played some more jazz chords, then tripped into some light bebop.

'It's wonderful to hear you play proper music. Dear?'

He kept his eyes fixed on the keys.

'Is everything all right?'

'Wonderful.'

'Did you get out today?'

There was sympathy in his mother's voice and it made him feel lousy.

'Anyway,' she said, 'all this mail just arrived. Thought some of it might interest you. There's also a postcard.'

'Oh?'

'From Prague.'

Monk sprang to his feet and grabbed the pile of mail off her. He threw it on top of the piano and sorted frantically through the junk arrivals, his chest pulsating hard.

'Your father used to sing it for me, did you know that?'

He couldn't find the postcard, so he started through the pile once more.

'In his more romantic days.'

247

'I can't find the postcard. What did you do with it?'

'I have it here, on the tray. I would have told you if you hadn't snatched the letters off me like that.'

He held out a hand. 'Can I have it, please?'

'Who's that?' His mother's face had just lit up.

'What?'

'Whose picture is that?'

Monk snatched the photo of Ellen from the piano top and put it in his back pocket.

'She looks nice. Does she have a name? Never mind, I know you don't like to talk about your girlfriends.'

'The postcard, Mother.'

'Will you do a full performance of the "Tristesse" for me some time? I do like Chopin.'

Reluctantly, Monk nodded. 'Sure, Mother. I'll play it for you some time.'

'How about after tea?'

'Can I have the postcard, please?'

'After tea?' There was mischief in her eyes.

'Okay, Mother, after tea.'

She handed it to him and, to Monk's utter disgust, he saw immediately that it was from O'Leary.

'Here's a mug of tea for you and some biscuits. I've already had mine. I didn't think you'd want to come up.' She went to the door and shivered. 'Lord, it's so *cold* down here, I don't know how you stick it, with the winter coming.'

She smiled sadly over at him and left.

Monk waited until the creaking on the stairs had ceased and silence had resumed. He went out and bolted the door to the passageway, which she'd left open as usual. He returned inside, weighed down by that sinking feeling, unable now to get her voice from his head, that haunting voice, plaguing him, afflicting him, vexing him. He fondled Rufus gently underneath his neck.

He looked at the front of the postcard. The picture featured a big central square with a jazz group playing in the middle: Staromestské Namesti. It was postmarked 31 October, a week ago.

Ahoy Monk!

How's it going back in damp Ireland?

Great news: got a permanent place in Jan's band. Know you'll be pleased for me. Musically, it's cool. Jan's got this great new pianist – Dmitri is his name. Makes such a difference playing with professionals.

Ellen joined me recently. Got this small but excellent flat in the Staré Mesto just two days ago – old part of town. Love it here. Music is everywhere – especially classical. She's in her element. Met some old Czech friends she knew from the Academy here. She's auditioning for this chamber quartet at the minute. Practises on this Kawai we hired. Very like yours, only it has a great tone. She's trying to get Ita to come out, but I'm doing my best to make her see the awkward side.

Ellen sends her regards. She hopes you weren't too upset when she didn't return your repeated calls before she joined me here.

By the way, she's pregnant! No big deal. Went to a clinic yesterday. She had a scan done. I saw it on the monitor. Over two months old. It's tiny. She's certain it's going to be a girl. We'll see.

Have a good one.

Dobry den, and best wishes to your knee.

Joel

PS We'll probably be back for a few days over Xmas. If you're down around the harbour be sure to drop in.